THE NATIVE COMMISSIONER

Sam Jameson was eight years old when his father George died in shocking circumstances. He decides, some forty years later, to finally open the box of his father's papers which his mother had passed on to him, and he left sealed for two decades. In trying to piece together a picture of his unknown father, Sam discovers a troubled, doomed, but extraordinary man – and an extraordinary story. George was a Native Commissioner in the old South Africa, deeply unsure of the morality of his work, but unable to escape it. The backdrop is the lush and harsh landscape of South Africa in the 1950s and 1960s, in the early years of apartheid ...

Shaun Johnson has for many years been a prominent figure in the South African media world, and an award-winning writer of non-fiction. He is currently Chief Executive of The Mandela Rhodes Foundation and lives in Cape Town. *The Native Commissioner* is his first novel.

THE
NATIVE
COMMISSIONER

A Novel

SHAUN JOHNSON

PENGUIN BOOKS

PENGUIN BOOKS

Published by the Penguin Group
Penguin Books Ltd, 80 Strand, London WC2R 0RL, England
Penguin Group (USA) Inc, 375 Hudson Street, New York, New York 10014, USA
Penguin Group (Canada), 90 Eglinton Avenue East, Suite 700, Toronto, Ontario,
Canada M4P 2Y3 (a division of Pearson Penguin Canada Inc)
Penguin Ireland, 25 St Stephen's Green, Dublin 2, Ireland (a division of
Penguin Books Ltd)
Penguin Group (Australia), 250 Camberwell Road, Camberwell, Victoria 3124, Australia
(a division of Pearson Australia Group Pty Ltd)
Penguin Books India Pvt Ltd, 11 Community Centre, Panchsheel Park,
New Delhi – 110 017, India
Penguin Group (NZ), Cnr Rosedale and Airborne Roads, Albany, Auckland 1310,
New Zealand (a division of Pearson New Zealand Ltd)
Penguin Books (South Africa) (Pty) Ltd, 24 Sturdee Avenue, Rosebank,
Johannesburg 2196, South Africa

Penguin Books (South Africa) (Pty) Ltd, Registered Offices:
24 Sturdee Avenue, Rosebank, Johannesburg 2196, South Africa

www.penguinbooks.co.za

First published by Penguin Books (South Africa) (Pty) Ltd 2006

Copyright © Shaun Johnson 2006

ISBN 0 143 02501 5

Typeset by CJH Design in 11/15 pt Sabon
Cover design: Flame Design, Cape Town
Cover image: Visualsafari/Images of Africa
Printed and bound by Paarl Print, Cape Town

For my brothers Barry, Rowan, and Craig

And if he does not remember them, who will?
J M Coetzee, *Boyhood*

I

ON the morning it all started, I woke and sat in one movement. I remember the feeling clearly; it was as if I'd been propelled upright by a forklift. The sunlight was bouncing gently off the sea and feeding through the gaps where we'd closed the bedroom curtains haphazardly the night before. Outside it was warm and still with wisps of mist burning themselves off the ocean surface as the sun spread over the hills.

The only sound in the room was soft breathing from the bed. I slipped to the floor, padded along the corridor and down the stairs past my son's room, then made my way over our veranda to the gate that leads to the sea. It was one of those limpid days; the flatness of the blue-green water stretched far out into the distance of the bay and I could see the outlines of the big ships on the horizon, jostling for access to the port. The local fishing fleet was also at work, seabirds watching. I fiddled with the rusted padlock, then jogged barefoot around the front wall to the cellar whose decaying wooden door faced the full salt blast of the swell below. I told myself I needn't be self-conscious about my tall barrelly frame, balding head, morning stubble and curious errand – there was no one to see me.

The cellar door opened easily. When my eyes had adjusted I saw that there, in the far corner in the dank half-light amongst gently rusting garden implements and the crowding flotsam of too many moves to too many homes in too many places, sat the box. It was propped up against a sodden wall on an ill-fashioned shelf comprising a broken plank resting on trestles from another time and purpose. The plank sagged in sympathy with the box of superannuated cardboard. It was a very long time since I had allowed myself to register that the box was still there, still unopened.

The privileged enclave in which we lived was motionless, the houses clinging to the slopes unroused, a pleasant surprise awaiting them when doors would be flung open to the dome of clear sky. The day had chosen itself well. There was not yet a sound to drown out the gulls' caws; you would never have known that a city sprawled not half an hour's drive away.

First I considered the box without touching it, respectful of its travel-weariness and fragility in this untended cavern. It was very large and, I allowed myself to remember, heavy. The tape that had sealed it for thirty-five years appeared to be holding, applied with vigour all that time ago as if to discourage any thought of reopening. On the sides were peeling stickers and smudged stamps, the insignia of removal companies, towns, countries, destinations; I had the sudden impression of a scuffed overused passport, no longer valid for travel.

I took the box in a fireman's embrace, gingerly, spreading my legs wide for purchase but not taking the full weight; just tested to see if it would hold together. It shifted shape and seemed to yield under protest with a wet tearing sound.

I left the cellar door open and retraced my steps through the mixture of low bush and wild seaside grass. I went up to the garage and rummaged until I found what I was looking for: a folding metal trolley like a railway porter's miniature and, from the toolbox, a clean sharp knife.

With the trolley wedged under the shelf in the cellar, it looked like there was a good chance of manoeuvring the box down slowly and I was pleased when this worked without any spillage. I could push it quite easily, and all that was needed was to keep it balanced because the sides protruded. I got safely through the gate and back to the bottom of the stone stairs leading up to the veranda. I turned the trolley around and heaved, bumping the small rubber wheels up each step, one by one. The slate flagstones of the veranda floor offered a wide flat expanse, like a giant's operating table. I tipped the trolley forward to slide the box to its final resting place, where it settled and waited.

My mother had spoken to me only once about the box; a few sentences I could still recall to the word. That was all those years ago when she gave it over to my care. She had known already then that age, poor health and the life she had lived were rubbing their hands; that she would soon begin the modern middle-class downward death journey from small townhouse to retirement village, to frail care centre, to a bed somewhere not home from which one day she would not stir.

Those are your father's papers, she had said to me, pointing at the box. I have decided that you should be the one to have them. Open it when you are ready.

There it was, older and more damaged like all of us who had touched it on its long elliptical journey to this shoreline. These African places had its contents passed along the way, the names a private family mantra: Babanango, Ingwavuma, Umbumbulu, Ndwedwe, Nkandhla, Tsumeb, Zoekmekaar, Kentani, Duiwelskloof, Pretoria, Johannesburg, Libode, Witbank, and finally here, way down in the humid south again, overlooking the Indian Ocean, back close by to where it all began.

I took the knife, made four long incisions along the lines of sealing tape, and opened the box. Then I exclaimed without meaning to, and hoped I had not woken my son or my wife still in our bed with the baby.

Inside was a rotting, fused mound of carefully ordered paper and memory trinkets kept closed for an adult life, her magpie's work, capable of calling back the unknown dead. Powerful smells of age, confinement, solitude, inattention. Resentful colours had run into one another, inks no longer manufactured, dyes not fastened. Some of what was inside was lost to decay, but most had survived. For me it was like the fantastical volcanic pipe of *Tsomsoub*, so virile with mineral wealth that it thrust itself through the crust of Africa's earth, demanding to be mined.

Somewhere inside all of this: the family secret, not spoken of for nearly four decades now. I had an overpowering sense of something having been rescued arbitrarily, at the instant before its predestined oblivion.

Still I did not touch what was inside. I got up from the cross-legged position on the flagstones which I would have to resume on countless days and nights of reading and sorting to come, of solitary quarrying and tunnelling, and looked about me. I stood for a long time staring out from where I lived; stood peering over an ocean at the bottom of a continent.

Eventually I decided I should fetch more tools for this private archaeological, anthropological site. I needed more boxes, the modern and smaller types to help excavate and then codify the big box itself. And garbage bags because surely, surely, there would be much whose time had come at last to be discarded and buried forever.

I thought then that I knew at least one thing about what might be inside, though I had never read so much as a word of the contents of the box. Inside was the presence of absence which had shadowed my life. I thought I must surely be ready now, with more than half my days certainly done, to confront what had happened in a small suburban house on a summer's morning in Witbank,

South Africa, in 1968; something that changed everything in an instant and forever. I wanted to release a story from a sealed box I had dragged around for decades, and which had in its turn dragged me like a sinker. I wanted to hear the voices of my father and my mother.

JUST BEFORE THEN

Ward, 1967

I WAS talking to a Mauritian man who's had a frontal lobotomy. He is a cheerful and interesting fellow and we've become quite good companions. I told him I should be going home soon to my family up far north from where we are now. Certainly not later than new year and perhaps even in time for Christmas. What a surprise that would be for them. My Mum and Dad could pick me up and take me to Glencoe via Babanango to get the train to the Transvaal. I said I was looking forward very much indeed to seeing my wife and my four sons. I said my friend and I probably wouldn't have many more chances to talk so we should make the most of it. He should tell me if I was boring him too much with my stories when Lord knows he had his own. Unfortunately my speech is still as rambling and unclear as if I had never learned any punctuation at school. But he said he could understand me well enough.

I told him my wife has been writing every day or nearly every day. He said I told him that already. He said he may have had things done to his head but he still knew what I told him. He said my memory actually sounds worse than his and I agreed. My faculties swim clear then cloudy. In her latest letter she said heavens how the week flew. And yet in another way it seemed months long because there was so much for her to get through. But she thinks it is good she is so busy because it will bring me home all the sooner. She went into the post office on Friday to send me a telegram. The queue was so long that she decided to skip it and have a call at half price instead. It is terrible without me there she says but she is prepared to pay any price to have me well. She says I must not worry if I am not discharged in time for Christmas as there will be other Christmases we can spend together. She told me about the neighbours leaving for the holidays because no one who doesn't have to will stay in the town of coal and steel. Mr and Mrs Claassens brought around some peaches and nectarines before they went. My stand-in at work was being very considerate. He said he had great regard for me and he has been good to her. Mr Pupkewitz asked kindly after me last week and he too sent his kindest regards. The Collinses will soon be on their way as will the Reverend and Mrs Miller as well as the Nicholses and Mr and Mrs Tomkins. Rina Goldman from next door sent Christmas greetings wishing me good health and a speedy return. She sent a lovely tin of biscuits and a card. My wife will miss her when she goes away on holiday again. Rina is a brick and her closest friend I think. I told my friend my wife is quite particular about her grammar and most often says *shall* rather than *will*. Our boys have been good under the circumstances. How lovely it will be when I am finally home and for the first time in ever so long we might have our four sons under one roof. She has decided to post our eldest boy's fiancée a half petticoat given to her last year and never used. Also a pink top her sister gave her which is brand new but she never wore as well as a few odds and ends. She says because it does not feel like a normal Christmas there will be no presents this year. What with all the expenses she thinks we can be forgiven. She does not know yet what they will do for Christmas Eve as she has not thought that far. It is probably too late to book for dinner at a hotel so she will possibly just buy a chicken. Even though there will be no presents she thinks she must do something as a token for the sake of the small boy. He has just turned eight and now notices such things. She went to a lovely church service in the morning. They will go to the 9.30am Christmas morning communion. She says she has received no letters from me this week but then again her *Reader's Digest* didn't arrive either so it must be the chaos in the post office. If I have a copy I should bring it when I come home. She will personally be very glad when the whole season is over. She has shelved all plans of Christmas cards too this year because of the money and because she has no time or inclination. But we shall write them together next year when all this is behind us.

I said to my Mauritian friend this is actually quite a beautiful place don't you think. Not where we are in this room and building obviously but this green city on the sea. It's humid and quite different to where I live in the coal town up north and probably more like the island he comes from. I said I liked this warm summer rain especially when you can do nothing more than lie and listen. He told me a bit about his home in Port Louis and his own family.

While we were talking we were sitting in the library or rather what they call the library which is basically also the lounge. The walls are painted the colour of nicotine like all Government institutions in this country. There are nice grounds but you can't go out with the rain. In the building itself there is not much room to move about. One must either be in the sleeping area or the lounge. And when in the lounge area on most uncomfortable chairs with only eighteen for thirty people not including visitors. Laundry is a problem and I have had to write to my wife to ask for clothes to be sent to Umhlali station where my father can pick them up. So far she has sent a mackintosh and a safari suit and some display shirts for the times we are allowed out. In here we're just in our gowns all day. We make our own beds and lay the tables in turn which is a bit of a comedown for me in life. There is no soap supplied and I had to manage on pieces I picked up in the bathroom until my sister sent me a cake of toilet soap. There were two other men in the room writing while we were there talking. There are all sorts here. We have the queerest characters. One a brilliant impossible man who will doubtless have to be sent to Maritzburg for further observation. He caused a commotion last weekend and I am afraid I allowed his conduct to affect me. There is a woman who used to work at Prynne's Outfitters whose slogan is *The Most Beautiful Shop In Africa*. A wonderful character. Story is she fell from a horse during her honeymoon and eventually had to have her arm amputated. Another woman here has leukaemia on top of the mental troubles. She tries to be so cheerful it makes me feel ashamed. Others from all walks of life including a doctor. I am fortunate in being in with Jack Hewson who in private life is an insurance agent. He has had a pretty full life. Some three years ago he had a motor accident and lost his money and lost his wife as a result of penicillin poisoning. He married at forty-six and had been with his wife only three to four years. Now he's in here broken down with the rest of us. I expect that most of the inmates will go home for the weekend and it will be very empty and eerie. Probably just me and Maurice the Mauritian. I hate this place but then I cannot say that I was overjoyed at the last one. And this one is much more affordable being subsidised as it is. Preferable for a long stay. I could not get well thinking of the fresh debts piling up day by day on top of everything else. What can one do? I hate being under obligations. I despise being penniless and embarrassed.

Maurice asked how my treatment was going. He explained he'd had his frontal operation done in France two months ago. Didn't work. If it had of course he wouldn't be here with us what with

Christmas coming and Durban being a long way from France and even Mauritius for that matter. He said they were going to try something else and he would just go with the flow rather as I am because really what else is there to do. I told him as much as I know or can remember at the moment about my treatment. I said even though I'm only forty-nine years old there are now things I do not remember or do not even know if I knew in the first place which makes me very sad and frightened. I told him I was sent to Pretoria to a nursing home in Lynnwood earlier this year a week after our silver wedding anniversary. That stay was about a month long. Then in October I was sent to that other place here in Durban. The expensive private one before this cheap Government one. At that place it was mostly pills. I couldn't recall the details. They still thought tablets would be enough and changed them all the time. I started to get more confused then and to have strange spells. On one occasion I was so embarrassed because I suddenly started shaking and shivering for no reason. I must have looked like a dog after it had been given a bath. It passed after a while. I said that there they also took my blood for calcium testing and looked for diabetes trouble. Dr Lukic said it was possible my problems resulted from something physical which is exactly what I have been saying all along ever since I had that first bang in my head at Duiwelskloof. I have very labile blood pressure right up then down and the doctor said this could cause spasms in arteries etcetera. It was at a hundred and ninety-eight over a hundred and ten then it dropped to a hundred and thirty over ninety. My dread was that I had calcified arteries though another doctor said that a look into the eye showed that no damage had resulted from high blood pressure. Dr Lukic said then he hoped that controlling the blood pressure would lead to improvement. I kept telling them it must be physical. Maurice said he hoped I was right. Then they said I must come here which I realised could not be good news and the treatments must not be working. Here they said there would be a psychiatrist and a psychologist a specialist physician and an occupational therapist. And there would be shock. Shock treatment. Oh my word I knew then how far things had gone. And I said do you know the damndest thing? As I sit here with you today I don't know whether I've had it yet or not. The shock treatment I mean. I must have of course but it might have burnt off some of my memory. The shock together with all the medication. I said they are now also putting me through narco-analysis which is a truth-finding test very modern and new apparently. They started on Thursday but I was in some kind of trance and could not answer them properly. There are times that I feel tolerably well but I am getting more listless each and every day. God it can't be like this always. I told my friend I like this young doctor who is kind and serious and very dedicated to his work. He seems very well up on the most recent developments in psychiatry and psychotherapy. Better than some others I had before who seemed to love themselves more than they did their patients. He must help me survive the next few years. The blood pressure came down to one hundred and twenty over eighty and he cut the tablet to half per day instead of two per day. He's the one who said I should be discharged soon. Hoorah! Although I know I am not yet well I feel I have improved. I still have great difficulty with memory and concentration but I am fighting to be well. I've seen far too many people who come back again. I see Dr Lukic tomorrow at 2pm and much will depend on the blood pressure reading then and what I tell him about the nervous feeling in my legs. This episode as such is at an end I think and maybe I have broken it. There is no longer the agony of being seized in an electrical field unable to move and your face frozen like a book cover of your mind. At one stage all this seemed too much to bear and I feared the very worst. I could not stop my mind from going to those dark places where it should not go. Now I have some hope that I will get through. When I need to think of peaceful things I picture my fuchsias and the garden at home and my family.

The man from Mauritius and I must have spoken for about an hour. Then I was suddenly too tired to go on talking and I thanked him for the chat and went to the sleeping area in the ward. My section of the sleeping area has screens around it to give some privacy. I keep all my letters in the tin cupboard next to my bed. There is the batch of letters from my wife which is thirty-seven in all and one from others which is about fifteen. I number the envelopes as they arrive. I take them out and reread them often to remind myself and keep up to date and to stop myself from slipping anchor completely. I told my wife she should not write so often when she has so much else on her plate but she said she worries that if she doesn't write every day I will forget her which is a strange and disturbing thing to say.

In the second batch there are letters from Mum and Dad who never mention why I am here and of course that is understandable from the old people. I feel terrible about the shame I've caused them. Their eldest son. And you can just feel it in their letters though they're trying so hard. They always write together on the same blue aerogramme always a short note from Dad and a longer one from Mum. In the first one Dad said he trusted I will not look backwards but will soon be my old self enjoying good health and that perhaps when this is over I can put in some time with them at Ballito Bay where they have retired. Mum says they wrote as soon as they heard from my younger brother who drove all the way from his farm near Babanango to the North Coast to tell them about me. I was born in Babanango. She said if I wanted to go there to rest they would be glad. She said the hot weather has come. It is such a change from winter when Ballito is cold and the sun starts disappearing at three thirty in the afternoon and Mum sits looking out of the big window at the sea with a rug on her knees and Dad puts on his Frank Sinatra record until it is time to turn up the old wireless too loud for the news. Mum said their thoughts and prayers are with me and that I will come out of this a hundred per cent. All their letters say more or less the same though there is different news about the family old Uncle Stanton and Uncle Barley and such and about the weather. Dad wrote to say he was pleased about my eldest son's engagement and that at long last we would have a daughter in the family after trying without success ourselves four times. In another one from last month Dad told me Mum was posting a parcel with a light jersey and a belt he'd managed to get in Umhlali which he trusted would meet with my approval. I can't actually remember whether it arrived and must ask the matron. He said they knew I was being moved to another hospital and they appealed to me to be really cooperative. In this way I would improve by the day and so I should pull up my socks not to mention my chin and get better. That's Mum and Dad all right. My sons have also all written to me. Of course even I can recognise how terrible it is for each of them in different ways at their ages to not have a father around. I keep all of their letters together in the second batch next to my bed. My eldest son wrote from the ship MV SA Lubombo where he is an engineer and is travelling the world to places like Las Palmas and Lisbon and London and Hull. Also Rotterdam Antwerp and Bremen and Hamburg. I like to imagine him there. As long ago as May he wrote asking if all was not well at home. Did they all know then already of the crisis I wonder? He said he realised how much we as parents have done for them and to what extent we have deprived ourselves for them. He said he loves us for it and thinks the only way to repay the debt is to try and do the same one day for his own kids. He thinks about such things much more than our other young ones. He has turned out very responsible and honourable and works hard though goodness knows he has had a hard time of it himself what with our lives being what they have been. I think I have been harsh on him and the others though I have not meant to. The girl he is getting engaged to is from Port Elizabeth and is a nice solid type of girl from a working family so I am pleased for him. The second boy wrote from Johannesburg to say things would all work out now and that next year everything will be better. I shouldn't worry about him not having a job even though he knows how much I do worry. His opening in life is just around the corner he says. When it comes there will be no stopping him he says which is just like him. He is an artist and wants to be in advertising though I have said he should stop chasing after rainbows and get down to accountancy or banking or commerce or something like that. I said he must not be very choosy and there was a man in here with me who could possibly help get him into his textile firm which has a number of subsidiaries. From the address on his letter my son seems to have been living in Hillbrow which is not surprising though it is a worry as he is a wild one. A place called High Hylton in Goldreich Street which must be flats of a sort. Still he has talent and has won a national art award which was reported in all the newspapers in the Republic. The judges said his painting was very adult and disturbing. Now he is doing batiks and my wife says he is going to go home to live for a while. I know the real reason is that he has run up debts of R100 or even more in Johannesburg but she is very protective of the boy. She is arranging a part-time job for him at a bottle store so we will just have to see what happens. My third son's written several times. His exams are drawing nearer and he is swotting maths exercise by exercise. Good boy that he is he says his brain is in working order. He's also helping with decorations for the high school matric dance. The theme is Ascot from *My Fair Lady.* Can you imagine that in the Transvaal for goodness' sake. He has just been confirmed in a suit they bought at Hepworths for R15.95 which he says is a nice dark grey. He says because of the storms every day the apricots are big and the peaches huge and the lawn is looking very green and class which must be teenager talk I suppose. Apparently even the tiny little new trees have fruit on them. The old hacked about peach tree near the Goldmans' fence is laden with peaches and the plums are ripe too. My vines are sagging with big grapes. The boy says he went with my wife and his small brother to see a South African film at the weekend. I wonder what that was. He has passed his test for a buzz bike licence though on the way back from an air display at the aerodrome just at the railway crossing the ball bearings went in the back wheel. He has worked on the roof to patch up the hole from the big lightning strike my wife mentioned in one of her letters. He told me about his visit back to Libode to see his old friends and they went to Umgazana Mouth where we had such happy times. He wishes I would hurry up and get better so we can once again be one big family. Even the small boy wrote. Mostly child's news. He has got a new tooth and won a Wicks Bubble Gum competition. Built a fort in the backyard and will be going to young Mark Goldstein's party where they are taking them to see the film *Kruger Millions*. The little man is making his own bed now. He is also making scrapbooks. He makes up stories all the time. They are all about the family including a drawing of our two cats. He has to go to neighbours every afternoon now to do his homework though he doesn't say which neighbours. Because his Mom is at work and his Dad is always away. But he has passed all his tests. He and his brother have lunch at the youth centre. Everything is fine he says. It feels like I have been away for years and he is missing me very much and hopes I will be able to come home soon. He wrote that his friends at school are asking where I am. I know of course that the whole town must be talking about me and I hope it is not too hard on the family. I have written to the two boys who are still at home to say how very sorry I am that I could not give them a father's time and attention and for my failure.

My younger brother being a very successful farmer doesn't have time to write much but he did anyway. He said kindly I have done the right thing by accepting that I must have treatment and that lots of people have my trouble though they don't publicise it because it is not really understood by the general public. How I agree with that. He wrote that the wife of a mutual friend has just been hospitalised for nerves so you see how nerves can play up. My brother is fit and resolute. He is happy with all he has achieved and I hope he will not always be driving himself as he has had to. We have talked straight and he has formulated some ideas about my precarious finances. He told me about his farm in old Zululand and how the Saturday before the most terrible wind broke trees and sent all the stocks flying. He was still trying to pick things up and hoped to put his cattle in the stalls soon. It had taken a bit of time to make the drains from the guttering downpipes. His piping has still not arrived in Dundee so he is relying on that little irrigation scheme going below the sheds. He thinks I know the one from the last time I visited. My brother also made the time to come and visit me here and brought my sister and her husband. I was pleased to see them but of course ashamed of where I am. I am not sure that I want Mum and Dad to see me here. Among the letters my wife forwarded was one from the dear old Transkei. Josias Makhubela from Maxaka Government School who I helped in my time there and secured an arable plot for him at Sipunzi. Now he wants to succeed Mr Mthintso as messenger of the court at Libode and needs me to give him a personal recommendation. He cannot know of my troubles of course and I must do this for him when I am able. Also a note from my friend Walter Fairbairn who says my wife told him I was laid up again. He writes well does Walter. Said that he like me has had his dream of a pilot's licence dashed by high blood pressure. He was all set for a solo in a Cherokee 140 when the medical came back unfit. Walter wishes me a quick recovery and return to the Highveld. He said the town plods along as always. His letter made me remember my high hopes when I went for those flying lessons. My new interest in life and then the medical rejection. I turned to pencil sketching but now that's gone too. Fanie Aucamp who is the regional director of my Department took the trouble to have a personal letter typed to me to say that all the members of staff were missing my presence very much. It was kind of him to say so. He said an interesting thing in this letter. He said I feel sure that you take far too much personal responsibility for the work we are now having to do. He said that in saying this he was talking from experience. He himself had decided that he would only do his best and not worry at all if something beyond his control was wrong. I should try this approach. It was not our fault that we're too old to get out. He said he was holding a special bottle of whisky for my return. Good man that Fanie. There are still a lot of them around even though often it doesn't seem like it. I have also just remembered that a Reverend Richards came to see me last week at this hospital which is in his parish All Saints and quite near the rectory. A fine chap whose visit I actually enjoyed. I think Reverend Miller must have got on to him which is kind. Mrs Miller is the one my wife says comes to the house sometimes after work and brings things for the boys. Reverend Richards told me he would be writing to my wife after seeing me and I hope he didn't say I look too bad. In this kind of situation one is at risk of letting one's appearance go a bit and some even look slightly slatternly at times which is depressing in itself.

I wonder how I am going to sleep tonight. Too often I find that just when the tablet should be doing its work I am wide awake like one of those startled bushbabies in the garden at Kentani. Later I'll have to go for a walk around the corridors to make myself tired. The other patients seem to have better sleeping patterns than me and I can hear some of them above the sheeting rain already in their beds though of none would I say they are sleeping peacefully. It's beginning to get dark outside. For some reason I am thinking about an outing we were taken on this week. We went to Tshongweni Dam. People looked at us. I suppose they had heard we were from the lunatic asylum.

Of course the person who is shouldering most of the burden of this whole ghastly mess is my wife and that after twenty-five years of marriage. But she seems to appreciate my writing and says she is sending me more paper and envelopes to make sure I write again so that she can open the letter box and see my handwriting there at the end of her day. For me I just have to be patient and hope and trust in her to see our family through. I picture her going to and from an office and I wonder how it will work out. Are we really coping financially I wonder and what about her health? I suppose she works on Saturdays also. She is so very small physically but strong-willed. I try to express my feelings to her in letters because

I am so bad on the telephone and anyway as we both know I am stiff and excruciatingly self-conscious at the best of times. I wrote to her to say that with the state I was in we had to accept that I could not continue with the work and there was no choice but to be taken away. She should be aware however that I know what a rock she is being and so does each and every member of our family. For you I have nothing but praise I said. It must be very hard indeed to do a six day a week job as the breadwinner and still try to run a house the way you know a house must be run. I said I so appreciated her letters and the effort she put into them to help heal my soul. I said I prayed she will have the strength to hold the family together long enough until I can get back and do my bit. I said I wanted nothing more than to get back soon and help her bring up our kids. I said teach me to be grateful. Help me to change. Bowls and reading. Let us live a quieter and fuller more selfish but not self-centred life. The garden for me. That's where I belong. I said here's to all this and to your spirit and courage. I wrote to her as from one who has not been able to one who is. I have had to talk straight about money too though I recognise that it might make her more frightened than the poor girl must be already. I have had to tell her that if I don't recover and am boarded out I get full pay such as it is for only three years followed by three months on half pay. And we must remember I have had four or five weeks' sick leave already this year. I have said she will have to save every single cent she can by taking lifts with the Goldmans next door and making the boys scrape the last butter off the foil etcetera. I have told her she must explain to our boys that we have no money though they must keep that strictly to themselves. I said my dear girl I must put to you the possibility of my never returning to work. Not just that I don't want to but that I actually can't. She might need to make the enormous decision to sell our house even though we still owe the bank so much on it. We have also got to pay back to her sister what we have borrowed and that loan I had to take from Mr Shlain. I told her I am very sorry and very humiliated to have to write these things but that is our reality. I was very frightened and pessimistic at that time. I said she was so full of energy that I thought somehow she would survive even without me but God forbid that such should happen. I said I love her and I love my kids and that I hope this love will lead us through. Then so that not all from me was gloom and misery I asked her to get Enoch our gardener to continue putting in plantings. He should also put in a few rows of mealies and patches of runner beans at places where they can climb. I said it's good to hear that there are no worms on the fuchsias and no aphis on the backs of the leaves. He should spray with Roger E which I keep on the top shelf in the greenhouse. One capful to three quarters of a watering can. I said she should ask Chris to help with watering by soaking one area and then the next day another. When I got home I would give him some holiday pocket money for this chore. I said please the fuchsias on the greenhouse wall must get water as that is where the Snow Queen is.

I said I thought I could read from her letters that she is enjoying working and being so busy. I said I was glad about that. Actually I hate the idea. I had always hoped my wife would play bridge in the afternoons and keep the home and family which is a big enough job. But I suppose I must accept it is good that she is busy with work and meeting people. I wrote to her to say please don't expect of yourself to be perfect in this terrible world and remember what landed me here. I of course still hope that I get so well that she can stop work again. I also had to warn her though I don't want to weaken her resolve that our income tax might be affected by her working. I enclosed a newspaper cutting which is quite frightening. She says I must stop worrying myself sick about money on top of everything else and that she is managing fine going carefully living on practically nothing and getting things straightened out. I know of course what she is trying to do in all these letters because they have a formula and I admire her for it. There is encouragement and advice to me sometimes quite strident even and there is a great deal of detail about the life I have left behind. I welcome the everyday detail from her because the ordinariness is important and it can be a life raft for someone in my situation. She never ever expresses fear though it must crowd her daily and she is unfailingly optimistic even though the tide has run against us so strongly. She wrote to me on my birthday to say I must never get too disheartened and never give up all hope. She and I were going to be happy again and we would spend my next birthday together when I am over all this misery. We would just forget it all like a bad debt and have many happy years ahead of us. Times like we had travelling last year and in the happy or at least happier places before that. We should plan to go to the peace and quiet of the Olifants Resort to rest and bask in the sun. That's a nice picture. I remember her other words too. We must be very sure this time. No more sorrow and illness in our lives. Stick it out. Talk to Dr Lukic. Dig deep and get your subconscious up to the surface. Take the fear and guilt and confusion out and look at them and you will be able to throw them away forever. You will free yourself of these evil things that seek to destroy you and us too. You are a good man though you doubt that yourself. We are all proud of you though you think we are ashamed. I still love you. Those were her exact words.

I am glad she has Rina next door to talk to. She is a very good person. Rina was the one who sent me chocolates and magazines by post. *Panorama* and *Scope* so anyone can see I am not exactly capable of intellectual pursuit at the moment. I handed chocolates out to the other patients and gave the staff two each so I am quite popular. Old Mrs Goldman's card was a beauty too and much appreciated. I asked my wife to say thank you for me as I will not be writing.

This cursed and crumbled year. I run it back and forth in my mind incessantly as I lie here. When things are darkest I'm afraid I feel it would be better if this planet was not populated with humans and was like the others rather. Just empty spheres in space. Or that if what someone once called the celestial joke of creating humans had to be made that we were all just one race in the world and the same colour and equal. Or that white people including my own people had never come uninvited to the black people's land in the first place. Or that someone had warned me not to love Africa and told me it could be dangerous to do so. Sometimes I think these thoughts are idle and sometimes I do not.

Because I am still confused and forgetful and because I cannot be like this when I get back home I am now writing some things down for when the relapses come. So far I have written down a total of twenty-two points to remember when I get home. My writing is squiggly and spidery from the drugs and everything but I can still read it and I have written on both sides of one sheet of notepaper so I can keep it with me easily in my pocket. What I'll do when I'm home is just as I feel myself beginning to plunge downwards I'll go somewhere quiet in the garden and pull these out to read them and ward off the blackness.

> A positive personality draws success, a negative one repels it
> Attitudes are more important than facts
> Formulate a mental picture of yourself succeeding
> Should a negative thought come to mind, counter it
> Inner peace, harmony, without stress is the easiest existence
> For sleep think of your mind as the surface of a pond
> Worry is the most subtle of all modern diseases
> Anxiety is the great modern plague
> Be bold and mighty forces will come to your aid
> Physical condition is determined by emotional condition
> Use peaceful words like tranquillity and serenity and placidity
> Do not feel responsible for everything
> Accept that what has been has been
> Try to believe in what you are doing
> Practise silence daily

I know these points should be obvious but I need them written down for the times when suddenly and uncontrollably they are not obvious to me at all. When hopelessness and meaninglessness and peacelessness descend like a shroud and you just want desperately to end it all. And then when the feeling passes you cannot understand how on earth you could have felt like that. And you thank heavens you did not act on it. With age you come to realise what a strange and wayward thing the human mind can be. I often feel like mine is missing a thermostat or something. I now understand perfectly what Churchill meant when he talked about his Black Dog following him around everywhere. Peace with myself says my wife is what I lack above all and I have to find a way of finding it. I have also written down some lines on courage. I can't remember for the moment where they come from.

> Let me not beg for the stilling of my pain but for the heart to conquer it. Grant me that I may not be a coward feeling your mercy in success but let me find the grasp of your hand in my failure.

Good lines I think. I am determined to get well now if only for my family. I cannot abandon them. My boys are so young and vulnerable and have no defences against what this blasted world has in store for them. I am not coming back here. I am going home.

Kitchen, 1967

THE minute I got back from the office I rushed next door to Rina's house – didn't even bother to change out of my work clothes. Now I'm home and can collect my thoughts while I do the ironing. What a week; thank heavens it's nearly over.

All day at the office I looked forward to seeing Rina again. And we had a great old yack, though as usual I did most of the talking. I'm so glad she's back from her travels.

I realised just how much I'd missed being able to pop over for a shoulder to cry on – as soon as she saw me she gave me a big hug and I said: coffee please, and make it strong, there's so much to tell.

She was home just in time to witness the annual exodus from Witbank – along come the Christmas holidays, and everyone just flees this town like they can't wait another minute to escape. I said this is a funny little town you and I have fetched up in, old girl, but I'm satisfied with it.

She hadn't heard about the new hotel, the Boulevard, where the grounds are being levelled, pavements and storm water drains etcetera all nearing completion, face brick wall with two foot high copper lettering – when it's polished that copper is going to glint; very effective. I said there's been quite a lot of new development, including the smart new Caltex garage on Voortrekker Road with petrol station and bowsers.

I often wish I could escape myself, these days; I really could do with a break from the doings of Mountbatten Ave, what with those amazing electrical storms on top of all my other troubles.

I still can't quite believe the lightning struck our roof the very day after poor George was taken away – such a horrible, violent, portent; it felt as if the whole country might explode, just like he says in his darkest moods.

The repairmen found a huge hole right through the corrugated iron directly over our lounge and ours was the only house in the whole town to get a direct hit; we even made the *Witbank News*! They worked all of two days before the ceiling and electrical board were repaired.

And those gallons and gallons of water running down the street after the meter got struck on the pavement; I'm rather hoping it was a proper strike so they won't be able to charge us for water this month.

It wasn't just us, though. The whole Transvaal had quite a time of it with the storms and I heard that houses at Robertsham were flooded to four inches and there was violent hail in Klerksdorp. Helen called to say they were nervous wrecks in Johannesburg and there were forty car accidents in the city and basements and excavations were flooded, poles even started burning.

The big storm we had here so petrified me that I jumped into bed and put a pillow over my head.

I remembered to thank Rina for the card she sent from her holiday asking how I was holding up and I said, actually, I've so much to hold together at the moment that I often don't know *where* I am – never mind how I am; just keep putting one foot in front of the other. But people have been very kind and helpful, with doughnuts, fruit from friends – and of course the biscuits from her.

Mrs Lyons, one of our church members and a good Sunday School helper, came over to me at Chris's confirmation morning tea to ask if there was anything she could do to help with Sam.

She'd heard I'd had to go out to work because of what's happened to George – it's the talk of the town I'm afraid, but suppose that's inevitable with a public figure. Now Sam's been going around to do his homework there in the afternoons. At least I have peace of mind knowing he's not in the house alone or roaming the streets.

The two boys are actually managing pretty well under the circumstances.

Chris is good to me and popular at school – he's heavily involved in arranging the matric dance. The girls in his class have made hundreds of roses from toilet paper, silver top hats from the cardboard inside the toilet rolls, and dozens of balloons to be dropped at the right time from the enormous fishnet the boys have been making night after night; they're also doing white paling fences and silhouettes of horses complete with jockeys.

I must remember to slip up to the school after work one of these days to have a peep at the result of all their labour.

His exams are going fine, he works hard, and still helps such a lot with the lawn and ironing and such even though he would obviously rather be tinkering with his buzz bike. Yesterday afternoon he and his friends were working on a repair job on the bike because of something mechanical that went wrong, the three completely engrossed and up to their wrists in grease. Sam, not to be outdone, was up to his own ankles in soil, building a fort under the apricot trees.

I'm glad that before the exams started Chris could go back to the dear Transkei and see the friends he still misses so much.

I think the littlest chap seems okay in spite of all the trauma in the house.

A couple of Sundays ago when Helen and Arthur came to visit, they helped him fill in a competition in the *Sunday Express* – just an easy question to answer and then luck of the draw. He asked them to post his entry to Cape Town and Helen put an airmail stamp on it the next day and we all forgot about it. Lo and behold! there came a congratulatory letter and a box full of at least one rand's worth of Chapelat sweets; you'd think he'd won the Durban July he was so happy.

Later he asked me an interesting question: Why did I win and not someone else, Mom? and I remembered our old family saying – Y's a crooked letter, and you can't make it straight – and that seemed to satisfy him.

Helen and Arthur are being so good, and I know they're trying to help without making us feel like charity cases, but I hated having to borrow money from them again, and on top of that they still do kind things like sending me a lovely set of stainless steel serving dishes. I'm going to buy them a Maria Callas long player for Christmas, just to say thank you though we're not doing any other presents.

I'm remembering that strange interlude when I took them to the station to get the last train to Johannesburg.

On the platform stood a young girl of about thirteen or fourteen. She came over to me and asked in Afrikaans how she could get into town. I asked if she was alone and she said yes, so took I her with us. She said she'd come from Brakpan and wanted to go to her sister in Botha Avenue, so I dropped her outside a row of miserable dark little semi-detached houses opposite the Orange Free State Butchery and she thanked me and walked away.

I felt like going after her to make sure there was someone at home, but one must not invade another person's privacy unless asked: poor little beggar – I wondered what story lay behind that; no child of that age should be arriving unannounced in a strange town in the dark.

I must say I felt a surge of fear for my own family just then.

Although I often feel so desperate that I just want to run away and pretend to be a new person somewhere, I absolutely must not fail now to hold this family together; I couldn't stand the thought of them alone with that hunted look in their eyes like that young girl.

There's so much sadness in life and so many people are frightened in ways one would never know; I always remember the aphorism my mother once told me: If you could read the secret history of your enemies, you should find in each man's life sorrow and suffering enough to disarm all hostilities.

Tomorrow when Rina gives me a lift in to town I'll hear all her news, which is so much more pleasant and exotic than mine – the Seychelles, excuse me!

I asked her if the news of our heart transplant had grabbed all the headlines while she was gallivanting overseas and she said oh yes, Chris Barnard was now world famous – imagine our country making world medical history, who would have thought. As George says, that is at least something for us to be proud of.

I got a letter from Billy this week, still at sea, for a long time this time, but our big excitement is his coming engagement – he really is a man now. George in one of his better moments wrote to say that when he was well again, he and I must sit with Billy and plan for his wedding date because we could probably make that the focal point of a Cape holiday next year, which would really be something for a family to work for.

Billy has a strong sense of the trouble at home and in his letter he wrote that seeing this year has been so very bad for us, the law of averages should now apply and things improve; he writes in every single letter or postcard, no matter how brief: Is Dad any better?

He's been on board ship five months and says he's very tired, working eight hours a day every single day since joining – no such thing as weekends off when a ship is on the ocean. Says he likes the life at sea but it's getting a bit too much; he was promoted to fifth engineer recently, but I have a hunch he's not going to stay in the navy all that much longer. They'll be in the Bay of Biscay soon and he thinks he'll spend Christmas deep sea, just south of the equator, and supposes that on New Year's Day he'll be in the Cape rollers three hundred miles from Cape Town.

He's due to dock early in January, then he plans to go to Port Elizabeth to see Sonya before coming up to us for about two weeks; what a lovely thought – me, George, Billy, Ryan, Chris and Sam under one roof after all this time.

Oh my Ryan: such a talented youngster but so troubled and *contra mundum* and a danger to himself; I think he inherited all George's fragile sensitivities, but none of his caution. Even the judges of that art competition said his work was not really youth art at all.

He has a recklessness and a self-destructiveness that truly frightens me and now he's left boarding school you never really and honestly know what he's getting up to in Johannesburg, though I always make a point of telling George that all is fine.

He is quite stern with the boy, I think perhaps precisely because he had high private expectations of him – as if, of all our sons, Ryan might be the one to succeed in the ways he himself feels he has not.

I would never say this to George in the current circumstances, but he is repeating his own family history – this is just what his mother and father did to him, and that always made him desperate for their approval, ending up feeling he was neither earning nor getting it.

Ryan's written to ask if I need him to come home – he says with Dad away again he thinks we need a grown man in the house, if you please! He wants to discuss this with me face to face as he is most concerned about his father, and my being here alone.

I think that's both sincere and also, probably, a way for him to save face with his friends because he's run out of money and has no job; I hope he has sown his wild oats and had a tummy full of Johannesburg, where I suspect he has been hanging around with a very bad bunch – on drugs, I'm sure.

I will say yes to him, of course, as it may be better for him to be in his own home until he is older.

I think he is happy at the thought of being home, and will be glad to have more time to work on his portfolio and do some batiks to earn extra cash; of course I know someone like him could never stay indefinitely in this *dorp*, but this break will give him time to marshal his forces and pay off his debts and help me out at the same time.

The younger boys too are so very obviously happy at the thought of him coming back, and that warms a mother's heart.

But the most important thing of all, for which I am so grateful, has been Rina's help in getting me this job with Mr Bernstein; we need the money desperately and thanks to her I've been given this chance.

Mr B knows I haven't worked in an office for twenty-five years but has been very patient and encouraging and it isn't as humiliating as I feared – not exactly the stuff of our family's earlier dreams, but there we are.

Luckily he doesn't know that my training a hundred years ago at that commercial college was hardly first class, but I'm actually learning quite a lot about secretarial work and bookkeeping – things are beginning to stick now and my brain is functioning; I think it had been beginning to rust!

It's a new life for me in a way.

I think a lot about the funny little cast of characters that now fills my days.

Miss Opperman from Ogies; I'm still not sure what she does.

The telephonist-cum-typist who has been said to be on honeymoon ever since I started and remains a mystery, something like a character from one of the Herman Charles Bosman stories who is always talked about but never actually appears.

A Mrs Potgieter, who has two young children and seems very nice, operates an accounting machine and certainly does not overwork herself – her husband is in the town planning department of the municipality.

Finally Mr B himself, forever coming in and out of the office like a tornado, switching everyone from one job to another – actually one never knows from one minute to the next what job one will do.

At the beginning I did a lot of typing, mostly the statements that need to have names and addresses on them before they make their way over to Mrs Potgieter's machine – I used an electric typewriter for the first time in my life; it is very fast and has a way of running away with you until you get used to it.

Mr B does the books and accounts for many places, the four biggest being the Curzon Hotel – our one, not the posh one in Johannesburg of course – Ballentines, Gemsbok Retreading, and Man About Town.

On one day I had to get through nineteen books of invoices from Ballentines, meaning that I checked the totals with strips done on the adding machine at the shop, checked invoice numbers, and on a good sixty-five per cent had to fill in surnames – the girls at Ballentines had failed to replace their carbons soon enough. As each book contains fifty invoices it means that I handled and checked almost a thousand as well as doing the switchboard and a few letters for Mr B.

Not too bad for a beginner, I thought.

I'm getting used to having to get up so very early, though now just about my only relaxation is listening to the nightly radio play in bed after I've washed my smalls, set out clothes and hat for the morning, written my daily letter to George, and before I fall asleep.

I'm too tired to read anything literary any more; I must ask Rina if we can go to the bioscope together one of these weekends.

The very hot weather and pressure of work seem to throw Mr B into a bit of a flap at times – he is helping the Curzon prepare to open an off-sales department. But I quite like the excitement; it takes my mind off everything else and that is good for me as I forget to fret. It's quite a mundane and probably meaningless way to spend one's life, but it is necessary and has the advantage of filling the days.

At any rate, he will suddenly call me to his office and ask me to do something like fix the mail and write up the post book, not registering that I've never done that before: on Monday he just blithely said, draw up a list of creditors as at February 28th for Gemsbok Retreading, be extremely accurate and don't forget to take into account post-dated cheques. My heart just sank but with a little help I did it and I now know considerably more about the whole set-up; I've done lots of extensions and totals of cash books without mistakes, cleared files and done licence applications, new and renewals.

I've started learning something about a trial balance and writing up on my own, so I'm coming on – it certainly isn't monotonous. I must gain all the experience I can, because it looks like I might need to use it for a long time to come if this family is going to survive, especially if it turns out that George can never work again.

I seem also to have become the staff representative somehow – a bossy nature, perhaps?

The ladies asked me to go and talk to Mr B to see if we couldn't alternate on Saturdays instead of all having to work every weekend; no one has any time to do their grocery shopping as we always finish after five on the weekdays, so I promised I would do so when the right opportunity arose.

It was a very rushed week with his temper very edgy and I didn't want to broach the subject, then on Saturday in walked Mrs Potgieter and said to me she was fed up and was going to resign because they had unexpected visitors from afar and she'd had to come to work.

When Mr B came in I cornered him and eventually persuaded him that two on and two off alternate Saturdays would be a good idea – he ended up by saying okay Mrs Jameson, you handle it whatever way you like, make your own arrangements.

I then went through and told the other three that it was all fixed and that two could be off as from next Saturday – they didn't believe it at first and then were so delighted that Mrs Potgieter said immediately, oh well in that case I won't resign; so I'm quite popular with the troops.

Mrs Potgieter's been helping me to write up the purchases journal for Gemsbok Retreading, March 1966 to February 1967, and that gives a rough idea of just how much backlog there is. And as I told George, he'd be surprised if he knew how many big nobs in this town owe hundreds of rands on their credit accounts to the shops and pay only occasionally in dribs and drabs, so ours isn't the only family that is financially embarrassed, it would seem.

He's a very decent chap, Mr B.

When he gave me my first pay cheque I asked him if he would please arrange to have PAYE taken off and he said he had already deducted it. I said, but Mr B then you have made a mistake because I have only worked three weeks, and he replied, I know that, it was no mistake, I have paid you for four weeks. Well that was a nice thing to do and it makes me feel good – he was satisfied with my work.

I decided to put the R94.80 into our bank and then withdraw R20 and put it into my savings account; that will build up nicely for the day when we have to meet our joint income tax.

I told George this, because he continually writes from the hospital how worried he is about income tax now that I'm working – he fills up letters with long screeds of calculations – and I hoped it would cheer him up, but sometimes I wonder in the poor man's state whether the feeling of personal shame doesn't outweigh the relief.

I told him very directly on the phone that this attitude was rot, and I wouldn't put up with it – somebody had to be bringing in extra money, and that was that. He just went quiet on the subject.

Rina kindly offered to let Ryan use their spare room when he comes home, but I said I think I'll move Sam's bed into my bedroom; he says he doesn't mind so I'll push the dressing table against the window to make space for it and Ryan can sleep in

Sam's room and work on his batiks. I'm going to ask Enoch to scrub the old table under the apricot trees and move it in; with the small reading light on the bookshelves and the windows wide for air, it will not be a bad studio for him.

Sam is still doing his little family scrapbooks. It's fascinating to see how he views the world. He presents us all as being famous for something, I don't know why, but which is quite funny given our actual circumstances. George is a famous gardener and I am a famous worker. Billy a famous sailor, Ryan a famous artist, Chris a famous motorbike rider, and so on.

Perhaps in his mind we need to be what we are not; he does seem to be a child who lives in his own imagination much of the time.

He wrote a short story called *The Horrible Greasy Fat Man*, which is hilarious. He writes a lot about the Transkei though that is a long time ago now; happy memories for him I think, and he constantly asks when we can go back there to live with his Dad: he has got it into his mind, and I don't see why I should have to take away any comforting fantasies at his age, that George's sudden absences are because he has to go back to finish some work in the old house in Libode.

This could cause problems, I know – his teacher told me she'd heard him giving this story out in the playground – but for the moment I am going to let it be. I still haven't got to the bottom of how he came by that black eye like a king-size golf ball; he says he collected a cricket bat in the face and I hope it was just an accident, as he insists it was. Says he was wicketkeeper and the batsman was a little too enthusiastic.

I did hear from Mrs Starky that some boys at school rag him about his father never being at the sports events, but I don't know if there's any connection and I've enough real worries without making up others.

Anyway, everyone at the school was rushing around madly for butter and such, and Mrs Craven had him flat out and well plastered – I suspect in the end he thoroughly enjoyed the attention once the pain had subsided, but he was very lucky indeed to escape with his eye.

I must remember to take him to the OK Bazaars for his haircut on Saturday, and I must get my own hair done before I start to look as worn out as I feel – the Jamesons have to keep up appearances, you know!

While Rina was away I went to the Scouts and Cubs AGM at the church hall. The business of the meeting over, the young scouts and cubs put on a small concert which everyone thoroughly enjoyed; as their acts were entirely their own inspiration and production it was quite fun.

The best effort was a Zulu war dance – this was Sam's class – mainly due to the enthusiasm of the performers; though their sense of rhythm was not too good and nor their voices, they enjoyed themselves so much that everybody else did too. At one point another group of children sang *Ten Little Nigger Boys* and Sam whispered to me furiously: Dad says that's a *very bad word*; the child doesn't forget a thing he hears adults say. And he's not a bit shy on the stage – he strides out and speaks up; should be quite adequate with a little encouragement.

It's hard to believe he has turned eight; how the years fly by.

I got a letter from my aunt in Port Elizabeth, which made me cry. Said she was thinking about me because on the wireless they'd just played *At the Balalaika*, which used to be George's and my signature tune and she could picture us dancing.

Also one from my aunt in Benoni, who really does care about me. She was so sorry to hear of our great trouble again with George's latest breakdown, and said medical science has advanced so much in the last few years, surely they must find something to cure brain affections too.

She said it seems women were meant to carry so many burdens in life – it was better I was working, for being alone all day in a house at present would be really bad for me while this way I could be at home for the evenings, which is most important for the boys, and I shouldn't worry too much about the eternal cleaning.

Of course Rina wanted to know about George.

I told her I'm really struggling and this time I have no idea how it's all going to end.

I said to be honest with her I'm terrified about what is going to happen to us and often feel angry with him for putting us in this situation, then I feel awfully guilty; I hate the thought of him in those horrid demeaning places – what a terrible position to end up in for a proud, good man.

I had a letter from a priest who had kindly visited him at the nursing home in Durban, saying he seemed reasonably well – what does that mean, *reasonably*? He wrote that I should not worry unduly as he felt sure that with a good rest and our prayers, my husband would recover completely. But of course he had to say that, he's a priest.

The most frightening thing of all is that George keeps writing to say that the doctors believe the cause of all this horror is physical, not mental, and so he thinks they are just waiting until they come across the right diagnosis and medication, or operation.

What George doesn't know is that this Dr Lukic has written to me himself. He says he is sure my husband's condition is not due to any organic disease of the central nervous system or other physical illness.

So what the doctor is saying is the exact opposite of what George is writing to me – he's deluding himself and it's just the same as it was with his work: deluding himself that he could somehow do the parts he agreed with, and avoid those he didn't. It's this kind of contradiction that is contributing to his condition, I'm sure, and unfortunately it just seems to be getting worse as time goes on.

I've given up the thought of trying to find another psychiatrist for a second opinion – I think I was clutching at straws – and it is the considered view of George's family that this doctor is the right man for the job; they are impressed with him even though he is very young. The doctor wants me to go down to Durban because there are some more consent forms I have to sign. I am terrified of these treatments, above all the shock treatment for which I had to sign special permission and clearance before they did it.

I fear from his latest letters it has made him quite unclear – and everyone knows what a clear speaker and writer George always was.

His side of the family is doing a lot to help, though they have their difficulties with me having never thought I really cut the mustard. His mother is hard with me, to the extent that George wrote to say he was sorry about how she had spoken to me.

But having said that, I suppose his parents, his brother and his sister have been going out of their way even though it is inconvenient and disruptive for them with their own full lives.

I wrote to his mother and father.

I told them not to worry about me, I am going to be all right, I was glad he was near them, I knew they would help him; that he is so tired and has fought against this thing so hard and so long, that he deserves to get well but this time it must not be rushed and every avenue must be explored. I told them he was so worried about them seeing him swing up and down uncontrollably, and that they needed to be gentle with him. He's desperate for their approval as I said, and this situation just takes it further and further away.

I sent ten rand as he requested, so he won't have to ask them for cash.

He wrote that he felt he was far too dependent on his sister Emma down there, but says as things stand we just have to bow to circumstances and make ourselves feel real gratitude – she's having to get him all the small things he needs, like toiletries. This is so difficult for me because Emma makes little pretence about my unsuitability for the family; sometimes I wonder if they think I am somehow responsible for what has happened.

She wrote to me in the middle of all this to say that although she was very sorry for me and she and her husband appreciated the fact that life was not at all easy for me, they had to give their views in a forthright manner. She said George was indulging in self-pity, she hoped I would realise that her letter wasn't easy to write, and that I should take it in the right spirit: I am only trying to help, she said, and trying to get to the core of your problems. She said we should face up to and accept the fact that there is no treatment and no medicine which can be a cure in this matter – it simply requires willpower.

This is the type of attitude I mean.

She said her husband, who is a big wig at Goodridge Tyres, was very busy, which I took to mean that he did not need George's difficulties in close proximity – but perhaps it was me being oversensitive by then. They are going to Rhodesia for Christmas to visit friends.

I am having to send clothes to George.

After work one day last week I shot down to Man About Town and bought a safari suit on appro which I hope he will like, a lovely drip dry, good quality with a cool loose weave. I told him it is a gift from the children and myself in advance of Christmas, with lots of love, and I sent it to Natal under registered post.

I'm also having to deal with George's office a lot, and they are actually being very reassuring and saying things are all right; the man who is standing in for him even went to the trouble of bringing George's salary cheque to my office – they're being issued on the fifteenth of the month nowadays.

Even a senior fellow in Johannesburg telephoned, stressing it was not an official call; he just wanted to know personally how George was. I suspected he was trying to find out how long he would be away, but he said I should not worry too much about that side of things, and he is arranging for a temporary assistant to pick up some of the workload.

George took this news well, even saying that with an experienced assistant he thought he might be able to get started again and manage. It was the first time in a long while that he talked about ever being able to go back to work again, so he must have been thinking in a better frame of mind – at least at the time of writing that letter.

I telephoned the head office and asked them to investigate his sick leave position.

A woman from personnel phoned back, very nice, and gave me the answers: as at the day he fell ill again, 24th October, he had seventy-one days sick leave due because of his long service – more than thirty years, to my surprise – and this will carry him right to the year's end. On 1st January the new three-year cycle of sick leave commences, so Pretoria says he should stop worrying and just get well.

I think that is wonderful and should ease a lot of his worry. But then he harbours so very much anger inside him – at himself as much as the Government – and of course he blames himself for not having had the courage to leave long ago. I've said to him this is a useless, circular way of thinking about things that cannot be changed, and I said will you now forget that you have a job at all – everything is being taken care of at this end.

A letter arrived for him at the house this week from one of the most senior men in the Department, which I opened.

This man clearly does not know what has happened. He wrote that he had just come from the Department's conference at Pietersburg and on one of the major items the Minister himself said they must consult George because of his knowledge of Zululand and Pondoland in particular, that he might have some solutions to propose about the problems that are developing – actually, precisely the problems George predicted in the first place. When might it be convenient for him to travel to Pretoria to meet the Minister?

What an irony. Suddenly they pay attention again to him and his views! It's a churlish thought, I know, but I'd like to see their faces if he turned up at the Union Buildings in a straitjacket. Anyway, I find myself in a pickle, not knowing whether to send the letter on or whether it will distress him further; it's just sitting there on the telephone table now.

I'm so glad the high summer's come even though the days are now such scorchers; I'm trying to keep up the garden for when he comes home because that's so important to him: he writes as much about his fuchsias as anything else. His Barbertons are going on blooming and the trees are heavily laden with fruit; I shall be able to make lots of lovely jam. The hydrangeas along the back wall look beautiful, too; they remind me of our Kentani ones in the Transkei and I must show George as soon as he gets back. And doesn't our little old Mountbatten Avenue look grand with its jacarandas ablaze right down the street.

I wonder where he will spend this Christmas in the end; there have been so many false dawns about him being discharged.

This time when he comes home, it will be for good, I just know it; this time is make or break – and this family is going to make. On the fridge I've stuck up a cutting I clipped from a magazine.

> Despair is sin, so never let it steal into your mind
> Though you've taken many blows and fate has been unkind
> things will take a turn if you can hold out long enough
> The outlook may be grim and gloomy and the going rough
> but when you reach the valley where shadows round you close
> it always comes out fine again for that's the way it goes.

Hardly up to the standard of my favourite Keats, I know, but it gave me a little lift when I needed one.

II

IT was a jolting experience, being able to eavesdrop on my
parents in my imagination like that. It was as if my father and
mother came fully alive in my head, as if I had been there in those
rooms with them nearly forty years before. At times I felt there
was something ghoulish and abnormal about what I was doing
– should I be fiddling with bones in this way? – and I wondered
whether this fitting together of fragments was recreating real
people, or a fiction of my own.

But in spite of my doubts I was in too deep to stop now; the
box could not be resealed. I had to find out. My behaviour became
obsessive. Almost every moment I had away from my office I
devoted to the reconstruction of the story; I could not stop. My
family felt the brunt of the compulsion. My wife was worried but
said she understood what was driving me, didn't mind losing me

for some time in this way, as long as I was sure that digging and raking in graves was healthy for me – that it was healing wounds not reopening them, that I was sure I would return at the end of the journey, and not disappear entirely. It would be awful, she said, if it ended up tipping me into one of my own periodic episodes of depression.

But I told her I was sure it would be to the good, that this was something I should have done a long time ago. She said only I could know whether that was true. My brothers and other relatives were sceptical – even alarmed – when I told them what I was doing, but they did not try to stop me. Eventually, when they got used to the idea, they began to send me bits and pieces, saved shreds of their own from those days.

By the time I was able to conjure the voices from the ward and the kitchen, I had already spent months on my project. I had read the letters from dozens of thick paper-clipped bundles, looked at hundreds of photographic slides neatly ordered in old-fashioned plastic circular canisters. I had pored over scrapbooks, yellowed newspaper cuttings, programmes and souvenirs of theatre shows long forgotten, speeches, stories written in another age. I had put together scraps of diaries, read school reports, seen medical accounts, old bills; I had fingered the faded insignias of rank from wartime. I had listened to tape recordings, hours upon hours of them, from an Africa and Europe of earlier generations; heard the scratchy radio announcements of the times, the voices of politicians long dead. I had touched locks of hair even, found amateur poems shyly written then hidden so long ago. I had immersed myself in this private cornucopia, an extraordinary archive of an ordinary family which happened to be my own; it had unlocked in me memories I did not know I had.

It was time to start the story at its beginning, and to bring it to its end. And I thought I knew enough now to complete the journey.

LONG BEFORE THEN

Zulu Lands, 1916

BABANANGO was one of the smallest places in what was then called the Union of South Africa, and here it was that George Jameson was born in the summer of 1916. The village was ringed by the battlefields where the impis of King Cetshwayo and the soldiers of Queen Victoria once butchered each other; places like Isandhlwana, Ulundi, and Intaleni. Blood River itself was only an arm's length away.

George was the first child of Milton Jameson, cattle farmer and trader; a jovial, tall, beefy, ruddy-looking man whose skin blushed a singed-looking pink in the African sun. Milton was also born in Zululand, one of the eight sons of Lucas Jameson, the first of the family to settle there. Lucas had been sent off to Africa by his father, the Dean of Chichester Cathedral in England, because it was supposed that the climate might help the boy recover from consumption.

Milton grew up in the village of Umzinto, when white settlement in Zululand was still very new. At thirty he married Enid, middle daughter of a well-to-do family from Greytown, and they went to settle in Babanango. In those days, across the old Zulu kingdom stretching north from the lower Tugela River to the southern border of Portuguese East Africa, were spread only a few thousand white people, mostly English-speaking but including some Boer farmers. There were more than a quarter of a million Zulus and, in the Nqutu district, also a small settlement of Basutos.

Zululand was a carpet of hills and plateaus rolled out from the foothills of the great mountain chain of the Drakensberg to the Indian Ocean. It was subtropical and green, well watered and wooded, a country of powerful rivers, wild game and thornbush. Milton Jameson used to say it was a place that got into the blood and the brain and wouldn't get out again. He had a poetic turn of phrase, and used to recite poetry in the evenings.

He said the history of Zululand was both tragic and romantic, that the human drama of the surrounding lands attached itself to all who lived on them, stayed even if they left. There were bleached human bones still to be found lying on the battlefield at the base of the Ghost Mountain nearby; no one would go near a mountain that was said to emit its own light at night, and make its own sounds.

In Zululand the only towns of any note were Eshowe and Melmoth, and there were many hamlets like Babanango, with a hotel and a general trading store for Zulus and Europeans alike, and not much else. It was a land in which cattle mattered a great deal to all the human beings living on it. These Jamesons were country people. They ventured into the province of Natal only once a year, travelling to Pietermaritzburg for the Royal Agricultural Show.

When George Jameson was delivered by a midwife in the main bedroom of the Babanango homestead, it was an event in the district. The Great War was raging in Europe and the birth of a baby was seen as a talisman of hope. It also signalled to the villagers that the Jamesons were staying, planting bulbs that would flower and trees that would provide shade only in future seasons. Impermanence was in the blood of white settlers; it was the knowledge that the place they loved used to belong to someone else.

George was promenaded in his baby carriage through the few streets of the village and there were admiring visitors to the house – the largest in the area, encircled by a wide open veranda with fine concrete pillars holding up a tin roof, and an imposing flight of stairs to the front door.

He came into a world made up of strange and magical words, many of them long and difficult to memorise. Umgungunhlovu and Isandhlwana, Dingaan's Kraal and the Tugela; Mtubatuba, Hluhluwe, Umfolozi, Pongola. Even the English names were mysterious: Ultimatum Tree, Coward's Bush, Fort Mistake.

At first they were all just like musical notes to him but these places, and especially the pure Zulu language spoken in them, became real to George long before the white cities of the Union. The other language of Africa he took into his heart was Afrikaans; it was as though in this place, English, his first, was his third.

He developed into a well-looking and quite strong boy, frontier stock, with a handsomely proportioned face topped by thick waves of light healthy hair. He was clever, sensitive, impeccably mannered, a perfectionist, hard on himself with a shadow of self-doubt and fearfulness.

The time came for him to be sent to Babanango Government School, where he topped his class. Though the class was tiny, it was his entire universe. He loved language and excelled at reading and recitation, grammar, composition and spelling, in English and Afrikaans. By the time he took his Natal Primary School examination, he was praised by his head teacher as a scholar of great promise, and it was decided to send him to Pietermaritzburg College as a boarder.

Fourteen years old and away from home for the first time, George was lonely and fragile but covered for it by working hard. In languages he outstripped the form; there were now more than twenty boys in his class. He played sport with enthusiasm, but was unexceptional. By the time he reached his matriculation year he took, with his father's support, the highly unusual decision to add an extra subject to his curriculum: Zulu Language. The school had to hire a special teacher for the purpose, who awarded his pupil ninety per cent in his final examination.

The headmaster scribbled on his report: First Class Matric – splendid. Great linguistic ability. A most able pupil and consistent worker. I expect him to do very well.

But this was 1933, in the years of the world economic depression, and although the Jameson family was not starving, choices were constrained. George had to forgo his dream of entering the University of Natal to take a higher degree in Zulu Language: what he had to do, his father told him, was go out and find a steady job that carried with it some income and security.

There was a fateful moment when wealthy Uncle Stanton, the patriarch of the extended family, considered making a loan to George to allow him to go to university after all, but he was a proud young man and decided that the obligation would be too great. The wily trader had in any case set conditions that George thought would keep him in the older man's thrall for the rest of his life. He declined to make that bargain.

George considered what he had to offer, and to whom, a callow white boy from a remote corner of remote Zululand. Facility with language, especially Zulu, was the only answer he could come up with. He wanted to cling to his dream of becoming eventually a professor of Zulu, or an anthropologist, or archaeologist; but those gentle pursuits would have to wait. He wrote out a job application to the Public Service; the Union Department of Native Affairs. In the Union of South Africa the Governor General ruled black people through this Native Department, with Magistracies spread across the land like the fingers of a splayed hand. George got his job, and started adult life as a knuckle on the smallest of those fingers.

In 1934 a letter arrived at the Jameson homestead in Babanango.

Sir,

I have the honour to inform you that it has been decided to appoint you to a Second Grade Clerkship on the Natal establishment of this Department at Ingwavuma on twelve months' probation with salary at the rate of £140 per annum. Kindly present your medical certificate to the Magistrate, Babanango, who, if it appears to be in order, will issue the necessary rail warrant for your journey to Ingwavuma. As your services are urgently required, I am to request that you will report for duty to the Native Commissioner, Ingwavuma, as soon as possible, advising this office beforehand.

I have the honour to be, Sir,
Your obedient servant,
R S Pendlethwaite,
Secretary for Native Affairs

Scarcely out of his teens, George set off for northern Zululand. Ingwavuma was even more remote than Babanango, more than a hundred rough miles to the north and east, on the very border of Swaziland and Portuguese East Africa. He was nervous of striking out alone, but also excited – he was ready to leave behind his boyhood. At Ingwavuma he launched into his work, and the schoolboy metamorphosed into a smartly attired figure of some gravitas. He appeared to be respected and welcomed by his seniors, and his perfect Zulu was remarked upon. He began to like the feeling of authority. A year later Mr Pendlethwaite wrote to indicate that George's probation period was over, and that he was to be given an increase in salary.

George was delighted by this and set about obtaining the qualifications in law which he knew were essential if he was to progress in the bureaucracy. Again he did well, passing his examinations at the first attempt. Pendlethwaite – his only connection to the imagined but as yet unseen metropoles – wrote from Cape Town to congratulate him on successfully passing the Union Civil Service Lower Law Examination.

After four years, George was diligent enough to earn promotion to the position of Clerk of the Court and Correspondence Clerk, Umbumbulu, above the Umkomaas River. He made the short trek with a light heart: he was no longer the most junior official in the Magistracy. He continued to gather qualifications as fast as he could, and sat several more examinations. In 1939 Mr Pendlethwaite wrote again, this time addressing George as *My dear Jameson*. Pendlethwaite offered congratulations on his achievements, and encouraged him to continue to study legal principles and the decisions of the superior courts throughout his career – this would be invaluable as he moved on to the higher posts in the Department.

George was flattered and encouraged by the attention from the rarefied heights. And after only a year at Umbumbulu, his hopes were rewarded. He was appointed as Native Commissioner of Ndwedwe, further up the north coast. The clerking days were over sooner than he had dared hope, and real responsibility was in his hands – entire authority, in fact, albeit in a small place. Now, when invitations to official functions came, they were addressed to him as The Native Commissioner. Things were going exceedingly well for a young man who'd had few options, and he allowed himself to dream of high office and honour.

Then the Second World War erupted in Europe, flinging into disarray the plans of countless young men around the world like George Jameson of Zululand. He enlisted immediately in the Natal Mounted Rifles and was made a sergeant. He expected to be sent to the North African theatre, along with all his white friends – they referred to themselves as Europeans more often than they did as white South Africans – where they would be called upon to prove their courage as men, fighting Nazism. He was proud of General Jan Smuts and the position he had adopted on the war. He felt youthful patriotism and even flashes of bravado. In his private thoughts he was frightened, because he did not believe himself to be naturally courageous, but he was ready, and pleased he had not been tempted to explore the *sotto voce* suggestion that his father and influential uncle might somehow arrange for him to avoid enlistment. The Union Department of Native Affairs granted him leave of absence.

He went through his combat training, read everything he could find about North Africa, and discovered that his childhood hunting forays had made him a superb marksman. He was ready to go to war. Though a gentle soul he was able, like so many other young men in the world, to make the adjustment. He told his parents he believed he would be capable of killing another human being if he had to, just as he had been able to shoot a hippopotamus at St Lucia when he did not want to. In his young and romantic mind he thought there were two fundamental rites of passage for human beings, rites that proved their individual worth: for women, natural childbirth; for men, combat in war. He daydreamed that he would return a victorious veteran, to be admired by his family and to find a pretty young wife.

But he did not board the northbound train with his unit. A staff officer at Natal Command headquarters withdrew his file from that of the pile of local recruits, and twice underlined the words *Exceptionally proficient in Zulu Language*. George's orders were countermanded. He was summoned to divisional headquarters, commissioned as an officer with the rank of lieutenant, and sent immediately to help found the Native Military Corps, a new unit of four black battalions being formed to provide military guards and garrison protectors, armed with assegais. At the base at Palmietkuil in the north east of the country, he did well enough to be promoted to captain. He had the rank, the uniform, and the men; he waited to see action.

As the wait dragged on into 1940, George was asked to give motivational talks at military functions. He was shy of public speaking, but good at it once he got going. At one event he noticed a dark-haired young girl, prettily petite, smiling as he spoke from the platform. When tea was served he approached her cautiously and asked her name. She was Jean Stockley, five years his junior, a clerk of the South African Women's Auxiliary Services stationed at Boksburg-Benoni Hospital in the Transvaal. She was smitten with the tall, dashing, moustachioed officer in his brown army uniform, and he determined to woo her. When his leave came he drove across the country to ask if she would go with him to visit his beloved Zululand. They went to Natal's beaches together; she shyly in a one-piece bathing suit, he in khaki army swimming shorts that reached to his knees, strong chest nonchalantly bared. They were photographed on a beach in wartime; under her hat she sipped bashfully at a cocktail through a long straw, and he towered over her, pipe in one hand and an arm draped around her shoulders like a bear shielding a small cub.

Jean was presented to the *faux*-dynastic Jameson clan. The family was accepting rather than embracing of her, as they had a sense of genealogical grandeur and she was from modest beginnings in Benoni, a *dorp* of the East Rand near Johannesburg. Jean said simply it was where she came from, she'd had no say in the matter. George's parents could not quite understand why their eldest son and heir would spurn the many attractive farm girls of the district who had considerable prospects of inheritance, but they did not stand in his way. The young man and woman were evidently in love and enthralled with one another, and in 1941 they were engaged. In June of the following year their marriage warranted a report in *The Star*, Johannesburg's main newspaper, accompanied by a photograph.

A PRETTY BENONI WEDDING
Captain George Milton Jameson
and Miss Jean Nora Stockley

ST DUNSTAN'S Church, Benoni, was the scene of a pretty wedding on Monday afternoon when Jean, younger daughter of Mrs M B Stockley and the late Mr W J Stockley, of Benoni, was married to Captain George Jameson, elder son of Mr and

Mrs M F Jameson, of Babanango, Zululand.

The bride made a charming picture in an exquisite gown of white needle-run lace, modelled on graceful lines with a full circular train and featuring the new low waistline, leg-o'-mutton sleeves and a heart-shaped neckline, worn over a foundation of georgette and taffeta. Her filmy tulle veil fell from a Court headdress of tulle and lilies-of-the-valley, and she carried a shower bouquet of white camellias, gladioli and carnations. The maid of honour wore a charming period frock of rose pink georgette, made with panniered skirt and gauged bodice, while the bridesmaids featured Empire waistlines, shirred bodices and fully flared skirts.

The bridegroom and all the men were in uniform. About 200 people attended the reception at the Benoni Town Hall, where Mrs Stockley received her guests in a handsome two-piece ensemble of pale cyclamen romaine, inset with lace appliqués. When the young couple left for their honeymoon, which is being spent at the Natal coast and in Zululand, the bride wore a modish powder blue bouclé suit, the jacket being trimmed with heart-shaped pockets and worn over a white angora blouse. Her chic halo hat was of powder blue fur felt.

Telegrams, read at the reception, were received from all over the Union. In addition there was a unique message from the men of the Native Military Corps, signed by Corporals L Dhlamini and M Luthuli, which read, in Zulu and in English: Wishing you matchless prosperity and happiness in your matrimony.

A year later Jean was pregnant, and in 1944 at the government hospital in Vryheid, Natal, gave birth to their first son Billy. When at last George was demobbed and transferred to the Reserve of Officers of the Union Defence Forces, he returned eagerly to his career. He found himself promoted to the post of Native Affairs Commissioner of Nkandhla, in the region of Zululand where he was born, and where his father still plied his trade. It was a big step up from Ndwedwe; in the arcane world of the Government bureaucracy, the equivalent of a gold star for a promising youngster, or a prefectship at school.

Nazism had been crushed and Field Marshal Smuts said the conclusion of the war provided South Africa with the historic opportunity of looking into itself and resolving its own injustices. This George embraced with all his young heart. At Nkandhla he and Jean set up their first home and befriended the few other young whites in the village. He began to build a library of Zulu texts which he annotated, and he gave a good account of the Jameson name in the district. His own little boy was growing and he and Jean had already decided that they would like to have a large family. She was happy making their home, nursing the child, and being wife to an up-and-coming young official in the area who was respected and popular and always invited to important occasions, in the towns and the kraals. She accompanied him to every function and made sure she did him credit. The frail little girl who had spent so much of her childhood in bed reading voraciously, her own dreams of becoming a ballerina defeated by slightness and occasional infirmity, had found a good man with prospects, principled and kind. They had a delightful son. Their world seemed in order, with purpose and pleasure.

George was proud – though inwardly ambivalent – to be awarded the War Medal and the Africa Service Medal. While he did not think about it as much any more, he struggled to shed the regret of not having fought at Tobruk with his friends, even if he knew it had not been his own choice. He found it difficult to stay in a room when others were recounting their war exploits, and he disappointed Jean bitterly by refusing to join the veterans' clubs which sprang up across the country. They did not attend the dances at the MOTH hall, because he said he would feel like a fraud; he'd had an easy war. He never wore his medals – in fact never took them out of the clear plastic containers in which they were delivered by the army. Jean quietly put them and their ribbons into a scrapbook.

Time passed quickly and peacefully at Nkandhla. George enjoyed his work, which he described as providing a bridge between the kraals, villages and towns of Zululand. There was still in the country a kind of post-war dazedness, torpor in the small towns. People of all colours and station just concentrated on rebuilding their lives. George thrived in these circumstances, and was proud to develop a reputation in the surrounding communities as a man to be trusted and turned to for help. His burgeoning Zulu-text library was gaining some fame in the area, and he was overjoyed when, at a village meeting, a senior headman referred to him as Professor. He began a respectful correspondence with the great Zulu writer R R R Dhlomo, and was so delighted to be taken seriously by him that he kept the letters in a special drawer in his study.

In 1948, at the age of thirty-two, George had been in his post for four years. His small family was thriving. He had every expectation of further promotion, and perhaps even a move to the Department's head office itself, now that he had proved himself in the field. He had read Solomon Plaatje's *Native Life* several times, had just finished studying Leo Marquard's *The Native in South Africa*, and had devoured all Olive Schreiner's polemical essays. He felt he was becoming truly expert in the subject of his work. He planned to write to Pendlethwaite again, to test the waters and see what he might have in mind now that Smuts had declared that the 'Native Question' was a national priority. He hoped he could play a role in this momentous matter. Jean gave birth to a second son, Ryan, at the government hospital in Eshowe, and the house was filled with the warmth of family.

Like millions of his countrymen, George was wholly unprepared for what came next. In the national election, the first since the war ended, Smuts was defeated and the National Party swept into office. The extended Jamesons, in the paternalistic post-colonial manner of the times, viewed the development as some kind of biblical catastrophe, sundering the natural order of things. They had thought that the Boer War put an end to such matters, they said to each other: Could this actually be true? George had never taken particular interest in party politics – though the views of his family and their circles were solidly with Smuts – but he recognised that this development might cause his own life to change in ways he could only begin to guess at.

He was by no means alone in the Public Service in wondering what the arrival in power of this different nationalism, itself born of struggle for survival and now preparing to cow others, would mean for him. The new regime said it would ring the changes in the Service it now controlled, and he guessed that the patrician, self-certain and self-satisfied British style – his own ingrained style and zone of comfort – would give way. Would Mr Pendlethwaite disappear and with him, to George's cast of mind, an old-worldliness and culture of what he called sensible liberalism? He had always proudly described himself as a liberal but not an *ultra*-liberal.

He felt deep ambivalence as Afrikaner power prepared to assert itself. He had since childhood sincerely and knowledgeably admired and loved the Afrikaner people and spoken the language beautifully – he told Jean he was proud to feel none of the superior prejudice many English-speakers affected – but now he was alarmed by the policies they would promote, and the fact that they would be free to promote them as they wished. These new leaders were not, he said, men like Jan Christiaan Smuts, whom he admired so much that he kept a bound copy of his lecture, *Freedom*, on his desk. In that book George had underlined a paragraph which came as close as anything else to serving as his own motto:

> *In a world of racial cleavages, in a world of growing economic nationalism and antagonisms, English and Afrikaans South Africans are busy closing ranks and building an enduring peace. Africa is once more true to her reputation for novelty. May she also yet find the formula of understanding and co-operation between white and black!*

He wrote to his parents: I may be wrong, but I fear these Nationalists will want to treat the black man as an unperson. This could lead to terrible things. And I don't know what it is going to mean for my job. Perhaps they will even want to chuck all us English out. And perhaps, even, I should get out and not be a part of what is to come? What do you think? He asked himself whether his easy love and respect for the Afrikaner might have been built on the assumption that his, and not their, people would always be in power.

Things did not change quickly, though he worried privately that even if the new rulers did not undertake a purge of the Service, they might leave him and his type to rot – or spin them further and further out into the peripheries. The uncertainty and shaky self-esteem that had been in his very tissue from childhood, began to press. He had no idea of what else he might do with his life: he had sought security, found it in some form, and all his actions had been predicated on the keeping of it.

In Nkandhla George talked tentatively to Jean about his worries and doubts, but they decided to wait it out and see what happened. They said perhaps it would not be so bad after all – he told himself he should not prejudge circumstances over which he had no control, as the war had surely taught him. He knew that this moment might be a dramatic stop and turn in the road, but for the present it was a matter of dealing with things as they came and not seeing patterns; that was the only way forward, as his father always said.

The new regime did not leave George to moulder. A letter arrived at his office in Nkandhla, informing him he was to be transferred with immediate effect. He was to be the Native Commissioner of Tsumeb, South West Africa, covering the entire district of Grootfontein. He had just finished studying Dhlomo's books *UCetshwayo*, *Indlela Yababi*, and *uNomalanga kaNdengezi*, as well as B Wallet Vilakazi's collection of Zulu poems, *Amal'ezulu*. His library was growing fast and he regretted that he was to be sent so far away from Zululand. But he was offered no choice and he, Jean, Billy, and baby Ryan had to prepare to undertake the great journey north.

George wondered what he should make of it all. It was a promotion, undoubtedly; Tsumeb was the administrative centre of a colossal district, and the town itself was on the cusp of importance. There must be some residual confidence in him in the corridors of power, he thought, if they were comfortable enough to entrust him with the posting. It could be an exciting experience, and even a chance to prove his worth to the new masters and perhaps gain respect as before. It was troubling that, unlike in days gone by, there had been no friendly and fraternal conversation with the Department, just a curt instruction, but it was a bigger posting and it came with a bigger salary. What could be read into that, other than that they had decided to keep him, that he remained secure?

Desert, 1948

THEY were headed for quite another Africa, George and the Jamesons. He began to read aloud to them stories of the great desert and the people of the open arid region known as South West, a South African Protectorate since the Germans had been driven out. It was in the far vastness of the west-of-south, near enough to touch the arc of the Kalahari. To its west, many hours' drive, the cold Atlantic. To the north, the colonial overlordship of Portuguese West Africa. To the east, beyond the Kalahari, the Bechuanaland Protectorate. To Jean it all sounded ominous, not romantic.

The family made the first of its epic journeys by rail. It took close to a week to reach the oasis town in the desert up north, and it was the purest hell – especially for Jean. She was disbelieving of the distance they had to travel, and petulantly declined to share George's interest in the places they passed on their winding, clattering way: Maseru, Bloemfontein, Kimberley, Upington, Keet-manshoop, Windhoek. Government officials travelled economy class, and George, Jean, Billy and Ryan were crammed into one compartment, stiflingly hot. They argued and bickered, and the changes of train at obscure sidings became interminable. Jean felt as if she was being sent to some awful *gulag*, and George was offended by her unwillingness to be optimistic, as he was having to put on a show of confidence himself. The South African Railways food was execrable and expensive, the boys whined when their parsimonious father would not fork out for more colddrinks, and the hamper Jean had packed was soon emptied. She was having to tend incessantly to the squalling baby.

When finally they got there George arrived not speaking the language of the Herero; he learned fast enough. To his library he added everything published by the anthropologist Phillip V Tobias of the University of the Witwatersrand, a man he admired and wished he could emulate. In Tsumeb he soon found he had greater freedom than he had anticipated. The radical changes in the policies and practices of his employer still had not come to pass, although an Act had been promulgated whereby the South African population was to be registered according to race, and issued with individual identity cards or reference books. The precise details were unclear to George, but the intent unavoidably obvious. The words *wait and see* were becoming a mantra in his life – a coward's mantra, he sometimes thought – and he knew this approach could not forever be without its misfortunes. Segregation had been in place for centuries, but this would take it to a new and, in his view, flammable level. How, he asked himself, could one manage fairly and honourably the interface of the races in such a deteriorating atmosphere?

But for the moment it was still the Union Native Department of the Union of South Africa that he worked for; the declaration of a Republic and withdrawal from the Commonwealth were in the future. The word Bantu, historically noble in his view, had not yet been commandeered by the State and made ignoble and insulting in its usage. So on he pressed with the work at which he was becoming ever more adept, and which came with ever-increasing authority and status.

In the oasis town George was indeed a big man. His letter of appointment placed him in charge of a sub-district of some eight thousand square miles, on which there were two hundred and nineteen farms. Sometimes he felt, with a degree of private pleasure, that these official dispatches read like orders to a governor of some remote outpost of empire; which in some ways they actually were. His own father had recently become interested in having the family history documented, and commissioned the College of Heralds in England to produce a family tree. It painted a picture of gradually fading gentility, a fanning out over the world which began in 1550 in the southern English town of Chichester and nearby village of Itchenor. George had pored endlessly over the enormous piece of parchment with its ornate and delicate calligraphy, fascinated as he was by the genealogy of others and now faced with his own.

He found, in addition to the grandees of Chichester, another grand ancestor, Sir Adrian Jameson, who had been a real Governor: of Ceylon in the 1930s, and Hong Kong in the 1940s. Tsumeb did not have quite that ring to it, George admitted to himself, but then it was not nothing either. He and Jean developed a secret dream. One day they would travel to Europe together, just the two of them, and they would visit all the places which had somehow produced pale people who would become Africans and come to live in places like Babanango and Tsumeb, hundreds of years later. They started a special savings account in a post office book, which they referred to as The Overseas Account. They calculated it would take ten years to save enough for two aeroplane flights and coaches and hotels and guided tours in England.

The posting being sudden, it was a frantic rush to glean some knowledge of the place he had been sent to. George found out: Tsumeb, from the Bushman word *Tsomsoub* meaning, according to some, place of copper. To others, a hole dug in loose ground; still others said it was from the Otjiherero, *Otjisume*, a place of frogs. He guessed that the form in which it appeared on the contemporary maps must be the spelling determined by German colonists during their times. The Tsumeb of his days was in the throes of becoming a boom town in a great hurry. Astonishing mineral deposits, famed from prehistoric times, were now considered to be commercially exploitable. In the 1890s a European explorer had heard of a pipe that broke through the earth and stood as a glittering outcrop nearly fifty feet into the air. The Hain//om Bushmen and Herero had mined it, and copper ore had been traded with the Ovambo at Lake Otjikoto. The adventurer was shown the way to the place and saw a sight the likes of which he said he would never again see in his life. The rush began at the turn of the century.

More than fifty years on an American company was establishing a gigantic lead mine. Railway tracks were being laid from Walvis Bay, fortune hunters and work-seekers were streaming in. The problems associated with the creation of an instant oasis in the desert were in large part the new Commissioner's problems. Among other things, housing had to be built for the thousands of labourers who had materialised in the town. George relished these responsibilities. The young and well-liked Native Commissioner, doubling, as always, as Magistrate, was elected Chairman of the Village Management Board. He was also Receiver of Revenue, District Accountant, Marriage Officer, Immigration Officer, and Representative of the Customs and Excise Department. He was Presiding Officer at mining inquiries, which became frequent. The census declared that Tsumeb was a town of two and a half thousand Europeans and five thousand Natives, and George was its king.

He struck up a great friendship with one his clerks, Jan van Doorn, who was based at a satellite station in South West Africa so small it made Tsumeb seem a metropolis by comparison. They sat together at the Minen Hotel, drinking *Cuca* beer from Portuguese West Africa and watching the dust devils in the distance. George made a note of one of their exchanges. GJ: I bet when you became a civil servant you didn't dream it would involve all this – everything except desk work. JvD: *Ja*, measuring the height of the river each day at midday, manning the water pumps, repairing the generators, reporting on the radio to Windhoek every morning and every night. And now you have me also looking after the camels – no one told me there were camels in South West! I'm a bloody camel vet most of the time, as they get those thorns stuck in their feet. They weren't made for South West, camels.

The two friends took to their frontier existence, dressing the part in bush hats and khaki jackets with epaulettes. They made forays into Ovamboland, travelling up the single road through Oshivelo to Ondangwa and Oshakati, and once as far as Ruacana. George admired the Ovambo stools, carved from single tree trunks, and proudly bought a pair for the house, which Jean immediately invested with the status of family heirlooms for a little group of unwitting itinerants that cared about such things.

George and his friend got into a scrape when a farmer, who he had fined a substantial sum for sharp practices, brought charges of his own that the two had hunted guinea fowl on his land without his permission or a permit – an allegation which was, in fact, quite true. A countryside compromise was eventually hammered out, involving placatory exchanges of biltong and the return of several guinea fowl carcasses. There was a simplicity to this life for people like them, and George did not spend much time thinking about what might be happening far down south in places like Pretoria, Cape Town, or Bloemfontein.

He took up two different causes: those of the Bushmen of the Kalahari and the *bywoners*, poor white tenant farmers. He regarded the position of the Bushmen as nothing short of tragic, and feared for their future as the steamroller of civilisation crushed their ancient desert lifestyle. He worked with the police stations on the fringes of the desert, supplying salt, tobacco and mealie meal to border posts, and eventually porridge once the nomads felt safe enough to venture out from their hunting lands. Whether this would help them, he did not know, and he wondered if he might not be creating a dependency that did more harm than good. He toyed with the idea of writing a proposal to the Department that a swathe of desert be declared a permanent reserve into which others may not go, but decided that this would not be well received by the policy makers.

The *bywoners* had approached him to rail against the unfairness of the rule which said that only landowners could hunt for the pot on the surrounding plains. We are the poorest of the whites already, they said, and now we must starve as well. They sent a delegation to the Commissioner's office in the town, and George received them personally to listen to their troubles. He found he agreed with their case and promised to investigate and raise the matter with Windhoek. A burly *bywoner*, Gerhardus Tromp, grasped his hand at the end of the meeting and looked George in the eyes with the passion of a frontiersman: *Meneer*, he said, if you do this for us, I say here and now that the first kudu I shoot will be yours.

George was successful in proposing the change and a fortnight later, while the family was preparing for its evening meal, a rickety truck pulled up in the driveway, driven by a grinning Tromp. On the back was the largest dead kudu bull George had ever seen, and Jean shrieked in horror – though Tromp took it for delight. The family spent the next week skinning the giant buck, and Billy ground meat for sausages until his hands were raw and his back ached. Jean hated the whole process and was reminded, by the gore and the stench, of how little she liked this place and this life. George was oblivious, just touched by the *bywoner*'s sincerity.

He did find Tsumeb fulfilling in many ways, working harder and faster than at any time before, and he enjoyed the respect in which he was evidently held in that isolated human microclimate. In the capital there was talk of a Commission of Inquiry into South West African affairs and an eventual grand plan to create reserves for ten ethnic groups among the black population. George thought it far-fetched and didn't pay much attention. The whole country, in spite of being nearly two thirds the size of South Africa itself, supported a population of under half a million, thinly spread over some 320 000 square miles of land.

George told himself it was a good thing he was posted so very far away from anything, especially the laws that were being rapidly promulgated under the rubric of the new policy called *apartheid* – which he referred to when he had to as *apartness*, thinking that less crude. Still the Department was leaving him alone to do things as he felt best, and he was convinced he was winning the respect of the black people in his district. He thought perhaps the South African electorate would see the error of its ways at the next elections, and return the more moderate United Party. That would restore things to the way they should be. The notion of majority rule was, of course, still so preposterous to a man of his times and station that it was not even aired in what he considered respectable circles.

For her part Jean was increasingly unhappy in the pressing heat and dust, out of place in the roughness and readiness of the mining camp aspiring to be a town, and resentful of their rude accommodation. Although the prospering settlement was quickly beautifying itself with trees and parkland and flourishing gardens, when she cast her eyes around she saw only mining headgears and desert beyond; it was not the type of place one conjured up in daydreams. The water was hard to the taste and the cost of living high because of the great distances goods had to travel to reach the shelves of Tsumeb's few stores. Still she played expert foil to George, making the best of the meagre social life on the desert's fringes. In 1951 she gave birth to their third son Chris, who was small and very unwell with scarlet fever, but fought his way tenaciously into life. They had been hoping very much for a daughter but were thrilled with their pretty new boy.

Young Billy was placed at the Newmont Mining School, but after a while George became convinced that the American syllabus was not appropriate, and so moved him to the only alternative in the town, *Tsumeb Afrikaanse Primêr*. The youngster had to struggle through in a language not his own. Billy was a great deal more unhappy about life in Tsumeb than he let on directly, though he found other ways of communicating the message. George and Jean were having to spend a great deal of time at the local hospital, waiting anxiously beside the doctors tending the sickly baby, and Billy was expected to suspend whatever social life might be available in order to babysit the difficult Ryan. One night Billy went to the family *armoire*, selected the husband and wife figurines which Jean had lovingly saved from their wedding cake, and beheaded them with a hunting knife. He buried the torsos in the tough Tsumeb soil. It was a long time before his parents found the defiled statuettes, and they never worked out exactly what happened though they had their suspicions. George worried that the path he had chosen was making life too hard for his family.

Busy as he was, George gradually began to have the uncomfortable feeling that this might not be more than a wayside in his career. He wrote to his parents that it was like being sent somewhere in a war that it was necessary to be at that time, but would always be a place that would be left for somewhere else. But for where and for what? He grew restless and incrementally uncertain as to whether all this was leading somewhere in some linear and logical way; this was in sharp contrast to his Zululand years. Certainly, there was no longer direct and collegial discussion with the Department about what he was doing now, and what he might be doing next. Neglect had its advantages but carried with it this blankness about what to do instead. He and Jean began to talk often about their feeling of unsettledness. The unthinking purposefulness of their more youthful years was fading. George said to her one night, but sensed she might not have fully understood what he meant: I no longer wake up in the morning and just charge at the job like a bull at a gate.

The nascent worries of Nkandhla were with him, try as he might to brush them aside. And when he had been in Tsumeb for nearly four years – the time had passed quickly at least – he began to pick up indirect hints from other Department officials that he would soon be moved again. He held out little hope that it would be a step forward. He was beginning to accept as reality that he was not now going to be admitted to any of those inner circles or achieve high office, and that his ideas about the interaction of European and African culture were not of interest to those who had assumed control. The word *failure* whispered itself loudly in his ear for the first time, though he clung to the countervailing notions of security and some stature at least. Gradually, from the changing style and measurably decreasing frequency of communication from his faraway superiors, he concluded that this chosen path of his might indeed be a personal dead end, a great mistake, as well as increasingly problematic morally; and that caused momentary panic. Perhaps, he thought, he had reached the point where he could no longer fall back on waiting and seeing. Perhaps finally he should get out while he could, dignity intact, and take his chances.

He made a big decision, in his way. On the 20th of April 1952, for the first time since he joined the Public Service, and deeply unsure of himself in private while putting on a confident air for the townsfolk, George requested a testimonial in the strictest confidence so that he could seek a life beyond the sway of Government. His putative patron was the Member of the Legislative Assembly of South West Africa, representing the constituency of Grootfontein. George was sufficiently pleased with what he wrote to have it carefully sealed in a plastic envelope. It read:

I have known Mr G Jameson for several years as The Native Commissioner of Tsumeb. Both as District Surgeon and as a member of the Village Management Board, of which Mr Jameson is Chairman, I have been closely associated with him. As Tsumeb has grown within a few years to be the second biggest town in South West Africa, Mr Jameson's duties are particularly onerous, and involve numerous problems of an unusual nature owing to the peculiar circumstances associated with a rapidly growing mine town. I am most impressed by Mr Jameson's ability to cope with all his duties in a highly efficient

71

manner, and still to establish a smoothly functioning Village Management Board. In spite of all he has to do, he remains at all times courteous, friendly and willing to assist the public. As a person who pays meticulous care to detail while at the same time possessing unusual organising ability, I am certain Mr Jameson would be most successful in any field for which he is qualified, and I wish him every success.

Emboldened, George requested a further reference, in August, from the Resident Manager of the Tsumeb Corporation Limited. He wrote that he would recommend Mr Jameson without hesitation for employment in any capacity requiring his legal knowledge, administrative, clerical and organising abilities. His manner, integrity and impartiality had made him highly respected by the public in general.

This too George sealed in plastic, and confidently sent both, along with a carefully composed covering letter, to several companies. He began to prepare himself mentally for a new career after eighteen years. But the next letter he received was from the Department. The now-familiar communication, otherwise known as an Order of Transfer, did catapult him to a more obscure place, as he feared. He was indeed being spun into the peripheries of the periphery that was Africa itself in the world of the time. He was to go to the district of Groot Spelonken, the village of Zoekmekaar, in the far Northern Transvaal more than a thousand miles away by rail, as the new Native Commissioner.

The packing began, and the absence of clarity of purpose and eventual outcome seemed more pronounced in the small household. Jean was relieved to be escaping the desert town, though by now it held some fond memories, but her overarching feeling was fear of what awaited. George told the family it was all to the good, but they were beginning to feel like rootless nomads and could see that he was not convinced himself. He wrote in his private papers: I feel like a man who in his life has struck coal, when he was searching for gold.

He was allowed to stay in Zoekmekaar for such a short time that they would hardly remember the village, or Billy the school. A bare year and another Order of Transfer later, the family bags were packed once more and George, shuffled far southwards to fill a vacancy as Native Labour Officer to the gold mines on the Reef, renewed his attempts to escape. He wrote to Anglo-Transvaal Consolidated Limited on the 14th of October 1953; the company had advertised for a Native Labour Adviser to the Group. He wrote from number 119 Cleveland Road, Kensington, Johannesburg, from a small semi-detached house built after the gold rush for workers streaming into the mining camp which was then exploding into a city.

Dear Sirs,

I am at present in the employ of the Union Native Affairs Department, where my rank is that of 1st Grade Native Commissioner. My duties in this post constitute liaison between the Native mineworkers and the Government on the one hand and the Mine Managements on the other. As Labour Officer, I am an ex officio member of the Native Labour Advisory Committee, which consists of four Government Labour Officers and three nominees of the Transvaal Chamber of Mines under the chairmanship of the Director of Native Labour. I have been the incumbent of my present post since 1st July last year and I have reason to believe that I was specially selected for it. My experience with Natives dates from childhood and, in my nineteen and a half years' service in the Native Affairs Department, I have had wide administrative experience, covering Natal and Zululand, the Northern Transvaal, South West Africa, and now Johannesburg. Although most of my service has been in rural areas, my four years' duty at Tsumeb introduced me to many new facets of Native Administration.

He had been teaching himself Sotho, a language he felt he did not speak well enough, and carried around with him the phrase book *Puisano: Ea Sesotho Le Senyesemane.* His aim was to be able to speak every indigenous African language used in South Africa, a feat he believed would be unique among white men if he achieved it. He informed Anglo-Transvaal that he was about to turn thirty-seven years old, with three minor children, of nine, five, and two. This time he gave as his referees the American Consul in Johannesburg, the Regional Magistrate of Johannesburg, and the Managing Director of the Tsumeb Corporation, who also wrote to say he wished George could come back to South West Africa; it was such a pity he'd been shifted like that.

George sent his letter and waited. He began to feel deep, contradictory confusion: he did not know any more where he belonged, and he was unreasonably moved to find that he was missed in Tsumeb, remembered there at least. He cursed himself for weakness and sentimentality. Anglo-Transvaal wrote back in November 1953, regretting to have to inform him that owing to unforeseen developments it had been decided to postpone indefinitely the creation of the new post. His application had been filed for future consideration.

He was assailed by a sense of hopelessness, entrapment, self-doubt. Perhaps it was actually nothing to do with the politics, he began to think; perhaps the truth is I am just no good. He was in the metropolis now, as he had once fervently hoped to be, but uncomfortable with his employers, and evidently unwanted. He was dispirited and unnerved by his failure to secure a position in the world outside the all-powerful Government. His last effort had been with Strathmore Management Limited, in 1954. He had secured an interview, but not an offer of employment. In 1955 he tried Anglo-Transvaal again, to no avail.

At this moment an alternative opened itself to him. Uncle Stanton, bachelor-potentate of his mother's clan, was no longer young enough or well enough to run his Babanango stores, and George was offered the family sinecure. Here was a direct choice, and one which had to be made. He enrolled with the School of

Accountancy in Johannesburg, studying every night, and received a diploma with a mark of eighty-five per cent. This would serve him well if he was to take over the Babanango business as, it appeared, his parents wanted him to. But as he thought about it further, he could not escape the fact that this would mean leaving the safety net of the Service, for all its frustrations and moral complications. It would also mean, for George's fragile self-esteem, abandoning his vocation, and being seen to have had to scuttle back to suckle at the family bosom having failed to make it in the outside world. He agonised with Jean over this decision, finally declining to his disgruntled uncle and closing a door he knew he would not again be able to open.

One day in Johannesburg, the Department called him in with the now familiar abruptness. He was told he was being sent back to the countryside, this time deep into the Transkeian Native Territories as Native Commissioner of the Kentani district. He and Jean, disoriented and anxious, spent hours discussing the development. At length they decided that perhaps the Transkei or Zululand, where they had started, was where they belonged, especially now that things had changed and were changing so much in the cities. George still had not been able to bring himself to tell her of the true depth of his multiplying doubts, and was frightened of the effect on the already fragile family were he were to explain this, while providing no solution or even plausible option. By this time there was a partial desperation in him, which he began to feel physically, and he found he had to expend increasing energy to keep it masked.

They decided, as they prepared to bundle their life together for yet another journey, that they would make the most of the Transkei. He said to Jean that even though he was not rising through the ranks as they had once hoped, and even though the political direction of the country was growing so worrying, at least they could try and do some good in the countryside. He could put his Xhosa to good use and for the boys it would be a lot like his own childhood in Zululand.

It was also a place of intoxicating history, he told them. They could visit the stream called Gxara, close to Kentani, where a hundred years ago the young Xhosa medium Nonqawuse had her tragic spiritual vision: that if the Xhosa people would show their faith by destroying all their cattle and crops, they would be rewarded by the driving away of the Europeans. The spirits living in the deep pool of the Gxara were wrong: the cattle, crops, and then twenty-five thousand people died; the Europeans stayed put and multiplied. In the Transkei there had never been between the Xhosa and the British the pivotal pitched battles to draw historical lines under moments of victory and defeat, but rather a series of small brutal wars culminating in the subjugation of the Xhosa by 1880, when they were made British subjects. The British annexed territory piecemeal, and began to establish what they termed white spots; places such as Kentani where the Jamesons were headed.

Soon the South African Railways vouchers were issued and the travel-weary Jameson family boarded another train, this one from Johannesburg station for the extended, cramped, noisy journey to Umtata; another journey indeed. George said it was like an inversion of the Great Treks – both the real one in the history books, and their own unhappily remembered marathon to get to the north in the first place. Nobody responded to his strained attempts at cheeriness, and for a long time in the compartment not a Jameson was to be heard speaking.

Courthouse, 1957

TWO years later, in the soft Transkei, on a Monday morning as hot as any he could remember, George stepped down from a khaki-coloured Government-issue jeep. Usually he would have been dressed in his short-trousered safari suit and sturdy boots for traipsing over gorse-covered hills to reach the deeper kraals, but this day was different and he was stifling in his best grey flannel suit, white shirt, red-striped tie and brogues.

He paused to look at this place: his courthouse in a village without tarmac, flag flying in the yard, white walls recently painted, clouds scudding magnificently, telephone lines bellowing the recent arrival of technology in a corner of a corner of Africa. He walked straight-backed across the recently swept dust yard in front of the courthouse.

Molweni madoda, he responded in the formal manner to the

murmured greetings of men wearing blankets draped over their shoulders and leaning on sticks as they conversed in groups. Although it was still early morning, the coastal heat had moved quickly inland and he could feel a film of sweat developing above his lip. He should have brought his hat out with him today. A crowd had gathered in the courthouse yard already and by the look of things it would grow much bigger: on every hill around, to the north and south, east and west, there were people moving in straggled lines. They were converging on the centre of Kentani village – *Centane* in proper Xhosa – the clans coming in force to the seat of European authority to listen to the airing of a grave matter involving all the great houses of the district.

George acknowledged the salute of the court orderly waiting in the meagre shade of the angle-roofed corrugated iron veranda, and entered the building. It was marginally cooler inside thanks to two clattering ceiling fans powered by an old generator in the shed to the side. He went directly to his own office, where he had placed the Department-supplied desk to take advantage of the view through the small steel-framed window, a view of round hills marching to the seaside which never failed to give him pleasure. This was an achingly beautiful part of Africa, in spite of its poverty.

Umtata, the only town in the Territory of any real scale, was many hours' drive away, and though the hills and valleys were dotted with huts, there was the occasional silence of the ancients. Where they were themselves, on the road between Butterworth and Qolora Mouth on the Wild Coast to the south, were only two marked settlements, Qoboqobo and Kentani. Of kraals there were dozens, but these were not listed on the Union Native Department maps. You had to know them for yourself.

The clerk of the court, arriving earliest of all at the courthouse, had set out the trial papers on the desk and George began to go through them methodically one last time before proceedings began. He knew some, but not all, of the young men by sight, and he was certainly familiar with all the kraals involved and their headmen.

It was a convoluted and gory business that had to be dealt with, and one which had caused extreme unhappiness and upset in an area which had before been at peace with itself for a very long time. That was why the State had to step in, in his view; that was what made the role of the European in Africa both valid and useful. This was a rare situation, in his experience, because most of the trials he had presided over in this place and the others before had been minor, petty, administrative affairs – this one looked like it would go to the heart of the lives of the people of these lands.

His worst fears about his work in the changing Department and country had not been realised, and for a long time now he had again been entrusted with the authority to rule in the manner he deemed fit. He retained some confidence in his ability and suitability to do that. But because he was for the first time trying a case that could involve the ultimate punishment, George considered it his solemn responsibility to know every possible contextual detail that might have a bearing on the matter. He picked up the familiar Government form, U.D.J. 15., The King *versus*, and noted that the trial was to be conducted in terms of Act 24/1886/150, as amended. He knew this law very well from his years of conscientious study, and was relieved that he would not be applying one of the many new ones issuing from Pretoria and the Parliament in Cape Town in an avalanche.

The messenger of the court brought tea in a tin mug on a tin tray. They exchanged pleasantries about the weather but did not discuss the trial, as that would have been improper. There was an air, felt not least by George himself, of mingled nervousness and excitement: there had not been a court case of this gravity in the area for many, many a year, and there was no certainty as to how it would all turn out. If it went badly, everyone knew, there could be bloodletting all the way from the national road to the ocean. And it was his calling, after all, to prevent such things from happening.

He heard the voices of Sergeant Thompson, who would be prosecuting for the Crown, and Mr Smyllie, who would be conducting the defence *pro bono* for those accused who chose to avail themselves of his services. Both nodded as they passed the door to his office, looking tense. George thought himself fortunate that this trial had not come when he had just arrived in the district in 1955, before he had studied its history and genealogies, found his feet and established a rapport with the chiefs and the people. It was going to be difficult enough as it was. When he was first given this posting, in charge of a vast area with a population of some sixty thousand, he had been assured that most of his time would be taken up with agricultural betterment measures, local government development, and education; the work of a Commissioner. The court work, that of the Magistrate, would be the least of it – and that was more or less how it had been, until this day.

Soon both the courtyard and the small sparse courtroom, whose doors had been opened to give access to the public gallery, were packed. The clans had gathered. A rumour raced around the yard and into the court: messengers on horseback had arrived to say that the Paramount Chief himself might leave his Great Place and appear at the courthouse in person. The tension grew stifling.

Sergeant Thompson? called George. Mr Smyllie? Shall we proceed? They made their way with due formality to their appointed positions in the courtroom, accompanied by the pronouncements of the clerk. George assumed his seat of judgment and moved his eyes around the room, trying to gauge its combustibility. As he had come to expect from his time among the Xhosa, it was extremely quiet for such a large gathering of people; the more serious the matter, the more the dignity and decorum.

The plaintiffs were already seated on their wooden benches, fidgeting and making eye contact with relatives and friends in the gallery, occasionally remembering to look up at the bench respectfully. George gave the instruction for the accused to be brought in, and this caused the first rippled intakes of breath, furtive greetings. The charge sheet was read out in all its calculatedly intimidating formality.

There were ten men on trial, all young, between eighteen and twenty-two years old. Five were from Ngcizela Location, two from Thakazi, and three from Qolora. Their names, as they appeared on the charge sheet, were Tanase Ntabaka, Tutu Wafiri, Ndodana Relefe, Sokevu Tshembe, Notyatya Qikanya, Noghume Ngam, Kotingana Mbali, Ziyekile Beshung, Xakisayo Maranyake, and Mdushane Beshung.

The Crown was levelling against the group charges of malicious assault with intent to do grievous bodily harm, which might be extrapolated to include attempted murder. The weapons used, carefully documented in the court records and on gruesome display in the courtroom, were battleaxes, iron-loaded sticks, and studded knobsticks. Mr Smyllie was appearing for nine of the ten accused, one having declined to be represented and preferring to speak for himself.

Because George had now mastered pure Xhosa as well as Zulu – as he grew older, his contempt increased for the pidgin that other officials considered sufficient – he believed he could tiptoe into the truths of the world under discussion. He would make a wise decision, he was sure of that; he was the right man for the job; in fact the Xhosa were fortunate it was him and not someone else. He liked to think that in his work he could enter places other Europeans would never know and perhaps did not realise they needed to know. He did not want or need to rely on an interpreter, who would insert an additional level of mediation between himself and the great unfinishable work of trying to engage Africa on its own terms – daunting enough when attempted directly. He made his notes in Xhosa.

In this trial he had to decide whether to call down the law's fearsome punishments on this isolated, proud, subjugated place. He had always said that in Africa there was the deepest duty to try to understand the *why* as well as the *what*, for what right did one really have to judge people according to one's own assumptions if you did not know theirs? He had never yet in his professional duties made a decision of which he felt morally ashamed.

The accused looked skittish and slightly bewildered, perspiring, save for number one, defiant in his compliance. They would have to wait their turn to speak, as it was their accusers who would first be called upon.

Plaintiff Sikutuni Cengima stood. I am an adult Native male, he said, yet uncircumcised. I have paid taxes for five years. I know the accused; they are of the same age group as I. On Monday the 11th of November 1957 I was coming back from the dipping tank. I passed the home of Bitsumi Sitswala. I sat and talked, telling him I was going to inspan oxen to plough. Three of the accused arrived and sat down. Accused number two was armed with an iron-loaded stick, accused number one had a hunting stick which was plain and short with a small knob. Accused number one came and sat next to me. Accused numbers two and three stood. I continued talking to Bitsumi and Vakemi.

I felt a blow on top of my head. That blow was delivered while I was sitting down. Then all three accused beat me with the intention of death. I was standing and falling. Accused number one had already stood up when he delivered his first blow. Blows landed on my head and body. I fell to the ground thrice. As a result of the blows I lost consciousness. When I regained my senses I was at Ntirara's kraal. I sustained seven open wounds on my head. I show the healed scars to you here today.

The plaintiff did this with ceremony and deliberation, and there were sympathetic murmurs from the gallery. He concluded: I was detained in hospital for a week. I have recovered now except I have lost the use of my right hand. I gave the accused no provocation.

The focus moved to the dock. It was the turn to speak of accused number one, Tanase Ntabaka, twenty-two years old. He was tall, lithe and startlingly handsome, with broad features like a larger-than-life sculpture. There was a tautness in the room as he got to his feet slowly; George sensed this immediately, the trial would revolve around this one. The young man had an aura of authority about him, and it was acknowledged in the bearing of his fellow defendants.

Ntabaka looked directly at George. He said: It did not happen in the way the complainants say it did. It was they who had the knobsticks, not us. He glanced contemptuously at his accusers and sat down again. Accused number two, Tutu Wafiri, nineteen years old, stood and said the same thing, using the same words. Accused number three, Ndodana Relefe, twenty-one years old, said: I deny what the complainants are telling you about what happened and how it happened.

Bitsumi Sitswala, small, younger, and trembling, was called to give evidence for the prosecution. He said: I am an uncircumcised male of Ngcizela Location. I began paying Native General Tax last year. I am of an age group just junior to the accused. On Monday the 11th of November 1957 I was at Domboza's kraal. The accused arrived. When Sikutuni arrived he sat next to me. He was saying that oxen should be inspanned, when three of the accused moved nearer. Accused number one was in the lead. He struck Sikutuni mightily with an iron-studded knobstick. The other two joined in. Sikutuni fell three times while the three accused were assaulting him. I fled. The three accused chased me for a short distance. We had given the accused no provocation. I fled because I was convinced I would be killed if caught. Sikutuni was taken to hospital; we thought he was dying. He sustained seven open wounds on his head, as he has shown you. His right hand was very swollen. He was hospitalised for some days in Butterworth.

When Sitswala had finished, Tanase Ntabaka stood again to speak. Every pair of eyes in the courtroom, including those on the Bench, was drawn to him. He paused and spoke matter of factly, almost drawled.

As I say to you, on that day I saw that it was they who had fighting sticks. After I had noticed this I finished dipping the cattle. When I was on my way home with my group, Sikutuni sent young Bitsumi to call us to a beerdrink at Domboza's. We were surprised and had some discussion about this. Then we arrived at Domboza's. We sat next to the stock kraal. Sikutuni, Bitsumi and Vakemi arrived. We sat apart because, as I have said, we knew of the sticks they had. I asked for tobacco. It was given.

Tanase Ntabaka paused again and spoke more loudly: Then I struck Sikutuni on the neck while he was talking to the other boys.

The gallery gasped. Even George gave an involuntary, unprofessional start. He had been expecting a denial, or at least an assertion that the others had struck first; but here was a bald and clearly truthful statement that would not help the accused's case at all.

Ntabaka ignored the reaction and went on: A general fight ensued. The two younger boys ran away when my party beat the others heavily. Sikutuni fell when I hit him. The others' blows also landed on Sikutuni's head and body.

There he stopped in his recounting of that day's violence, and became reflective as if rewinding the memory in his mind to an earlier point.

But there is another thing, he said after a short silence. There were many grown men at the dip tank that day. I did not report to them that I had seen the three boys were carrying dangerous weapons. I failed to do this. I should have done so; it is they I should have reported to. That is where I was wrong. We would not be here doing what we are doing today if I had reported in the proper manner. I repeat that I carried only a plain stick and so did accused number two. Accused number three had an ordinary hunting stick. It was Sikutuni and his companions who carried dangerous weapons.

At this point Ntabaka sat down again. All his movements and actions had an unexpectedness about them. Both prosecutor and counsel for the defence, startled by the turn the evidence had taken, said they had no questions. George raised his eyebrows. Accused numbers two and three, not shifting their gaze for a moment from Ntabaka, intimated they had nothing to add at that stage. None of the accused had any witnesses they wished to call upon. The plaintiffs looked away.

George thought it opportune to call the lunch recess, not

least to give himself a chance to think. The gallery emptied, all at once noisy as it regrouped in the yard, and the accused were removed under guard to a holding cell, really just a tin lean-to in the yard. The plaintiffs avoided the clustered clansmen and moved some distance away, under a stand of trees. He closed the door to his office and cranked the telephone mounted on the wall – the party line system ubiquitous in Africa's rural areas – and asked the operator to connect him to his wife. Jean answered on the first ring and asked him how he was, how it was going.

It's more complicated than I thought, he said, I can't put my finger on it any more plainly yet, but I know it is not going to be easy to know what is the right thing to do. There is quite an extraordinary young man among the accused; I don't think I've met him before.

He said it might go on for a long time, too, that was his sense of it. How were the boys? She should explain that they might not see much of him that week. Then he would take them boating on the Great Kei, which flowed to the ocean not far to the south along the coast. She said she'd do so. And I know you'll make the right decision, my dear, she said.

When George called she was in the isolated house, large and pretty, situated a mile or so from the village. It was whitewashed and red-tin-roofed, provided by the Department for its pleni- potentiaries in such places. Actually, it was a delight to her after Tsumeb, Zoekmekaar and Johannesburg. The property was surrounded by established trees, dominated by an ancient yellowwood which offset the garden planted and tended by him; him with his uncomplicated love of gardens if nothing else.

Alongside the dirt lane leading to the house ran a dense forest, source of endless excitement and night time terrors for the younger boys. Whenever the coast was clear of grown-ups, they entered the woods with pellet guns and emerged with birds and small game for secret, unhygienic barbecues. A steel and wire gate opened on to the sandy driveway, and one had to walk around the rainwater tank to get to the front door. There was no electricity and the toilet was a long drop, situated so far out into the garden that the young boys were too afraid to use it at night, opting for potties whose contents were then emptied surreptitiously on George's hydrangeas each morning to remarkable fertilising effect. From the front veranda of the house there were wide-angled views of the ocean, sixteen miles distant as the crow flew. The family cat once walked the entire distance back to the house from the beach, earning an honoured place in district folklore.

Young Chris loved the house though it scared him at night, particularly when George and Jean went off to meet friends for drinks at the Rex Hotel in the village. The spookiness he felt and imagined was heightened by the fact that in the terraced garden was the grave of the young daughter of a previous Commissioner – considered by the Xhosa to haunt the house, and bring bad luck. The boys were convinced of this when on one awful day George accidentally reversed over the family's dog, sleeping behind the car. As he leapt out and tried to extricate the agonised animal, it bit him viciously and locked its jaws around his wrist in a death-clamp. George needed the doctor to remove it surgically, needed stitches, and the pet needed a gravestone. The boys decided that would be the only bad luck of this family's tenure.

They were growing, developing individual personalities, two of them now old enough to be well aware of their surroundings. With the Jamesons being undisputedly the number one family in the village, both Billy and Ryan became leaders of their own gangs, which alternated in using Chris as a hostage at their hideouts. The two older boys were sent to boarding school in Butterworth. Billy, the uncomplaining stoic, made of it what he could, while Ryan, natural rebel, vented his displeasure but was accepting of his fate. The toddler Chris revelled in the bucolic pleasures of village life. Yes, I think we feel happy here as a family, Jean said to herself. They acquired a lime green Ford Consul, to replace the old Austin which had expired after a return journey from Kentani to visit the family in Babanango.

Are you opening the library today? George asked gently into

the telephone. She had badgered him into having constructed a tiny one-roomed building in the village, with a single door and five small windows; Kentani's first and only library. There the books, few as they were, were catalogued and indexed to Mr Dewey's highest standards. Yes, she answered, there is a lot of interest in it you know; people don't have to be illiterate just because they live in the bundu. Well, he said, have a good day my dear. I must go back into court. Say hello to the boys for me. He replaced the heavy black receiver and made his way back along the corridor.

As soon as the court reconvened, George announced that there was a need to proceed speedily with the evidence, as there were so many people involved and it could take a great deal of time for every person to say what they needed to say. The process dragged on in the Kentani courthouse, hours turning into days, each of the complainants and each of the accused telling their intricate story in the same formal and formulaic way. The public gallery remained full and silent. There was further display of ghastly wounds. By the Friday, George had a good idea from all the evidence of what had actually happened and when and where, but that was all: it looked, unfortunately, like just senseless violence and savagery, which was how it was being presented in the local newspaper. There had been a suspicion expressed at some stage by Sergeant Thompson for the prosecution that it had to do with money, beer, or women – but everyone, plaintiffs and accused alike, dismissed these suggestions out of hand, scoffing at them and shaking their heads.

It was only much later, at the end of the next week when the trial was coming to its close, that some hint emerged from the layers beneath the life of the people of the kraals, on which George was to pronounce judgment.

The epiphany came, unsurprisingly, from accused number one, indeed the dominant figure in the small drama. Tanase Ntabaka, who confessed to the beatings but implied without saying as much that there were reasons which were not being aired in the alien courtroom, began to speak of the why of the matter. George knew that in the strict terms of the law, it was an absurd situation: Ntabaka was pleading not guilty, and at the same time admitting quite freely to the serious assaults – more, attempted murder – of which he was charged. In his own mind he was not guilty because there were reasons. In the court's mind he was obviously and precisely guilty as charged. But he was undeniably impressive; the only one to decline having Mr Smyllie defend him. As the final summing-up sessions began, George asked Ntabaka to complete his evidence and tell the court anything he felt had not been adequately covered in the drawn-out proceedings.

He rose and said this: I am accused number one on both counts. I am not represented. What I have to say is that on the 11th of November 1957, we did strike Sikutuni and the others. If we had been able to, we would have killed them. Then he fell silent. George looked at him from the Bench, thinking he must have finished and that the case was over; he would merely change the plea to guilty. But Ntabaka had not finished.

He said: However, I think I have not explained matters fully. On the day we went to the dip tank, the day I have told you about before, we saw the sticks they were carrying. This I have said also. After dipping we went to the stream to wash our feet. When we were ready to take the cattle home Bitsumi arrived with a message. I asked him why Sikutuni and the other boys were calling us. Bitsumi answered: They ask that you come and drink beer with them. Wafiri said to me, they usually drink alone, why do they call us today? I advised him to leave such thoughts behind and said that we should go and partake of the beer as invited. I had made my decision already.

We arrived at Domboza's house where the beer was. I suggested that we sit apart from each other as a precautionary battle measure. This I have told you also. Those others then arrived. One came and stood in front and shook his head and muttered, and then said: These boys are sitting badly. I have explained that we sat apart so that we would be better able to fight as I had seen their dangerous weapons, and this was the decision I had taken.

They came and sat among us. It was said that beer should come. Beer was brought and partaken of. I saw that accused numbers two and three were not drinking because they were frightened. I took a tin can and called accused number two to come and have a drink. I then called accused number three to have a drink. We sat talking and smoking. Then as I have said, I stood up and struck Sikutuni without him being aware. Afterwards we took our blankets and went home. Soon after our arrival a horseman brought a message that we were required by our headman. We went to the headman at Ntirara's kraal. Men were gathered. Accused number two and I explained what had happened. This is what we explained.

Sikutuni and party had dangerous weapons. I am the leader of the faction of my age group in this district, and I am due to be circumcised this year. By carrying dangerous weapons in my presence, Sikutuni and his group were purposely issuing a challenge to my leadership, and that of my group. They are denying this in this court here of yours, but they are lying and you do not know enough to know it. This was what was happening in the places we have mentioned, the dipping tank and the kraals. As the headman and the elders understand, I could not allow such a challenge from Sikutuni, or from any of the others. A point had been reached from which I could not draw back; this is understood among our people. I am a leader and a leader's duty is to keep the peace. Sometimes he has to make war to do so. This is our way. It is the custom of our leaders to take notice only if someone appears to be on the point of attacking you, and I am such a leader. This I think you need to understand. I thank you.

George found himself staring at Ntabaka, some previously unutilised synapses connecting in his own head, realising that he needed time to think through the disjuncture between the young man's self-evident truth, and that of the court with all its self-invested pomp in this dirt-poor place. On an impulse he asked Ntabaka whether there was anything else he would like to say before judgment was pronounced. Ntabaka considered this and then nodded guardedly. He drew himself up to his full height, with a look of genuine enquiry on his face.

He said: My Lord, I understand that we will be found guilty of these beatings we have been talking about all these days now and that we will be punished. This I understand. But I wish to ask this: *What has it to do with you, Sir?*

From that day on George would refer to this moment as *Ntabaka's Question.*

For George it was as if his lifetime of meandering, cross-tracking certainties and doubts clanged together in a cacophony of sudden clarity. He could barely hear himself speak as he acquitted accused numbers four to ten, for lack of evidence. His head was ringing as he heard himself convict numbers one to three, as he had to. He handed down the lightest sentences that he could in terms of the law – six strokes each. He had the sense that Ntabaka shrugged dismissively and fatalistically when he heard this, but it could have been his imagination. All the Xhosa left the courtroom in a great hurry, apparently relieved that this unavoidable part of things was out of the way, that no unbearable injustice had been ordered by the other law, eager to go back to the kraals to determine the next steps in the saga in their own manner.

George went back to sit alone in his office, managing along the way to look convincingly magisterial as he told the court staff they could leave, he would lock up. The night, which fell so quickly upon the hills of the Transkei, was coming, but he was not ready to go home. He needed time to think on his own, and drew up his chair at the window to smoke a cigarette with a shaking hand and try to grasp at his own conclusions.

He concluded that this day, this accidental trial over which he had been called to preside, was truly the first time since he embarked on his career that the uncertainty which before had nagged sporadically, now really gnawed at him like a constant and ravaging illness, if still not fully clear in its meaning. He sorted out and sifted through his own thought processes. Since 1948, he agreed with himself, he had worried primarily that his own advancement was being seriously curtailed by the political change in the country. But now he could not avoid questioning the career itself, the point of his working life, inside and outside of himself; he questioned the meaning and validity and morality of everything he was doing and everything he was standing for, everything about himself. He felt come over him, not dilettantishly now, a sense of hopelessness and purposelessness that weighed a ton, and he said out loud in his good English accent: It's all wrong. It was a physical feeling in his chest. Then George, who used strong language neither in public nor in the home, swore fiercely. He found, to his surprise and annoyance, that he was weeping.

Where is the country boy from Babanango now, he thought, the one the teachers said would go so far? This was how far he had come, and gone; presuming to judge Tanase Ntabaka and having him futilely whipped. What right had he to judge anything at all about these people, never mind the effort he was so proud of putting into understanding them and learning their languages? It was a right conferred by conquest alone; that was the only historically accurate thing you could say about it. He recalled having read with fascination, when he was first told that Kentani was to be his next posting, that it was in this precise place that the very last battle of what the Europeans call the *Kaffir Wars* took place. It was the ninth and last of these wars between the British and the Xhosa. He had read that on the misty morning of the 7th of February 1878, an army of Gcakela warriors threw itself at the earthen fort at Kentani. Inside the rough fort were some four hundred white men and three hundred Fingos, fighting for the Europeans. The Gaika section led the charge, and it turned into a rout; the effective end of Xhosa resistance. The chiefs fled to hide in the forests, and over the Great Kei. Kentani was a white town now, and became the administrative and trading centre over which this Native Commissioner would preside eighty years later.

Suddenly George stood up and stopped this train of thought, as if dropping a dam wall into a fast-running river. With a conscious effort of will he dismissed the doubts and the defeatism. He told himself to get a grip on himself. After all, he had always said his work was for betterment, that the world was not perfect, that the advantages and advances of European civilisation could be shared without the destruction of Africa's own. He still believed this – had to, he realised, for the alternative was chaos for his family – but the truth was it also suited his missionary's mien. Still he could feel there was air escaping very rapidly from his conviction; it was going flat. I call myself an African, he thought, and I feel myself to be one. But what do those people in the courtroom call me? It was a pathetically small personal struggle he was playing out, objectively speaking, but dignified by the fact that it was the beginning of an honest debate about the very life, or death, of a human being.

When it was fully dark he stood up, put on his jacket and began to lock up the courthouse. I will not lose my way in these thoughts, he said to himself angrily, I must get on with what I believe in, what I am trained for, paid for, and suited to. What vanity is it that makes me think I might be right and everyone else wrong? I love the Xhosa and I know it is their country, but surely they are not yet ready to govern it without us? He resolved not to burden his family with his now-dangerous apprehensions; he was sure the doubts would retreat in the morning.

He drove the short distance to the house, which was filled with light and the voices of his wife and three sons. He was able to re-enter his own small hermetically sealed world and soon sat talking happily, for the first time in days, about plans for the fishing expedition to the river mouth and news of the neighbours; he let float away the thoughts of what was being said in the encircling kraals.

They were all together that night; a rarity. Jean roasted a chicken and served hearty helpings of vegetables overcooked in the English manner, even though they had been freshly grown in their own garden. The two older boys were happy to be free, albeit briefly, of their boarding school in Butterworth, and the youngest one delighted in the presence of his big brothers.

After dinner, replete and nostalgic, George and Jean settled in the lounge, gathered the boys, and reminisced. The darkness was deep and enfolding outside. Dates and places are important to this family, George said, because for a nomadic family like ours there are so many of them to keep track of. Billy, remember you were born in Vryheid, Natal, 1943. Ryan, Eshowe, Zululand, 1948. Chris, Tsumeb, South West Africa, 1951. Those are the places that will be on your passports one day and you must remember that while there are many who will boast about coming from big places, eventually you will know the value of the fact that there are not many with those names that you will have on your passports. You must be proud of those names and places.

George stopped and went to refill his brandy glass. The boys were sleepy but they knew that there were few enough nights like these, when they were all together and their father was in the mood to talk. Jean wanted to excuse herself and go to bed but knew too the value of the moment. George spoke to them again about his childhood in Zululand, about him and his father shooting the hippopotamus whose magnificent teeth had been made into the ivory dinner gong that stood on the sideboard. About the days he traded with Bushmen, about horses; about cattle, cattle, cattle. It's said of farmers like my family, he told the boys, that all they do is eat, and watch cattle – that's all they do, and it's true. Thank God, we find we are just like the Xhosa! He talked of the dignity and wisdom of Africa that, he was beginning to understand, should not be judged according to smug assumptions of superiority; of how you should not even think of dealing with a man unless you genuinely respected him; about the wicked sin it was to call a black person a *kaffir*.

He talked a great deal more than usual and said finally, when it was clear that all must sleep: Another thing I have learned, my boys, is that fear of failure in the eyes of others can be a terrible thing if you let it dominate your life, because then you are always living in fear about your pride, of being embarrassed or humiliated or shamed. Who says one human being can go through his life without making mistakes, even moral ones? I have found that sometimes when you are absolutely certain you are right, you are very possibly wrong – and you should try not to be afraid of being wrong. Now that I am older I think one should expect in this life to make mistakes – and then the question becomes whether it was an honest mistake, and whether you have the courage to stop repeating it. Jean and the boys did not quite know what George was getting at, but understood that there was an important mulling over occurring in his mind.

The trial preyed on him unceasingly, so much so that he carefully kept the transcripts and went back to them often. It seemed to him to touch the heart of the contradiction of this sliver of Africa ruled by Europeans, the contradiction in which he was embroiled and complicit and that fascinated and repelled as well as confused him; that had an element of absurdity, difficult to isolate within day-to-day reality as it went on, carrying one along.

A year later George sat down in the Kentani house and wrote with his elegant fountain pen in longhand a short story about an unusual decision he had taken. He had decided, when a further matter of the kraals was referred to him as magistrate for trial, not to hear it in terms of normal European law.

XHOSA TRYSTING

By G M Jameson
Kentani, Transkei
18/11/1958

This is a story of the Transkeian Native territories, situated on the temperate fertile eastern seaboard of the Union of South Africa. It is based on proceedings in a Court of Law during 1958. It is a story of the Xhosa Bantu people who, despite the fact that airliners fly overhead daily, that passenger liners are continuously passing close inshore and that all kinds of vehicular traffic is used over the many roads that now criss-cross the Territory, choose to live as their fathers and grandfathers and great-grandfathers did before them.

Meet Noluthu. She is twenty-five years old, barefooted, draped in skirts, bodices and dresses of blankets, and on her head is a black cloth turban. Each and every item of dress is such as to be identical to that of every other married woman's. All her blankets are coloured with red soil dug from certain specific places. It is this custom which long ago caused ignorant outsiders to call these people Red Kaffirs.

To the European aesthetic Noluthu appears to be dirty, and to the unenlightened she and her people are without morals. Neither is true.

Noluthu has status at her husband's homestead of three thatched round huts. It is that of a wife and, moreover, that of the first and senior wife. Duma, the son of Skena, paid a dowry of eight head of cattle to her father and she partook of sour gourd milk at her husband's kraal after the wedding feasting and ritual. Even if Duma should later acquire sufficient cattle to pay as bride price for a second wife, her status will not be altered. It will, in fact, be enhanced.

Noluthu bore first one and then a second child, but both died in infancy. She is sad that this happened and at times wonders as to who may be using evil magic against her or her husband's family. She is young, however, and feels consoled by the fact that she will doubtless bear more children. The fates – or, to be more accurate, ancestral spirits – will take care of that.

Duma left for work in the city when Noluthu was nursing her second infant. His farming is no longer sufficient for him to be able to maintain a family, now that there are Native Taxes that must be paid to the Government. Even his great interest in cattle husbandry is actuated really by a desire to be regarded as rich, and to be able to muster together another bride price. It is also very essential, of course, to have stock to slaughter on the occasions of feasts deemed necessary for the solicitation of the spirits.

Duma works on the Reef, in Egoli, Johannesburg. His scale of earnings appears to be low but nevertheless, after an absence of say a year, he will come back and be able to stay at home for a year or more. Not only will he have provided for the sustenance of his family but, possibly, he will have enough extra money to be able to buy stock.

Noluthu's life is simple in the extreme and she is happy. She has no wish for a sudden elevation of her living standards. She wants to be left to live according to custom and she ensures that her behaviour follows its strictest dictates.

Mpetha is an older man than Duma and he has reached the stage that he no longer goes to the industrial areas to work. His sons and relatives will help in the event of his experiencing shortages. With some eight head of cattle and ten sheep in his stock kraals, and a wife and daughter running the household of the huts, life is good indeed.

Mpetha has a liking for Noluthu. If she were his paramour she would make a white smoking bag which he would carry to all feasts and beer drinks. It would be known then that he was party to an affair and that would better his status in his friends' eyes. Not for him any loose relationship with the unmarried mothers living at their parents' kraals, or with widows. His mind is set on an affair with Noluthu.

Custom allows such adventures but custom also punishes those unheeding of its dictates, those who are not wary and even those who are unfortunate. A game it is, and it must be played according to the rules and craftily.

A direct approach to Noluthu is unseemly in the extreme and she would spurn it. Mpetha goes to Nofukuda, Noluthu's husband's elder brother's wife, and requests her to make overtures on his behalf. The message is carried but Noluthu is still too grieved by her second child's death to consider such a proposal. A month later a second proposal is likewise declined, but this time Noluthu asks for time to consider. The third proposal is accepted and Nofukuda carries the message to Mpetha. Nofukuda has not acted alone. She has confided in all the grown women of her husband's family's kraal. In due course the senior woman of that kraal will ask to receive a half crown piece (two shillings and sixpence) and this will be spent according to time honoured usage.

Nofukuda has completed her role of go-between, and now Mpetha will arrange for one of the younger women of the family to become the appointment-maker and, from now on, he will meet Noluthu at times and places arranged by his appointment-maker.

Mpetha will give presents to Noluthu, to the appointment-maker, and to the women of the kraal. He hands the half crown to Noluthu to give to the senior woman, who will repair to the nearest trading station to buy tea and sugar. Noluthu and Nofukuda will enjoy these at a tea party which the senior woman will then hold in her hut.

For four years this relationship continues, with frequent meetings during Duma's absences at work, and infrequent meetings while he is at home. Mpetha's wife asks no questions about the new smoking bag that he now flaunts at festive gatherings.

Duma has been home for six months. Thrice Mpetha has sent messages but thrice Noluthu has declined appointments because of fear of detection. She accepts the fourth invitation. The time is to be the next morning, and the place the natural forest by the stream below her kraal.

Next morning Noluthu goes to the dry lands to pick weed vegetables and gradually makes her way toward the appointed place. Mpetha has kept the appointment too, but Duma has been watching. Nearer and nearer he crawls. He surprises Noluthu and her paramour.

In the act of fleeing, Mpetha grabs for his white tobacco bag but Noluthu has grabbed at it too, and, in the struggle, the cloth handle has broken and remains with Noluthu. Mpetha outruns Duma who, had he been able to come within striking distance, would have marked Mpetha by a blow on the head. Custom allows this and prohibits the marked man from retaliating in the circumstances. Noluthu, now the dutiful wife, hands the cloth handle to her husband. Her honour is now at stake. If her affair with Mpetha has not been conducted according to custom, she will be delivered back to her own people with a demand for the return of the dowry. She stands in danger now of dissipating her status, of becoming one of those other unmarried mothers or widows living at their parents' kraals.

Not for Noluthu such dishonour. She will produce the smoking bag handle and any other trinkets that Mpetha has given her, and she will tell the whole truth to prove Mpetha's guilt. Nofukuda, the go-between, and the appointment-maker, and the women of the kraal, will all tell all they know. They have nothing to hide and nothing to be ashamed of. In fact it was to meet just such a contingency that they assumed their various roles.

So she goes with her husband to Mpetha's kraal. Duma says no word to Mpetha. He leaves his wife there and returns home to send messengers. Custom does not allow Duma to speak to Mpetha directly in these circumstances; bloodshed could ensue. Two messengers produce the smoking bag handle to Mpetha. Noluthu makes her accusation and a claim is put forward for damages amounting to three head of cattle or thirty pounds in cash.

But Mpetha cannot answer such an allegation concerning, as it does, his whole family, unless adult male relatives are present. This answer satisfies the messengers who, however, decline to escort Noluthu back to her husband. At noon the messengers return again, and again they find Mpetha without his brothers. It is only on the fourth visit that Mpetha is found to have with him another of his father's sons and only then are the messengers satisfied to take the woman home.

Protracted family discussions and a hearing at the Headman's court fail to resolve the dispute and eventually one qualified European judicial officer, two qualified attorneys, one interpreter and some twenty interested Africans, in all solemnity and in a dignified court atmosphere, hear every detail recounted. Mpetha is finally informed that the listeners are in agreement that he should pay over to Duma three head of cattle or thirty pounds.

Duma returns home with his wife, and Mpetha goes away satisfied that he has had a good fight and that justice has been done. A qualified African medical practitioner, an African teacher and the interpreter, who hear the result of the proceedings, are agreed, too, that justice has been done.

Such are the intricate systems of Africa which are being brought to a close by the highroads of 'civilisation'. And who among us still dares claim that our law truly understands or knows what is best for Africa and the Africans? That we are qualified to judge?

Later George delivered his story as a speech at the Rotary Club of Umtata, where it was uncertainly received. He did not share it with the Department. And soon enough there was little time for further rumination as the machinery of the system whirred again into sudden life, shifting its moving parts. Jean was eight months pregnant when the official brown envelope arrived at George's office – he could barely stand to open it, let alone tell her of its contents. His tour of duty at Kentani was at an end; he was required to present himself on the 1st of December 1959, a few weeks hence, at Duiwelskloof in the far north, the Transvaal. It was now an immutable fact that they were using him to plug inconvenient holes in the Service whenever and wherever they arose, and entirely heedless of his own wishes. There was another Jameson home to be dismantled, and another to be constructed.

It was undignified and humiliating, but there it was. And the political changes had filtered down, finally: the Union Native Department was no more, replaced by the Department of Bantu Administration and Development, and it was the Civil Service now, not the Public Service. He was a Bantu Commissioner now, not a Native Commissioner. His worst fears were coming to pass on all counts: what kinds of laws was he going to have to administer in future? He had made a grave mistake in Johannesburg when he decided not to accept the offer to run the Babanango stores, but it was too late to reverse the decision; too late, too late. Eventually he had to show Jean the letter from the new Secretary of the Department.

I have pleasure in informing you that the Honourable the Minister of Bantu Administration and Development, on the recommendation of the Public Service Commission, has approved your promotion to the post of Senior Bantu Affairs Commissioner, with a salary at £1860 per annum (fixed) on the establishment of the Bantu Affairs Commissioner, Duiwelskloof. The transfer is at public expense and you should indicate in writing that you are conversant with the provisions of Public Service Regulation No. 181 and all code instructions in connection with the transfer of Public Servants. It is trusted that you will be happy in your new sphere of employment.

It's a promotion, Jean, George found himself saying again. Not much of a promotion, God knows, and yes the boys will miss the Transkei, but it's a promotion. Come on, he said, let's treat it as an adventure, as we always do. It's a beautiful part of the world, up in the Northern Transvaal. Perhaps it will be my last posting, and we can settle. I can teach the boys to hunt.

As before, he did not know whether he himself believed what he was saying, but they determined to face once again what lay ahead for them, if only because they were small people in the world and did not know what else they could do.

Devil's Gorge, 1959

DUIWELSKLOOF had no hospital. Jean was sent ahead on her own from Kentani to give birth in Johannesburg. On the day the new baby was born, George, Billy, and Ryan had already started their new life hundreds of miles up north from the Transkei; up in a place where the vegetation grew as if it was equatorial jungle and the flame trees blazed back at the sun above them.

Ryan wrote to Jean from the new fastness: Dear Mom, So glad to hear it's a healthy little boy. I suppose you are disappointed it's yet another boy, but we're not. Dad says we should call it Samuel Arthur Jameson. You should see how many telegrams he's receiving from Kentani congratulating both of you. We are painting the house inside. We are looking forward to your arrival.

When finally they were all together up in the valley and the shock of yet another unexpected gypsy trek was fading, George and Jean found to their mild surprise that they were invigorated again, quite enchanted with the place and allowing themselves small dreams of new possibilities. What an extraordinary human reflex this was, George wrote, this incessant attempted renewal in spite of whatever has gone before. In the early Duiwelskloof days they spoke quickly and excitedly and laughed a lot. This was the mysterious land of the Rain Queen who never dies, land of legends. It heaved and steamed with history still making itself.

The small houses in the settlement were face-brick and white plaster with metal window frames and red tin roofs. The gardens had wire fences; the popular palisades of the bigger towns had not yet reached that far. The village was only about forty years old, the roads mostly dirt. There was a hotel, a long lazy single-storey structure with an extensive stoep and pot plants at neat intervals, and a boisterous bushveld bar. In spite of the move, in spite of her new baby, Jean felt young enough again and full enough yet of life and hope. Even in that heat and obscurity she turned herself out as if for a promenade. She had brought her elbow-length gloves for special occasions that might occur. For an ordinary day she had black heeled shoes, a shaped long skirt and a twinset, topped off by her fine dark hair permed into tight rows of curls. Sometimes she wrapped a silk scarf around her head fashionably. She was tiny, far too small for those epic surroundings, standing barely five feet tall with her delicate angled pretty features and pale skin.

George's hair was flattened and tamed with Brylcreem, cropped short and plastered with a side parting to keep things in a separate and orderly diptych. He wore his brogues, loose-fitting suits and cool white shirts with the sleeves rolled up, showing the deep demarcated tan of his African youth. The picture of him entering middle age was of a tall man, six foot, very erect and proper in his bearing, ageing handsomely in a sandy-coloured, unspectacular way.

The family posed for a photograph with the Ford Consul drawn up on the thick green lawn as a backdrop. Billy, seventeen years old and a cadet at the South African Nautical College at

Gordon's Bay in the Cape, wore a smart striped blazer and sported a haircut as close to ducktail as his socially conservative parents and the college would tolerate. Slight and fair-skinned and very blond, in stature neither short nor tall, he was a true commingling of his mother and father and, as the first born, occupied a special place in the household. He was an attractive boy with a sensitive face that communicated a vague combined sense of uncertainty and determination. He was old enough to remember all the gypsy journeys, and the countless schools, never attended for long enough to make lasting friendships or excel in syllabi that shifted like dunes in the desert.

Ryan and Chris wore shorts and long red socks, pulled up to just below the knees. It was clear that Ryan, entering his teens and a boarder at Capricorn High in Pietersburg, would be taller than his big brother and his colouring was quite different, almost Mediterranean. His straight dark hair – all the boys had inherited Jean's fine strands rather than George's thick waves – was schoolboy-short but arranged for effect. He was good looking and aware of it. He had a dazzling smile, enhanced by a jaunty slight gap between his front teeth. Even in a still photograph there was the hint of a swagger in the way he stood, but his deep pooled eyes belied the overbearing confidence. He was a strange, troubled, angry, dislocated, brilliantly gifted boy who seemed to feel he had been placed among the wrong people, in the wrong place, by some monstrous mistake that no one but he had noticed.

Chris at nine years old was small physically – he had his mother's bones – but startlingly beautiful. The shade of his hair was at a midpoint between those of his brothers, and he had sweeping eyelashes that had caused other mothers to stop their prams on the pavement and coo. Despite his scarlet fever at birth in Tsumeb, he looked strong and fit, a coil of alert energy and purpose with a ready smile. He had a fierce determination in his compact bearing, almost daring anyone to take him on. He was at the local school in Duiwelskloof, but very unhappily so: it was a place for big-boned Afrikaner farm boys, not little descendants of English forebears.

The handful of English boys and the couple of Jewish children of the village were relegated to a separate class. It was planned for him to go to school in Tzaneen the next year.

The baby was still in swaddling clothes, too small for any distinct or lasting personality traits to be discerned yet. Surprisingly big and fat for the issue of such lean parents, with miniature tree trunks for legs, he was gurgling and happy. He had bright blond hair which sprouted as if it had been irrigated, blue eyes, and through the infant pudginess you could just about discern a fusion of family features. He delighted in the big family around him, and the attention showered on a *laatlammetjie*, a late lamb, born nearly twenty years after his eldest brother.

Jean had scrubbed the little freshly painted house from ceiling to floor; it was the first thing she had done after being discharged from the hospital. She had buffed the formica tops of the chipboard cupboards in the kitchen, wiped the varnished pine table and polished the Marley Tile floor. She nagged George to raise the matter of the leaking roof with the Department, though she knew how he hated asking for anything for himself. The house was plain and poor but it was shining. In the miniaturised universe of the village it had some gravitas: it was, after all, The Residency, seat of the only authority around.

While Jean preened the inside of the house George hurled himself, as always, at the garden. Soon neat flower beds and horticultural order were gestating within a tiny fenced-off square in the wild landscape. On the weekends, he said, he would make furniture in the shed, using the tambotie wood you could get there in abundance. First he would make two chairs for the lounge, then a drinks cabinet with a mirror for a shelf and clear glass in the front, and a kist for keeping all the family mementoes Jean collected so obsessively. He had brought his old box of chisels for the purpose, along with a wood plane, and had developed a technique for creating rounded effects using pieces of broken glass. He and Jean were having another optimistic go at making something of life, counting the blessing of four healthy boys, their own relative youth, and an income that remained steady if modest. All this should be enough to go on, George thought, as long as he could keep his own demons at bay.

The older boys had read in a book from his library that the first Rain Queen fled mighty King Monomatapa in the sixteenth century, stopping in mid flight in this area with her tiny Balobvedu tribe. They chose a grove of cycads – the Latin name is *Encephalartos transvenosus*, George informed them, as he did with every plant species they would ever see – not far from where this little dislodged family would now try to make another home in Africa in the middle of the twentieth century. They had also been reading Rider Haggard's *She*, in wonder. They would be able to explore the Zoutpansberg and the surrounding foothills of the Drakensberg, which reared up above the village. They could not know how soon they would be journeying again, and so once more they set about trying to take root in strange soil. George had entered his forties and was resigning himself to letting go the dream of escape, resigning himself to the tides and eddies which determined his family's encirclement in its small world, its incessant wanderings.

That is how it was at the end of the 1950s in that particular place on earth. It was intoxicating in its dilatory way and the feeling rubbed off on the boys. The music was Buddy Holly and Elvis for them, Sinatra and Dean Martin and Ray Conniff for the parents, blaring out tinnily from the gramophone as they sat on the small stoep and considered the riotous sunsets of Africa right on the Tropic of Capricorn. They knew some joy then. George and Jean drank their gins and tonics, more and more and then far too many of them, as the temperature climbed to thirty degrees and beyond.

Once again they were far away from anywhere else, that was true. But they loved the unfamiliar, exotic names. The closest town was Tzaneen, more than ten miles away. Mooketsi was nearer but didn't really qualify as a town. Bandelierkop was nearly forty miles distant, Makhado fifty, and Pietersburg even further.

To the north and west ran the fabled Limpopo. To the east, past Letsitele and Giyani, the Kruger National Park – which, as every white South African schoolchild had been taught proudly, was bigger than Wales. Forever etched in the memories of the older boys was a week-long safari along the very northern borders of the park with George's agricultural officer, the mysterious Mr Mentz. He was a German from Tanganyika who, George thought but did not pry, had his farms expropriated after the defeat of the Nazis and was now working for the South African Government. George thought it prudent not to discuss politics with the tough old man of the bush. The point of the safari was for the Commissioner to investigate claims that hippopotamuses straying out of the park were destroying crops of both the neighbouring white farms and kraals, and putting children in danger. They camped out in the starlight and huddled around the fire with the roar of lions in the nearby bush. Chris was too young to be allocated a rifle, and too small to see over the long grass in the riverine areas; the grass was taller than him, so he had no chance of seeing the animals making all the noises around them. This most African of experiences was both thrilling and terrifying for him. One night they slept in a crude treehouse, and found in the morning that elephants had uprooted all the vegetation around the makeshift hut below. Mr Mentz and George shot two hippos, to the mixed awe and revulsion of the boys.

Around Duiwelskloof itself, there was fold upon fold of forest, cool and shaded and mystery-filled. Tzaneen was a lovely subtropical place, the undulating hills swathed in citrus trees. A book they had bought said it was possible to visit not far from there the biggest baobab tree in the whole country, more than three thousand years old, more than fifty yards around at its base. There were places to commune with the ancestral spirits, George's abiding fascination; places like the Phipidi Falls of the Mutshindudu River. Below the falls, he told his sons, the pools were called *Guvhukuvhu* and in them lived *dithutwane*, half-human immortals. They should never scoff at other people's beliefs, he said, especially if they involved the unknowable world of spirits. The minds of the boys were imprinted, impregnated, with African magic. There was Magoebaskloof, with the Debegeni Falls hidden in the woods, the Schelm Bos, and the long soft stretch of water that was the Ebenezer Dam, rolling like a poem.

There was still wild game aplenty, and every home in the village had a gun rack. George kept rifles, pistols, and a shotgun, much to Jean's distaste.

George regaled the family with tales of the old settler times, before the village became a proper village, when it was just a stop on the great Zeederburg Coach Company route through the Lowveld, financed by the imperialist colossus Cecil John Rhodes himself. There were places where you could still see the remains of the old pioneers' track. The coaches used were exactly like those of the Wild West – the very same manufacturer, in fact, George told them – and once there was an attempt, very much unsuccessful, to have zebras pull them. Duiwelskloof once had its very own highwayman, his name enough to make the boys whoop with delight: Dick Turpend. He wore a mask and held up coaches, but with markedly less success than his fabled faraway near-namesake.

The settlement graduated in time to the status of a railway siding. Duiwelskloof had its moment in the Anglo-Boer War too; the famous firefight of the Bushveldt Carbineers happened right there at the old farmhouse, leading to a firing squad for Harry 'Breaker' Morant. The Jamesons had read the whole story many times. Morant, by his own admission, executed twelve Boer prisoners and went to his death insisting he had been acting under the orders of the man who now had him shot. Shoot straight, you bastards! were his famous last words, and they appealed so much to rebellious Ryan that he carefully painted them on the satchel he would take to boarding school.

Duiwelskloof itself was known by other names among the Venda, Shangaan and Sotho people of the valley and mountains. Many called it Ngoako Ramalepe, but it was thought to have got its Afrikaans name – in English, Devil's Ravine or Devil's Gorge –

from the combination of the steepness of the land and the rich red mud which churned into gluey quicksand in the rainy season, in old times making the task of the transport riders both dangerous and devilish.

The place had the fecund smell of heat that is African alone. Heat mixed and stirred with eucalyptus, and hanging fruit, and soil. The colours could be blinding; there was wild bougainvillea, frangipani, poinsettia, jacaranda. George took the bigger boys on long instructional hikes, speaking in his beloved Zulu, Xhosa, and Afrikaans, languages not his own but in which, as he often said to them, he preferred to think or sing. He sent a respectful message, from the modest courthouse over which he presided, to Queen Modjadji's courtiers. Yes, she would be glad to receive the Commissioner, they replied, and he bent over books for hours to try to understand this part of Africa at least as well as he believed he did the others far to the south. He felt in part worthwhile at this time, and the trial in the Kentani courthouse receded.

He made Billy, Ryan and Chris learn the names of the tree species – there are more than three hundred, he warned archly – and intentionally frightened them with tales of the leopards concentrated around there more than any other place in the entire world. He taught them about Makapansgat and the anthropological discoveries by Professor Raymond Dart, thirty-five years before. He was in a reverie when he talked of the ruins of southern Africa's first kingdom, at Mapungubwe where the Limpopo and the Shashe Rivers meet.

They befriended Astley Maberly, eccentric illustrator and chronicler of the wild nature of those places. His farm, Narina, was close to Duiwelskloof but hellishly difficult to get to. Just the way it's supposed to be out here, George said. He was in awe of Maberly and they were kindred spirits. The farm was a menagerie. Maberly spoke to animals without embarrassment and George wished he too could be that relaxed about life.

At the beginning of 1960 George decided that the rather ramshackle Duiwelskloof Commissioner's office complex in

Botha Street should be upgraded, and he had the Government Clerk of Works and a Departmental inspector come to the village from Pietersburg. The building in which he worked was just like a larger version of the houses, really; there was not an abundance of inspired architects in the area. He submitted plans he had drafted himself, and noted that pipes were rusted through, the roof leaked, and the benches in the waiting rooms had broken off from the walls. Eventually permission was forthcoming from Pretoria for him to proceed with a Minor New Works Programme, in terms of the provisions of Circular No. DPW No. 3 of 1957, and the project pleased George, an inveterate fixer of those things he could fix. His plan catered for an office for the Assistant Bantu Affairs Commissioner, the Accounts Clerk, and Public Spaces – by law divided into separate waiting rooms for whites and non-whites, a fact which he accepted without protest. He submitted a meticulously typed Improvements List:

A = Public space
B = Writing platform
C = Writing platform
D = Office space for Grade II Clerk
E = Public Space
F = Counter for public use
G = Counter to be removed
H = New counter for public use
I = Entrance flap to be provided
J = Racks for tax and population cards (Hardboard)
K = Partitions between offices
L = Office space for Clerks
M = Teak panels to be replaced by glass
N = Portion of veranda closed in and used as office
O = Two louvres to be built into hardboard walls
P = Awning to be provided over window

This, he felt, would make the Commissariat's physical appearance more congruent with its august function in the village. He had a harder battle, however, in trying to make a case to the bureaucracy of the necessity of installing electricity at the courthouse and offices. In his drawer he found a letter drafted by his predecessor, but never sent, to the Chief Bantu Affairs Commissioner in Pietersburg. The man had written: I have to state that the reason why electricity is required in the public offices at this station include, *inter alia*, provision of light for later afternoon and night work, especially in winter, as at present paraffin lamps are used and have often had to be taken into court. The strong room and two record rooms have inadequate outside lighting and require inside lights as well. Also, this is a tropical area and at certain times fans are necessary.

George took up the challenge and permission was eventually granted; by the end of that August the offices were paying £2.10 per month to the Village Council for the privilege of this modernity. In these small things he took pride. He went to work each day at the same time – early – but his return could not be predicted as he had to travel the District, except when the court was sitting in Duiwelskloof. He found his work interesting because it was varied and there was so much of it. He was mightily relieved that in this place it was not his main task to deliver court judgments; the authority he carried meant that his advice was sought on a splendid range of matters to do with development; roads and dams and cultivation and irrigation and the like. His interlocutors were chiefs and farmers and small businessmen, often at the same time. As always he liked to think that he was dispensing, if not wisdom, then at least fairness. Once more, he was left by the Department to get on with the job.

He did inadvertently make himself unpopular with local police officials, who were opposed to his plan for a new housing scheme to replace the Duiwelskloof Location and cater for a growing black population. There was no question, under the new Group Areas Act, that races would live in anything but separate locations, but George felt everyone should have decent facilities, at least. First he commissioned a health report from the local district surgeon, who wrote that current conditions in the black location were wholly unacceptable. His report said the houses were so close to one another that only one person could walk between them at a time. There were pools of fetid water and no drainage, and residents were forced to live with a permanent stench. The houses were heavily overcrowded and the latrines provided were quite inadequate for the numbers. When the tropical rains came, a tributary of the Brandboontjies River burst its banks and flooded the township. George's ally concluded that the conditions were so bad for the black population that it was the urgent responsibility of the authorities to rectify the situation. It was becoming an ideal place for the spread of epidemics, especially *longtering*, phthisis, which was rife in the area. He did not think the current site could be upgraded, and believed the only solution was to allocate new and better-located land, and build a proper village.

Armed with the report, George proposed the purchase of an unoccupied farm and the construction of a new township. This was the kind of project he loved. But he was bitterly opposed by the District Commandant and village Sergeant, who complained to his superiors and warned that this new Commissioner was dangerous: he would encourage more Bantus to pour into Duiwelskloof if it became known that luxurious accommodation was available. George responded with a long appeal to the Chief Bantu Affairs Commissioner in Pietersburg. The situation of the two and a half thousand inhabitants of Duiwelskloof Location was shameful, he wrote, and he urged the acquisition of the farm. The location community itself was fully in favour of this and he had consulted the leading figures. After a long delay the Department told him his proposal had been considered, and rejected. This was a blow to his standing in the tiny community, but he knew it was hopeless to pursue it, and he felt again the oppression of his impotent power.

George experienced different friction with the townsfolk when he refused a demand by the owner of Castle Wholesalers for annual compensation for the use of a road leading to the location. The owner said this road passed over his land, and he should receive an amount of £7.10 each year from the Bantu who used it. George wrote back to him, the letter lacking his characteristic courtesies: With reference to your letter of the 25th ultimo, I have to inform you that as the road in question has been in the undisturbed use of the public for more than fifteen years it cannot now be closed and it is not understood how you can demand an annual payment from the users.

The family was no longer welcome at Castle Wholesalers. The boys found this confusing but were learning that there were some subjects on which it was unwise to question their father.

Now increasingly isolated within the village, each evening George and Jean listened together to the news on the transistor radio, feeling as far from the events of the day as truly they were. They heard that Mr Khrushchev had visited Budapest, and Egypt had resumed diplomatic relations with Britain. The Shah of Persia had presented his bride-to-be with a ring of diamonds, sapphires and rubies. Gold was up to £12 10s 3d per fine ounce. A pack of twenty-foot long killer whales had been spotted off Fish Hoek, in Cape Town; they wondered whether their sailor boy Billy knew that, being on that ocean so often. Elizabeth Taylor was recovering from double pneumonia, they were relieved to hear, though in truth Duiwelskloof had not been aware of her illness in the first place. Senator W J L Pretorius of the National Party had addressed a public meeting to further explain the Immorality Act. They were reminded that their Prime Minister was the severe, to their thinking almost maniacal, Dr H F Verwoerd.

George and Jean sat and talked often and long into the night about the places they had lived in before that one, about who they were and who those were that went before them; gently they recapitulated the long curious zigzag journey, like the jottings of a heart rate monitor, that they had taken together across the breadth and depth of Africa's southern stretch before fetching up here in the Devil's Gorge.

They were not old, but not young any more either. They were both delighted to have a new baby in the home; the disappointment of the final failed attempt to have a daughter had dulled. They had put on the mantelpiece their favourites among the many congratulatory telegrams they received after Sam's birth. Transkei friends: Congrats on Kentani souvenir! From his staff in Duiwelskloof: Congratulations on a full tennis team! The extended Jameson clan sent good wishes from Babanango, Johannesburg, Durban, and other places.

With his own career becalmed, an underlining event had just occurred on George's side of the family: his big burly father was about to retire after trading and farming for more than fifty years in the Babanango-Qudeni district of Zululand. George's mother Enid – clever, cantankerous, acerbic, hard as stinkwood and with a waist-length mane of sun-bleached white hair which she insisted on having combed by her granddaughters – had decreed that she and Grandpa Milton would build a house overlooking the beach at the tiny settlement of Ballito Bay on Natal's North Coast, to which their children and grandchildren would be summoned each Christmas to account for themselves. George dreaded this: he could not quite imagine that the old man's working life was over, and it made him fear that his own perceived failure would be paraded at the family gatherings. But there it was in the local newspaper: Mr Jameson Snr told a reporter he would henceforth be pottering around with his Barberton daisies in his seaside garden, and was certain that Zululand would get along fine without him.

One night in the Duiwelskloof house, George smiled at Jean. Sitting thus on the very Tropic of Capricorn, the sun gone down, boys sprawled in the lounge, baby asleep, the cries from the bush growing ever louder, he fetched one of her scrapbooks.

I was still Lieutenant Jameson when we got engaged, Jean, d'you remember? Of course she remembered; it was her memory of life at its most beckoning. She held the scrapbook tenderly in her hands in the cramped lounge of the house. She knew the contents of that old wedding report almost by heart. Over the years she had read it to the boys more often than they cared to remember. They always gave her a gentle ribbing but knew that on this if nothing else they had to indulge her. When she read it out aloud in the latest strange place, they knew, she was marking the new territory with her old memories, like a rhinoceros spraying.

Seventeen years and so many places later, the words still brought to her face a beatific smile and about this George felt proud and proprietorial. He looked at her in encouragement. He listened to her precise clipped way of speaking, diction as clear as royalty's, but located by the flattened and foreshortened vowels of English-speaking white South Africa. While she was reading the boys shrieked out their favourite lines from the old report: Leg-o'-mutton sleeves! Two-piece ensemble! Smart hat! It is at times like this, she responded indulgently, that you boys can understand why your father and I tried so hard to have a daughter who would grasp the importance of such matters, unlike you philistines.

There was a pause in her reading. George looked enquiringly at her over his glass, then with tenderness and nostalgia. He nodded gently and waved his hand in a forward movement saying, Go on, my little Jean, go on. Eventually she put the scrapbook down carefully. She was quiet for a time and all that could be heard was the buzzing of insects in the bush. Then she said, these days a mere wedding is unlikely to get a mention in the newspapers, let alone the full treatment. It was somehow softer then, even though it was a world at war. This world of ours now is very hard, in every way.

She brightened up. But isn't life funny George, she said; we used to joke about how we came from small places like Babanango and Benoni and now here we are in Duiwelskloof, the smallest of all? Perhaps we are meant to be in small places. There is a good life to be had in them, if only one is allowed to stay long enough.

With Tsumeb, Kentani, and the rest a fading memory, the Duiwelskloof days passed happily enough at first, local contretemps notwithstanding, and there were tentative feelings of semi-permanence and security. After six months they made a journey to Pietersburg to have Sam baptised in the Church of the Province of South Africa, Diocese of Pretoria. The ceremony was performed by the Archdeacon of the Northern Transvaal, at Christ Church. The sponsors were Uncle Arthur, Jean's sister's husband, who drove up from Johannesburg, a Duiwelskloof neighbour, Doreen Harries, with whom Jean had become friendly, and Billy, who travelled from Gordon's Bay. It was the 8th of May 1960. They visited Ryan, the reluctant, truculent boarder at Capricorn. When they got home it was just Chris and the baby with George and Jean; just the four of them in the Residency then, and soon it would be three, the house feeling empty except during the holidays.

George was beginning to think a lot more about the four boys he had brought into the world, and of what kind of father he was being to them. Secretly he felt he was not a natural father, though he was so fond of his sons, and they of him. Certainly, he gave them time, but he thought the attention he offered was limited because of his troubled engrossment in his own thoughts and doubts; in that sense, he thought, he was himself perhaps not fully grown up, and might never be. But he could not fail as a father, even though he was not sure he was worthy of the role. He told himself he had to make a point, at the end of each week, of carefully thinking through how much attention he had paid to each boy. He thought of his own childhood, racked with doubt and self-consciousness, and hoped he could still help his own boys to have it easier.

In Billy he saw much of his own sensitivity, in Ryan a strange non-conformist intensity he did not recognise at all, and in Chris a determination and single-mindedness that reminded him of his wife. The baby he just enjoyed, spending hours on the weekends teaching him to stand up straight on his outstretched arm, finding he could roughhouse without worry – the child loved being held upside down and swung about, gazing at his father with frank adoration.

In the holidays Billy was overjoyed to be home – he had been lonely at the nautical college – and to be able to tell of his experiences to an attentive family gathered in the small kitchen while Jean fried bacon and eggs, the boys' favourite. His brothers wanted to know about the ship on which he was being trained for a career in the Merchant Navy, and he gave them loving detail. Ryan was persuaded to talk about Capricorn, where he was seeing out the year with ill humour before going to the prestigious St Martin's in Rosettenville, Johannesburg. This was an extraordinary development for the family: Ryan had seen an advertisement for an art scholarship in a newspaper, applied without telling anyone, and won it. His success was reported in *The Star* in Johannesburg. George didn't know whether to be proud, or ashamed that his son appeared not to need him – or even his permission. He ended up feeling both pleased and inadequate. School was not nice at all, Ryan told them, and he couldn't wait for the day when it broke up and he could get out of there once and for all and go to Johannesburg where he said he belonged. He brought home an article in the *Impala* magazine about his winning the scholarship, and said he was quite a celebrity in Pietersburg. Everyone said he mustn't forget them when he became a city slicker, but that was precisely what he intended to do, he said cruelly – forget them. George and Jean exchanged worried glances, but Chris, at nine years old, listened to his brother's tales as if they were storybook adventures.

George busied himself with the pleasures and complications of being father to a big young family, and told himself again that the work he was doing was tolerable. It seems to be going okay, he said to himself, and he was thinking less about the indeterminate anxiety of Kentani. It is all right, he said, we're doing all right.

But it was not all right.

After nine months in Duiwelskloof, on a bright Thursday morning, both incrementally and suddenly, in the form of something that had been stalking him and had decided to emerge from the bush, the shadow came out from behind their sun.

On that morning when George woke, he found the shadow had crept across his face and stayed there. He could not lift himself from the bed. He had felt down, to be sure, but this was of an entirely different order. He was trapped as if in a field of electrical current. He could not feel anything wrong with his limbs. But he couldn't move. Panic welled volcanically in his chest but he did not call out. Jean was in the kitchen feeding the baby and making breakfast. Chris was moving about noisily. George did not want to speak to anybody but he knew he could not just keep lying there.

The light was streaming through the bedroom window and he could hear the sounds of birds and animals, but they were distant and filtered because of the electricity sparking around in his head. He was supposed to drive to Gravelotte that day, and then to Marulaneng. But he could not move, really could not move.

Eventually Jean came into the bedroom with coffee, wondering aloud and cheerily why he was still in bed, being such an uncharacteristic lazybones. She stopped dead when she saw his face like a stretched rubber mask on the pillow. George! she said. What is it?

He shook his head and his tongue felt thick and swollen, too big for his mouth. There were tears coursing down his cheeks.

I think I have had a bang in my head, he said at last. She sat on the bed and took his hand, terrified by the torrent of torment and sadness and fear that was swirling behind his eyes.

She held his hand for a very long time and they did not speak. Eventually his eyes closed and he drifted into a strange sleep, breathing unevenly and letting out what sounded to Jean like gasps, or small sobs. She left the room quietly and telephoned George's secretary, saying he would not be in that day – he must have a stomach bug or something. No, they didn't need the doctor to come around to the house, they'd just see how things went. All his appointments should be cancelled – and probably for tomorrow too.

It was dark outside when George finally rose from the bed, unsteadily, like an invalid. He had slept the entire day. Jean, Chris and the baby were sitting in the lounge in silence, dinner plates on their laps, when he came through in his dressing gown. They stared at him. I'm very sorry, everyone, he said, I don't know what came over me but I'm better now. It's a lovely evening, please don't let me spoil it. I'll be fine – I must have picked up something in the bush, a tick bite or some such.

Please don't go to work tomorrow George, Jean said, please go to the doctor.

No, no, he said, really I'm fine; just need some fresh air.

He walked out into the clear night and sat on a rock in the garden, where he stared out beyond the fence into the wild plains and scrub, ghostly in the moonlight. Jean quietly put Chris and Sam to bed and kept a silent vigil until finally George came back inside. He raised his eyebrows and tried to smile at her: Don't worry, my girl, just a bad turn, mind over matter; won't happen again. I'll be right as rain tomorrow and can catch up on all my meetings.

But the truth, which only he fully knew, was that this had been coming for some time. He had been fending off its flurries. Several times he had found himself suddenly and unexpectedly immobilised – at his desk, driving his car, in a meeting, on waking in the middle of the night. But it had always passed quickly and he had made himself forget about it. There was certainly something wrong with his head, but how did you tell that to the country doctor who doubled as a vet and was more concerned with blood, surgery, amputation – ailments of the flesh? So he had hoped it would go away, had hoped it away, but it did not go. He had tried to read up for himself in medical books, which he kept at the office so as not to excite the family's curiosity, or alarm them. Clinical depression was the term that seemed to come closest to describing his unwanted malady as he understood it, modern words for what they used to call melancholia in the old days.

He tried to think himself through why it would be that he should suffer from melancholia. There was nothing obviously physical, nothing wrong that you could see and touch. But he had read of a theory concerning pressure being exerted invisibly on the brain, something not right in the skull that caused a kind of short-circuiting. That would explain his mystery and his misery.

Certainly, he felt, it could not be just in his mind. He loved his wife and his children dearly. He knew how lucky he was to have them. It was true that he was a disappointed man and anguished about the work of his life, but he and Jean had talked about that endlessly, contextualised it, accepted it; surely that alone could not have so wholly poisoned his subconscious. There must be something else wrong with him. He did have times when he unwillingly struggled to understand what was the purpose of life – he had always been a diligent rather than a deep churchgoer, and the truth was that religion had not provided for him a sense of spiritual equanimity – but he failed to see why he should be special in this regard. Surely most people wrestled with the human condition. Was it perhaps something he had inherited, something genetic?

It was also true that being unable to discuss his episodes of depression with anyone – certainly not with his mother and father, who he felt were disappointed enough in him already – could be exacerbating things. He could not really talk about his feelings of confusion and entrapment in his chosen calling, either. He could not imagine discussing that with his colleagues; it would be professional suicide. And did his own family even understand what it meant that he had been sent here, had to bring them here, in this manner? Were the boys aware that not only was his dreamed-of career sinking like rainwater into the dry earth, but that he didn't believe in it any more? But what at his age was the alternative? The time for alternatives had passed. He had a wife and four young boys. And he had his pride, if not the courage to break his bonds and strike out for meaning. They had so very little money, but what if that turned into none at all?

There was no possibility that he and Jean could entirely disguise what was happening, and an unspoken insecurity began to pervade the home – not all the time, but sporadically, hovering like the animal in the bush. Only Sam was unaware of it. Jean and Chris began to watch George warily, fearfully, solicitously, for signs of an attack – usually prefigured by periods of brooding silence, when he seemed to look right through them. When Billy and Ryan were home they too knew that something was changing. Billy wrote from college, unintentionally infuriating his father: Are you back to normal, Dad?

George became sharper with the elder boys. Sometimes, just occasionally, they felt they did not recognise this man as the father they knew. He and Jean began to argue episodically, never violently, but often viciously and woundingly. George accused Jean of thinking him a failure, and wishing she was with someone better. The house was so small that everyone could hear. Chris covered his head with a pillow. It was not bad all the time, but it was bad more often, and the tension seemed to build until they were circling each other like scorpions, trying to say as little as possible for fear of being stung.

George did not suffer another fully formed collapse in Duiwelskloof; there was not the time. They had not been there for even a year when the next transfer came, as always in the form of a registered typewritten letter on the Department's official notepaper. This one, George felt, was the most insulting yet: again no explanations, no preparatory telephone call, certainly no consultation: just the imperious impersonal language of the bureaucracy. They were to be uprooted yet again – so much for the Devil's Gorge – after such a short spell, simply because there was another remote post to be filled and the Department believed from past practice that he could do the job, and could be relied upon to accept the instruction without complaint or troublemaking.

And now that he was gradually acknowledging the extent of his secret weakness, of which the Department knew nothing, he would be doubly reliable this time and even thank them as he packed his angry bags. He was on his way back to the old Transkei. He cursed himself for not having had the courage to get out. But again they ritually listed the good things, buoying each other up, and again they prayed that this time, at last, there might await some permanence and settledness, contentment even. George determined to rid his mind of its affliction in a place he knew and loved so well.

Wild Coast, 1961

LIBODE was a speck of a village a hundred miles farther up the Wild Coast from Kentani, between the capital Umtata and the seaside resort town of Port St Johns. The rough road that passed through it led to Mlengana, the magnificent and sinister Rock of Execution which, George said, the Xhosa chiefs used to dispatch their enemies in olden times. Pondoland was another potent place of Africa, a countryside of breast-shaped green hills and rivers disgorging into lagoons and sea, where there were too many people with too little money on too little land, where cattle were a common sight on the pure sandy beaches.

The family occupied The Residency in the village. Billy was completing his studies at the nautical college, and Ryan had begun his scholarship in Johannesburg. Chris went to the local farm school, and Sam was becoming a toddler. Although this was a village quite without electricity, the Libode homestead was an imposing, sprawling thatch-roofed house built in the shape of an L, warranting its own noisy generator. It was by far the grandest the family had ever had, with acres of wild garden for George to tame. There was a hotel, his courthouse, a general store, a sports club, a village doctor called Marius Marnitz, and an abattoir which provided morbid fascination for the youngsters of the village, imagining what went on inside and regaling each other with ever more improbable tales of gore.

Hillside kraals ringed the settlement. It was a pretty canvas, with not much on it; George was relieved to be back among the Xhosa where he felt at home. Though the indignity of the Duiwelskloof transfer rankled with him – being shoved like a bloody draught on a board, he said – he believed good could be done while his writ ran in a small place like this. He seemed to be freeing himself from the paralysing attacks of the mind, and there was a sense once more in the family of a fresh start in a place they loved.

Jean was amused to see him becoming patrician as he grew older, his own family genes pressing to the surface. At the age of forty-three he seemed to be revelling in being head of a big family, and when the boys were in the house during the holidays he took to standing in the front garden and bellowing: Jim! He said it was too difficult to try to remember all the names, so he mustered them rather in this militaristic way: when they appeared and lined up in front of him, he pointed at the son he was looking for. Dinners in the evenings were formal affairs in the dining room, for which they all had to change into proper clothes; George wore a wing collar. He devised a technique to ensure that they developed the correct straight-backed English posture: if he saw them slouching in their seats he would get up, fetch from the drawing room a smooth polished wooden rod, and slip it horizontally behind the back and under the armpits of the errant boy, who had to finish the meal as if impaled on a stake; like a scarecrow, or Christ on a crucifix. Postures improved markedly.

He was a disciplinarian but not an ill-tempered one. He

despised childish sulking, and invented a new term for it: *bottomlipitis*. Bottomlipitis was banned in the Jameson home. If a son's transgression was grave, the punishment was a doleful journey to the lower garden, where George picked a long switch from the willow tree, and commanded the boy to dance as he laid about his ankles but never drew blood. He corrected the older boys' diction incessantly, and Jean subjected them to spelling tests. We may not come from the wealthy side of the family, George said, but we come nonetheless from a family of gentlemen and I'll not have you forget it.

One night George went into Sam's room and told him he was too old for a dummy. Did Sam agree, he asked, that he should throw the dummy out of the window, into the wild garden? Sam said yes, because he worshipped his father. Three hours later the Xhosa house staff were searching the flower beds and the lawn in the pitch darkness, led by George with a paraffin lamp.

Far away from this rural nest it was an alarming time in the country. What was being decided had dire consequences for the Transkei, would have consequences for the work of a Commissioner. George followed the news reports avidly and worriedly, scanning each edition of the Government Gazette. A Republic had been declared, the Union dissolved, and Dr Verwoerd had taken South Africa out of the Commonwealth. Apartheid was being dressed in the clothes of a philosophy, not just a utilitarian set of ruthless controls as before. Its logic demanded that the Native Territories move from being protected reserves to putatively independent countries, postage stamp nation states. This George could think of only as folly though he could not say anything about it without placing himself at a risk he was not prepared to take.

The Transkei now covered an area of 16 000 square miles, and was home to a million people. A Bantu Parliament – the *Bunga* – had been installed in Umtata. George had much to do with the characters in the drama, as Pretoria interfered in matters of chiefly hierarchy to advantage their chosen man. Kaiser Matanzima was someone he mistrusted entirely – the feeling was mutual – who was preparing for political battle with his traditional superior, Paramount Chief Sabata Dalindyebo, as well as Victor Poto, Paramount Chief of the Libode district and George's closest friend among the Xhosa.

George was of an age with Kaiser Matanzima. And he had heard of another man, born two years after himself at the nearby village of Qunu which he had visited: his name was Nelson Mandela, and in George's understanding he seemed to be the charismatic leader of the group of revolutionaries now on trial after their arrest in Johannesburg. The Sharpeville massacre had occurred, and the resistance movements had been banned. George felt that disaster was brewing in the land, but in all honesty didn't see how the whole mess could possibly be unravelled, things having gone so far. When he looked at his country's future, he saw only an angry blurred ball of confusion where once there was such optimistic clarity in his mind. He brooded on this in the home.

George kept photographs of the *Bunga* building, and formal groups outside it; a sort of toytown Parliament. The caption to the formal photograph hanging on his office wall identified, in the third row: Chief Z Sigcau, Chief B Sigcau, Chief V Poto, Chief S Dalindyebo, Chief K D Matanzima. George appeared in the middle of the front row, with the most senior white officials.

In Libode, *Ntabaka's Question* came back to harass him virulently. He sensed far greater resistance from chiefs and headmen than in the Kentani days, and was not sure what this would lead to. He recognised that whatever else it turned out to be, the time in Libode might offer his family the bucolic idyll they craved, but it would not come with political or moral quietude for him.

As before in his life, George threw himself headlong into those aspects of his work he liked and was comfortable with, and his garden. He blotted out what troubled him. The preparations for elections in the Territory meant that the Department had been given unheard of funds for betterment in the district, aware that it would be exposed to the glare of attention as never before when reporters, observers and officials descended at the appointed time. George oversaw the construction of new roads, especially the upgrading of the treacherous Mlengana stretch, which became known thereafter in the family as Dad's Road. Also a project to encourage contour ploughing for crops on the hillsides that displayed the effects of soil erosion like open, dry wounds. He found time, too, to refurbish the courthouse complex, renovate the little school and sports club, and to begin construction of a rudimentary golf course for Libode, its breathtaking setting making up for its roughness. The greens had to be fenced to keep off the cattle, which made for the interesting sight of white men in deepest Africa in plus fours, waving putters in the air as they clambered over the wires that separated them from the results of their approach shots. The Xhosa women, in particular, found this weekly tableau quite hilarious.

They spent the early 1960s doing these things. George built a beautiful, expansive rock garden below the house, and an impressive aviary which became the talk of the district. The lawns flourished under great willow trees and soon the flower beds were bursting, as if he was able simply to transport them from place to African place. He grew vegetables, and the Commissioner's radishes were in great demand. Jean said she was tickled pink to have a homestead of such gravitas, with its dining room for official entertainment, seating twenty. The roof was rethatched and the walls were painted. George and Jean played tennis on Saturdays in immaculate whites and posed for portraits in the garden with their wooden rackets. George built a swimming pool behind the house, in truth more of a hollow concrete block above the ground with a standpipe to fill it from the rainwater tanks, and the children of the white village made a noisy daily pilgrimage. The Residency was a colourful place, full of life, and as always they enjoyed being the most important family in the village. They made friends with the well-known trading families of the area, the Spriggs and the Horgans. Sam was treated like the prince of some impossibly tiny principality.

George was able to indulge his odd love of wild hailstorms,

wandering out into the garden in the night time, catching hailstones in his bush hat and singing riotously in Xhosa, watched nervously from the open front door by Jean and Sam, peering out from between her knees.

Once a month they drove to the muddy banks of the Umgazana River, as it was known by the whites of the Transkei. It was in fact the Mngazana, George explained, the little Mngazi, and in the 1700s it housed the Great Place of Chief Sango and Gquma, the famed European castaway queen of the Wild Coast. It was in his considered opinion the most beautiful place in Africa; a Xhosa secret shared with only a handful of privileged whites. The combination of green hills, majestic shadow-casting rocks, pure beaches, thick mangroves, and mysterious islands in the lagoon was for George an evocation of paradise. He said he would live there forever if he could, cut off from humanity's doings and as close to pure Africa as it was possible to be.

Having made their way down the short but dangerous road from Port St John's, they climbed into a small wooden boat with peeling paint and a single outboard motor, borrowed from Dr Marnitz. Jean arrived looking incongruously chic in the surroundings, scarf tied around her head, angular dark glasses and a dark brown leather valise. The boys were covered in mud in minutes, but she was not. They made their way a few miles down the river to its magnificent mouth and lagoon. Their destination was a whitewashed hilltop cottage, with sweeping views of the ocean and the hills and valleys. There Sam gambolled naked with the Xhosa children and their cattle and dogs, and George took photographs of his youngest son's very white backside. One picture in particular was shown to all friends and relatives: Sam, naked but for a straw hat, holding on to the fence on the hilltop, gazing down at the exquisite river mouth where his brothers cut an arc through the water in the small boat, and the green hills of Africa rolled away into an endless distance. The first sentences the little boy spoke were in Xhosa; he found the language's clicks easy and melodious, and determined in his childish mind that the natural order of things in the world was that there were very many black people, a very few white people, and although they lived in different places they all cared a great deal about cattle.

Sam was a happy child. The Xhosa women called him *Mafuta*, the fat one, with open affection. He loved fishing in the river and estuary, albeit without skill or success. On one of those weekends George took pity on him and contrived that his brothers distract his attention while he attached a minute dead fish to his hook, and then shouted at him to reel in. Sam was unfazed by his catch's lifelessness, and carried the prize around until its smell caused Jean to intervene. As a dare one day, to the horror of Chris and Sam, Ryan ate the raw river shrimps they had collected for bait and cackled with satisfaction into their astonished faces. I am a Xhosa chieftain, he said, this is my land, and you are my subjects.

After a year at the Libode school, Chris entered standard five in Umtata – another Jameson become a boarder – and being a naïve country boy he was much unnerved by both the girls and the doings at the big school and in the town. Nevertheless, he was able to spend extended time at home in the village. Ryan was settling, in as much as he would ever settle, at St Martin's in Johannesburg. Billy continued his stint in far-off Gordon's Bay, and Sam became used to being the adored only child in the house.

George was relieved by the absence of the extreme attacks of anxiety, and honoured again his promise to himself to concentrate on his four boys. He forced himself to focus on their doings and thought processes, even if they were mundane compared to his own meanderings of the mind. But he understood that this time was a hiatus: however much he tried to hide away, matters of his work would place the family in shadow again. He took a telephone call from Umtata. The Chief Magistrate of the Transkeian Territories came on the line with momentous news: the Minister of Bantu Administration and Development himself wished to pay an inspection visit to Libode. George, who conceded in himself a tendency to be cowed by authority, was in two very different minds. On the one hand this was big news indeed for the Libode district and intricate preparations would have to be made for visits to the Paramount and lesser Chiefs, the courthouse complex, as well as a reception at The Residency for the Minister and his entourage. The village would talk of little else as soon as the news got out. On the other, he knew he would not be able – or willing – to speak plainly of his true views.

Jean revelled in her role as chief social organiser of the biggest event in Libode's history. The entire village was roped in. The day came at last, and George was pleased when all went as planned, everybody playing their scripted parts to perfection. Sam was presented to the Minister and did not misbehave. George was indeed given no opportunity, and created none, to debate the political blueprint of the Government. He carried with him from that day a fleeting, shaming image: his face reflected momentarily in a mirror in the house, smiling ingratiatingly, close to obsequiously, at the powerful politician. That night he rose from their bed, took the mirror to the woodshed in the back garden, and shattered it with an axe. Jean cleaned up the mess in the morning and irritably dismissed questions about it.

George's new friend Dr Marnitz sent a handwritten letter from his surgery to the Commissioner's office. Dear George, he wrote, Just a short note to congratulate you on the great success you made of Friday's event. It speaks volumes for your organising ability. Really a good show! Another letter arrived two days later, on the official notepaper of the Office of the Chief Magistrate, Umtata. Dear Mr Jameson, it read, I would like to convey to you and your staff my sincere congratulations on the efficient manner in which the administrative and social arrangements were made during the recent visit of His Honourable the Minister for Bantu Administration and Development. I would also like to thank Mrs Jameson and her helpers for the excellent refreshments provided by them. His Honourable the Minister has expressed his thanks for the satisfactory manner in which the proceedings were conducted.

George turned his attention back to the people of the kraals and tried to keep out of the way of the turning cogs of power as much as possible, at least until it was unavoidable. He dwelt again on family matters, and the brood for which he was responsible. And he derived satisfaction, even joy, from his continuing acceptance in the kraals – the new policies had not entirely poisoned his friendships. He received a letter from a minor chief at Misty Mount, which he brought home proudly to show to the family.

The Commissioner (Nobangula), Libode

Your Worship,

I feel I am duty bound to express my heartfelt gratitude for your having attended the ceremony of the unveiling of the tombstones of my family. This marks a prodigious stride of destiny of the bridge between the Europeans and the Natives. This again has honoured the occasion, warmed by your paternal generosity which will remain indelible to the minds of them that attended. Your speech was educative and it is the talk of the home. I am the most fortunate person who had been honoured by your presence and that is the pride of our family.

> Who is the honest man?
> He that doth still and strongly good pursue
> To God, his neighbour and himself most true
> Whom neither force nor favouring can
> Unpin or wrench from giving all their due.

I hope that these few words of gratitude will kindle your heart with the glorious fire of charity and service.

I am, Your Worship,
Your very obedient and worshipful servant,
Mxolise Qoboyana

Jean heard from her Duiwelskloof friend Doreen Harries – she was one of the few outside the family who had been aware of George's breakdown in that distant village. She enquired kindly after his health, and reported that the drought in the Northern Transvaal remained acute, with acres and acres of gum plantations dying. She said George's successor had also suffered a nervous breakdown. She said: Seems to go with the Service these days!

A letter came from the O'Kiep Copper Company, thanking George for hosting their representative during his recent visit to the area. The Company had always been very proud of its good relationship with its Bantu employees, and with the villages in the Transkei from which the majority of the men originated. They had sent a representative to strengthen this goodwill, and the kind assistance extended enabled him to complete his task in a very satisfactory manner. George was forced to think about whether it was a good thing to facilitate distant employment for the clansmen as migrant labourers, or not. He understood the tautologous reality: they needed money because they now had to pay Native Taxes. They paid Native Taxes because they now earned money. Only a fool couldn't see that Separate Development was also the development of a most useful labour pool for others who were not the Xhosa people. He decided that if that was the reality, then at least he was helping the people to be able to pay the taxes which they could not avoid paying – whether he was there or not. The justifications went round in circles in his head. He stopped thinking further about them then. ·

Soon there could be no more avoiding the Government's plans for the Xhosa homeland, and it was overshadowing the more peaceable doings of the kraals. A resolution was adopted calling on Pretoria to declare the Transkeian Territories a State under the control of the Bantu people; a draft constitution was prepared. At the opening of the national Parliament in January, the State President said the progress of the Transkei to self-rule was the most important development of the times, and the model for the resolution of South Africa's racial conundrums. The Prime Minister said consultations were under way to finalise the constitution – meaning an election in 1963 for the Transkei. George, having been in those consultations, shook his head impotently.

The elections came. George was easily convinced, because he wanted to be convinced, that his friend Victor Poto would defeat Matanzima. The long weeks of preparation and then polling became a blur, because in his heart George knew the outcome. Still, he had to address dozens of community meetings in the kraals, to explain procedures to the people, and assure them that their choices would be honoured. The meetings always looked the same: a rude table, covered by a white sheet, set up under a tree. The headman flanking him, as he stood there in all his evident Europeanness in spite of the perfection of his Xhosa speech, sweating in mandatory suit and tie, more often than not with one of his own sons standing next to him, similarly besuited. In one photograph even Sam was there, a happy bottle-blond translucently white child in the Wild Coast heat, strapped to the back of a grinning Xhosa matriarch, surrounded by ten thousand tribesmen.

One particular image broke George's heart. It was captured in a photograph of a very old and wizened Pondo man, dressed in his single threadbare Umtata suit and battered hat, being dragged to a polling station on a sled of woven branches by two scrawny oxen led by his grandchild. It was too far for him to walk from his very deep kraal and he was smiling broadly and toothlessly and waving his pipe at the camera because he had been told he was about to exercise his democratic rights for the first time. No one who saw that picture needed to have explained to them the betrayal of belief that was occurring.

The election was over soon enough, and George would have liked to forget about it as fast as possible. Chief Poto had come inconveniently close to actually winning, meaning recounts and legal obfuscations before the Government could declare Matanzima the victor, and Chief Minister of the Transkei. *Ntabaka's Question* set itself squarely and sourly in George's gaze, and all of a sudden he knew he could not now stay in this new Transkei, though he loved it so and did not yet know how not to. His immediate response was to rebury himself in the work he could bear. He hosted the American Consul in Libode, who wrote to thank him for a most interesting and informative day spent in the Libode district. The Consul said he had greatly enjoyed getting out into the country, seeing the beautiful agricultural lands and, in particular, attending a meeting with the Africans from the location, headed by Welcome Singana. He asked George to pass on to Headman Singana his thanks at the earliest opportunity, and said it had been an honour to be introduced to Chief Poto. It had been very kind of Mrs Jameson to provide tea in both the morning and afternoon, and he certainly admired their beautiful house and garden, and the work George was doing.

Billy had, as George expected, made it through nautical college. He was now in Port Elizabeth, working as an apprentice in a power station. Here was another odd impact of the imposition of apartheid, like a tiny footnote in the greater scheme of things: because the country was now out of the Commonwealth, ties with the Royal Merchant Navy had been severed, and the South African Merchant Navy did not have many ships. So he couldn't get a place, as he had expected to. The power station was the next best option. George saw parallels with himself. Billy wrote often from the suburb of Walmer, where he had digs.

In 1963 Ryan wrote from St Martin's in Johannesburg. The school was beset with problems, escalating into a crisis. Most of the boys were leaving, because the masters had lost control of the situation and teaching was in chaos. Anyway it must settle down, said Ryan, either that or bust. For himself he intended to stick it out and get his matric unless it got much worse. They shouldn't worry about him. Of course George did worry about this most complicated of his sons, furthest away.

For Chris, the schooling roundabout spun on: it was decided that he would go to board at George's old school, Pietermaritzburg College. George worried about the expense, but was confident that this was the right thing to do. Chris hated his first year at the college – he was one of the 'new gentlemen', juniors who were fair game for the older boys – and to make matters worse he was not from Natal. At this time he prayed that the bus or car in which he was returning to school from the holidays, would crash. But he knew better than to make his parents aware of his true feelings. Instead he sent them a cutting from the *Natal Witness* about Cuthbert and Robert Jameson, relatives. Apparently, he said, some lions were starving way up in Northern Bechuanaland and when these Jamesons returned after a day's hunting in the bush, they found the hungry lions had gnawed big holes in the wings of their planes, and couldn't take off. It was thought that this was the first incident of its kind in Bechuanaland. Chris scribbled on the cutting: What kind of weirdo family are we?

The following year George wrote a note to himself which he kept in his desk drawer:

<u>South Africa: 1964</u>
Population: 17.5 million
Bantu: 12 million (± 70 per cent)
Transkei: 1 million (± 6 per cent)
Libode: 100 (0.000571428 per cent)

He was putting himself in his tiny context, but passions were strong in the smallest of places, and he happened to be the lord and master of this one. He found himself at the centre of a controversy fought as fiercely as if it was taking place in the cities. The rapid political changes in the Territory had been too much to absorb for some inhabitants of the white spots, and in Libode some townsmen rebelled against what they saw as the loss of white authority. In the *Transkei Territorial News* of 30th April 1964, George was the subject of the entire front page.

PONDOLAND UNDER COMMISSIONER AFTER
BOARD RESIGNS: *LATEST DEVELOPMENT*

THE affairs of Pondoland are now in the hands of Commissioner Mr G M Jameson, following the resignation of all the members of Libode's six-man Village Management Board.

This is the latest development in a civic controversy which has split the village and led to the repeated resignation of members of the Board. Different aspects have already led to criminal court proceedings and it is understood civil court proceedings are still pending.

Earlier this year four members of the Board, Mr A V Pushkin, Mr E Friend, Mr R van der Maas and Mr R C Pugh resigned, leaving everything in the hands of the Chairman, Dr M B Marnitz, and the Deputy Chairman, Mr D M Church, until an election meeting organised by the Assistant Magistrate of Libode, Mr P A van Horen. This meeting was held on March 26 and the four members who resigned were the only men nominated and so were elected.

There were stormy scenes at the meeting, Dr Marnitz said he would lodge an objection and that the matter might go to court, and there was a brief scuffle outside the meeting during which, it is alleged, blows were exchanged. Two days later Dr Marnitz and Mr Church resigned. On April 15 the remaining four men resigned, leaving Libode without a Village Management Board at all. In terms of the law, the Provincial Administration asked Mr Jameson to take over the function of the Board and accept appointment as District Commissioner of Pondoland, in addition to his other duties.

Mr Jameson has all the powers and functions of the Village Management Board and he will run the town in the Board's place until a new Board can be constituted. It is understood Mr Jameson will probably remain District Commissioner indefinitely.

Paramount Chief Poto sent a messenger on horseback from his Great Place to The Residency: Could he help Mr Jameson ensure that his villagers behaved? George thanked his friend for his concern, but declined the offer – he would sort out his own errant tribesmen, he replied, just as Chief Poto did his.

The working life of an emperor-in-miniature, such as George had become, was inordinately busy. But the turn of events did not change his mind: his goal remained to once more evacuate his family, and try life somewhere else. As a back-up, as always, he had been studying by correspondence at night, and passed the first year of a law degree at the University of South Africa, as well as achieving a distinction in Xhosa Language to go along with his qualifications in Zulu.

Their outward life continued and appearances were kept up as he hatched his latest escape plan. He and Jean were guests of honour at the Umtata Choral Society's presentation of *White Horse Inn* in the town hall of the small capital. The normal admission fee of one rand was waived for the Commissioner and his wife. The Umtata Round Table invited them to *The David Roy Show, Dancing & Cabaret Plus A Beauty Contest*, at the Hotel Imperial. Their social life was busy if not elevated. In October George placed a notice in newspapers in Umtata, Durban, Cape Town and Johannesburg: Golden wedding. Jameson-Roseworth. Married by Rev. Parkinson, at St James' Church, Greytown, Milton to Enid, on 30.10.1914. At Home, Ballito Bay, 31.10.1964. Congratulations Mum and Dad, from George and Jean, Emma and Keith, Gary and Jeanette, and all the grandchildren.

George loved Sam with a pure joy. He taught him, from a treasured illustrated book on display in the lounge, the Latin names for his favourite flowers: pansies, morning glories, golden showers, black-eyed susans and the like. Sam memorised the Latin, and George proudly made him do a show for every visitor to the house. Sam turned four in the garden of the Residency, surrounded by all his Transkei friends. He sliced his big toe in half, right through, vertically, with George's spade – trying to learn to be a gardener like him – but the injury was gruesome rather than dangerous. The family car made the journey to Umtata Hospital at record speed, and they could never remove the bloodstains from the back seat.

It had been decided finally that Ryan should extricate himself from the wreckage that was St Martin's in Johannesburg, and join Chris at Pietermaritzburg College to complete his schooling. This move went smoothly, to George's relief. Chris was doing very well in Mathematics and Arithmetic but told his parents he was struggling with Science. He was delighted to have his older brother at the same school, and said Ryan had been very nice to him, even introducing his younger brother to his new friends. He was in open-mouthed awe of Ryan's magnetic attractiveness to the girls of Maritzburg. They just follow him around, reported Chris, and Ryan doesn't even seem to notice though the rest of us have never seen anything like it. When he chose Holly to go to a session with him at Warner Beach instead of Margie, Margie cried for days. She told her friends Ryan was the most beautiful young man in Natal, if not the whole country.

What he didn't tell his parents was that within days of Ryan's arrival at the school, he had become a legendary rebel. He had doctored the conservative school uniform – adding pointed toecaps to his shoes, ditching the regulation shirt and the like. He and his gang shinned the drainpipes of the hostel each night to go out on the town, and Ryan developed an astonishing capacity for alcohol consumption and brawling.

The brothers being as different as could be, Ryan soon began to excel in Art and English, and to fail dismally in Mathematics. He was battling temporarily with Afrikaans, he said, but only because he had a childish teacher; a minute little man with a mind to match – a mental pygmy, was Ryan's scathing phrase. In Art and English he was far ahead of everybody, he said, and he was doing well in sport too – he'd played the college number six at tennis and wiped him out quite easily. In the Art classes, he had to admit, it was a bit pathetic to see some of the chaps copying his techniques, but the masters knew which were the originals. He wrote that he and Chris were getting on better than they ever had, and he could assure his mother and father that his younger brother was working hard.

Towards the very end of the tumultuous year, the Secretary for Justice himself wrote on the new official Transkeian Government notepaper: I wish to place on record my appreciation and thanks for the part you have played, and are still playing in Pondoland, and in managing and reconstituting the Libode Village Management Board. A copy of this minute is being forwarded to the Secretary for Bantu Administration and Development, with the request that it be placed on your personal file.

George wrote on the bottom: Mr Poswa. *Noted.* Type copy and place original on my personal file.

But beneath it all he began again to have his days of despair. He finally plucked up the courage to tell Jean he was sure they must leave the Transkei, and he should seize the chance while he was accidentally in such good standing with the Department. She was devastated. He wrote to Pretoria, the first time in his career that he had actually asked to be moved, saying he believed his work was done in the Transkei and that he would appreciate the opportunity of a fresh challenge. He did not presume to say where.

One day George said to Jean that he sometimes no longer knew whether he believed there was any chance of real acceptance for the white man in the black man's land, or for the black man in the white's. And as you could not keep people in their own places, or others out of them – everything all over the world was too far gone for that – it would be better if there was only one race; whatever colour emerged from the merging of black, brown, white and yellow. He went on in this vein: If you are like me and are told you do not belong here in Africa and are not wanted here, where do you belong? I cannot just pack up and go home: where is my home but here? I am nobody's settler. I have never set foot in England in my life. Did my great-grandfather know what he was doing in sending his son to live in Africa? What did my grandfather and father do by staying? What have I done to my own sons? I have made them love this place, without warning them that it might be a dangerous love, and an unrequited one. I wonder where they will be when this century ends. Will they still be Africans, still in Africa? Will there still be a place for them? Will they be bringing still more of us African Jamesons into the world in the year 2000, when I will be an old man of eighty-two? Do you know, Jean, that when I think about it carefully, the people I have met in my life whom I most admire have black skins? Why is that?

He could not resolve these things in his own mind at all. And in these times all talk at the white clubs in the Transkei was of Poqo, a militant African nationalist group which George's contemporaries thought of as a kind of Xhosa Mau Mau, and shivered. They had read their Robert Ruark in those parts. The murders at the Bashee Bridge seemed to presage something similar in horror to Ruark's expertly crafted stories, precisely intended to terrify white people in Africa like them.

When Matanzima was finally installed, George sat at his desk at the Commissioner's offices and thought about the decision he had made. As he worked through it, he concluded that he had three choices, of which he had selected the third. The others were to accept what had happened in the Transkei and to try to help to make it work as best he could – his voice could still be a voice of reason and fairness, though it was drowned out most of the time. The second was to resign and wash his hands of the whole unpleasant experience, and again take his chances on finding other employment somewhere outside Government. The first option was seductive, requiring no specific new action and no risk. The second, he concluded to his disappointment, he had not had the courage to grasp. The third kept intact his current safety net, such as it was. He recognised with regret but self-knowledge that he was indeed a man of limited bravery. He comforted himself with the fact that the path he had chosen was, at least, the safest option for his family.

He was indeed in good odour with the bureaucracy, and his request was received politely and acted upon quickly. In fact, wrote the Secretary, you were due for a promotion and we have a senior vacancy up north, in Witbank – a complicated situation, and a position which we need to fill with an experienced fellow of top calibre by the 1st of May 1965.

When the news had been circulated around the family, Billy wrote that he was glad to hear Dad was happy about the move, and that he knew two chaps who worked at Witbank power station; they said it was a nice enough place if very industrialised. He said you never know, but that if Dad stayed at this post long enough, it might be possible for him to get a job up there too and be close to the family again.

Ryan wrote: I hope you are pleased with the promotion to Witbank, Dad – I have heard it is an okay place, and not too big or small. Perhaps it's good, too, that Sam will have the choice of a bigger school than Libode! Sam was too young to understand that they were leaving his beloved Transkei forever.

Young Chris wrote from Pietermaritzburg: Witbank? Where is Witbank? I've never heard of it!

III

I KNEW I had now reached a place of great significance on the journey, and it scared me – so much so that I stopped abruptly. I blurted out to my wife that I thought I might not finish the damn thing after all. She looked at me nervously and said but why, after all this time and effort? It was not an easy question to answer, and I had to think carefully. Eventually I said to her, there is something different about the story's telling from here on, and I'm not sure I'm ready for it.

I had realised that I'd been hunting and gathering facts, dates, details, like finding a child's puzzle pieces lost under a sofa, for months, trying to work out what happened when, who had said what – all at one remove. It was my family's saga, to be sure, but until this point I had been too young to be fully in it, to fully feel it, and that protected me somehow, gave me a shield or a second skin. Now I understood why, after flowing and flooding and gushing, the story had all of a sudden dammed up when it reached Witbank. I had come to the precise stage where my own memories began to merge with those I was reinstating, patching together, imagining out of a box: from here on I had seen everything and heard everything.

Was I ready to release my own memories, packed away and pushed down for so long? What would I find there? Would I be the same person when it was done? For several weeks I left my pile of paper in my study, busying myself with other things and trying not to let it glare at me, accusingly incomplete, every time I came home; I hate not finishing what I have started. But much as I tried to let my work put the story in its place, it pulled at me like a dog tugging your sleeve. I stopped speaking about the story but could not stop thinking about it – and this triggered in me sombreness and dark moods that upset my wife and worried me.

Eventually I decided that the answer had to be yes; the memories had to be set free, the compulsion was too strong. I said to myself I now had the tool of recollection – childish and imperfect, to be sure, but vivid – to add to all the reconstruction. Just finish the story, I said. I fetched the pile of paper. I took leave from work.

Once I was back into the floodwaters, a new sense of urgency overcame me: I became terribly impatient when I found that the box, full as it was, still had some holes in it. My mother had hoarded plenty of documents from the Witbank years, but there were unsatisfactory, tantalising gaps along the way, suggesting to me that in my father's troubled state he must have begun not to write things down so diligently, so there was less for her to squirrel away. In Witbank the papers became more wayward: swathes of rich detail interspersed with silences, holes.

My obsession with filling every gap led to sporadic forays into amateur detective work. I became an odd fixture at the National Archives in Pretoria, demanding access to obscure files from obscure Magistracies in that monstrous place on earth my country had once been. To my own surprise I turned up more than three thousand pages, official documents and letters signed by Commissioner G M Jameson, and handwritten notes and reports in the fountain pen script now so familiar. The old documents were brittle but perfectly preserved, in their proper categories and chronologies, and I was comforted to feel that I was salvaging a little more of him. So, I thought with satisfaction, my country respects history and, as weighty and comprehensive was my mother's box, still there was more if you had a reason and the will to keep digging.

I also traced the psychiatrist who had treated my father, and wrote to ask whether I might talk to him; the young doctor now an elderly man. There came from Dr A J Lukic a courteous, infuriating, and, to my mind, overly defensive reply.

> Unfortunately, I am unable to recall without clinical records or notes at hand your father's case. I had started practice in July 1966 and any contact with your father the following year was so long ago that records would have been destroyed. Despite establishing a good therapeutic relationship with one's patient, it is not possible at times to elicit the underlying thought processes that result in their actions.

I had his address so I went and stood outside the building from which he practised. I stared at the windows for an hour. I wanted to barge in and say: This is not good enough! But at last I turned around and walked away. Those doors that didn't wish to open, I would not force.

I travelled to look at the places where my family had lived. Many of the old houses were still standing, but I resisted the temptation to knock on doors and ask to see inside. During this time I was living like a ghost. I was hardly at home. Eventually, one night when I was back in Durban, my wife sat me down and said, this must stop. You could spend the rest of your life hunting for things that may or may not be there. Don't you feel you know enough now?

So I stopped my searching, and allowed myself into the story. I released my memories, so long suppressed. I let go of the twenty-first century and swam back into my missing middle years of the twentieth. I allowed the rest of the story to wash over me and out of me.

BEFORE THEN

Coal Town, 1965

WE have never lived in a place like this, and my father has never had to do work like this. The English-speaking whites of the town pronounce it *Whit-bank*, the first syllable like the sound an owl makes, while the Afrikaners say *Vit-bunk*, and they are right; they made up the word, and the town, after all. White Reef is an acceptable translation, and it is a harsh place of coal and steel, the reddened face of industrialising South Africa.

We approach Witbank after two days' dusty journey by car, me strapped in the back seat and my father and mother in front, suitcases and boxes everywhere else. I have held in a pee for four hours or more – I've learned that in Afrikaans this is called *knyping* – because I am unwilling to do anything that might set things off. My mother has snapped and sniped at my father the whole way, predicting an accident because there is so much packed in the car he can't see properly out of the back window, reminding him that he had refused to send some of our possessions by rail, because of the cost.

From the national road the town seems to lurk behind its shield of black coal dumps, malevolently observing our arrival. The fields on either side of us are as brown as the Transkei's are green. Neither of my parents says a word. My mother arches her eyebrows and pinches her lips. I steal a look at her and then at my father, who grips the steering wheel and stares straight ahead seeming not to be blinking. We move into a hotel. It is all my mother can do not to cry at the contrast between the cramped, shabby room, and the thatched elongated spaciousness of the Libode Residency. She unpacks, sighing, and I sense my father cannot wait to get away from us. He says he must find the Commissioner's offices, even though it is a Sunday, so he'll know the way there in the morning.

Though winter is coming I am in my country shorts and ugly special boots to stop me becoming knock-kneed. I am five and a half years old. When I go with my mother to the corner café for provisions – the hotel does not serve dinner on weekends – the townie children look at me oddly and smirk. I know no one, my parents know no one, and already I have no idea of what to do or who to be in this place.

In the morning my father leaves for his new office before daybreak; still they have hardly spoken to each other. My mother and I go to the park. I try out the swings listlessly, and she sits on a bench glaring into space and seeming to curl her nose at the acrid air of the coal town. The countryside all around is said to be beautiful – or so we have read – but that must be far away from these coalfields, at whose epicentre we sit in the town. I have never been down a mine shaft, but feel I now know what it must be like. Days pass and we settle because we have to. My mother takes me to join the public library; the public swimming pool will have to wait for summer. I drive her to distraction with my talk about Libode and the Transkei.

On the 14th of May 1965, an article with a large photograph appears in the *Witbank News*: Mr G M Jameson has been appointed as Bantu Affairs Commissioner, replacing Mr J Chesterton who was transferred to Evaton. Mr Jameson hails from Libode in the Transkei where he was Bantu Affairs Commissioner and Magistrate.

My father plunges into his latest world, leaving us to make do as best we can. He ruffles my hair occasionally, as if suddenly remembering I'm there. I cannot know it, but he has realised almost immediately, with a horror that makes him nauseous, that the job that the 'experienced fellow of top calibre' is required to do by the Department is both enormous, and appalling. This is what his decision in Libode has led us all to, he realises with a sense of pre-emptive guilt. This is quite, quite unlike the pastoral idylls that have gone before, for all their complications.

The Bantu Affairs Commissioner and Magistrate of booming, entrepreneurial, hard-working, ugly, ruthless, exploitative, seg-regated Witbank in 1965 is required primarily to control the movements of tens of thousands of black workers – to meet the needs of the explosively growing collieries and other heavy industries as they expand, and to ensure that if they contract, unwanted workers do not stay in the town. It is more intricate than that, of course, but my father thinks this pretty much sums it up, and it is the true face of racial social engineering on a wickedly ambitious scale. He is awestruck when he grasps the sheer audacity of the grand apartheid plan: that there will eventually be *no black South Africans*! In Witbank, workers from, say, the Transkei and Zululand, as well as Portuguese East Africa and Malawi, will be lured at certain times, repatriated at others. Gigantic townships are being built and every attempt is being made to see that compounds are constructed along ethnic lines: black South Africans according to their language groupings, and so on.

With the bilious belching smokestacks, thrusting mine dumps like the work of mutant moles, dirty blackened sky, incessant noise of construction, and great tides of new arrivals like advancing divisions in wartime, my father says the scene makes him think of Dante's bleakest passages, or a Hieronymus Bosch nightmare, transposed on to an African plain. And he has chosen – chosen – to be at the centre of it.

It is his most pessimistic vision come to pass; not only is the work abominable, but it is of such volume as to be overwhelming, with almost no relief in terms of what he considers real upliftment projects, the dispensing of fairness and justice, and all the other straws at which he has clutched for so long. He will be working fourteen hours a day if he is to do this job he has sought, and from which comes the income to support us. He will be processing thousands of official documents each week. Worst of all for him, he feels he cannot blame anyone else for his predicament: not the Government, not the Department, not the industrialists, not even his lily-livered English-ancestry compatriots, most of whom he thinks have quietly stopped being serious about political opposition, choosing to let the Nationalists do the dirty work while they themselves accumulate wealth speedily and tut-tut about the new laws. No, it is he who has asked for this and he has got it, all on his own.

When the shock of the enormity of his situation has passed, and my father has dismissed as too humiliating his first impulse to resign within days of our arrival in Witbank, this man who is often indecisive makes a series of quick decisions. He will as far as possible shield us from the reality he will be facing each day at the Commissioner's offices. He will do the work he has to do as humanely as possible, and help as many people as possible. He will treat the work as a prison sentence he must serve each weekday, and in the evenings and on the weekends he will try to devote himself entirely to us, forgetting himself and what he does. He will try his utmost, as he has always promised himself, to create a family atmosphere of stability and nurturing kindness. He will see this out for five years, which will bring him to the earliest age at which he can retire without sacrificing his pension, and then he will finally get out and try to put the great mistake behind him.

By then his three older boys will be making their various ways in the world on their own, and he will have only my education to worry about. They should then be all right, and he can perhaps still even do some lecturing and writing in his retirement. This is possible, he says to himself, I can do this. This is George Jameson's emergency survival plan in Witbank.

The human instinct, the renewal reflex, hunts out help, big and small, in its attempts to survive. For all the horrors of the situation, time passes quickly and my father's decisions are holding. The work is as he feared, but he thinks it can be borne. And although not even its most loyal inhabitant would describe Witbank as an attractive town, it has its compensatory human warmth and all the pleasant middle-class amenities that attach to a settlement of its size. If I can only hang on, he thinks, we can make a life here while we have to.

My parents buy, with a mortgage, a small house on suburban Mountbatten Avenue. We all know it is ugly, cramped, and soulless, but we do not say so. The first thing my father does is to commission a group of Ndebele women to paint the whitewashed courtyard walls in their startling and meaningful patterns of blue, red, yellow, green and black. This is certainly a first for Mountbatten Avenue, and indeed the whole of white Witbank. Of course he will be able to transform this garden too.

Chris will come up from Pietermaritzburg and enrol at the brand new Witbank High School, within walking distance from home. My father says it is a perfectly acceptable institution – one he has himself been asked to open officially in May 1966, along with the Director of Education. He and my mother join the tennis club on the edge of town, and we make outings to the nearby dams. My parents meet some people they like and make new friends. My father excitedly decides he will take flying lessons. He tries his best to make the most of what they have, though he misses the very different interaction between white and black in the countryside.

Surprising Ryan springs another surprise. His entry in the national youth art competition is selected as the clear winner out of eleven thousand entries. There are photographs in all the newspapers, and it is announced that the parents of Ryan Jameson (17), pupil at Pietermaritzburg College, will be asked to attend a ceremony at the State Theatre in Pretoria to accept his award. Ryan's piece, a human horrorscape in black and white, throws the judges, who say it is not youth art at all. Another of his paintings wins a Royal Natal competition, and his first batik is exhibited in a Johannesburg gallery. In his letters Ryan is matter of fact about it all, and my parents are again proud but slightly confused. A friend of theirs who lives in Johannesburg writes effusively: How proud you must be of Ryan! What a thrill it will be for you to go up on stage in Pretoria! His picture was certainly the most ambitious in the whole competition, and most competently done. There is no doubt now that he is an exceptionally talented artist, and I do like his bleak humour too.

His painting appears in the *South African Digest*, and the local newspaper treats the matter as highly significant for the town's cultural coming of age. *Honour For Young Witbank Artist*, runs the headline, and the report omits to mention that Ryan has never set foot in the place. It is duly recorded that Mr and Mrs G M Jameson were guests of honour at the function in Pretoria, presided over by the Mayor, and addressed by a Professor from Pretoria University. The Professor commented favourably on the painting by Ryan Jameson. It is reported that Ryan is hoping to go to the University of the Witwatersrand next year; also a surprise to my parents.

One evening in the lounge of the house on Mountbatten Avenue, at the regular time when I am in my pyjamas and my parents have what they call their nightly 'spots', my mother points to an advertisement in the *Witbank News*. Witbank And District Musical Society, reads the notice: Choir and Orchestra Rehearsals continue satisfactorily for the concert scheduled for next month. A well-balanced programme has been arranged and the concert will be staged in the Taalfees Hall commencing at 8pm. The organisers are particularly anxious to keep to schedule and the public attending this concert are kindly asked to cooperate by being in their seats before eight. The concert will start dead on time! Commissioner Jameson will be Guest of Honour. My mother says: Oh Lord.

When it becomes clear that I am uprooted like a weed and wilting with loneliness, they make a plan for me. Because the nearby junior school will not admit someone so young, they appeal to the Mother Superior of the local girls' convent, who they have met. It's an unusual situation, she says, but yes, she will let me join their grade one class; I will be the only boy among the six hundred girls of the Convent of St Thomas Aquinas, Witbank, but it will help me through the year until I am old enough to go to Robert Carruthers Primary. Having grown up in the Transkei believing the world was made up of very few people who looked like me and my family, and very many who looked like Chief Poto and his family, I now enter one in which I am the only male in a great sea of females. But I am no longer lonely.

The work rears up in front of my father like a swaying snake. His eyes seem to be receding in their sockets, and he never sings his Xhosa songs any more. In the month of our arrival he had been appointed to the Location Advisory Board in the main black township. He attends his first meeting and is especially welcomed by the chairman and the secretary. Mr Jameson comes as our leader, the chairman says, and we will work smoothly with him. He invites my father to say a few words. He says: Mr Chairman and members of the Location Advisory Board, thank you very much indeed for your welcome. I found your discussions very interesting. I am thirty-one years in the Government service, with wide experience but not in the urban areas, and I have already seen in my first few days that I have much to learn here. All I can promise you is honesty and my very best efforts. Thank you very much.

He registers that dealings here between powerless black men and powerful white men are conducted in a formally bureaucratic manner – every exchange is through the Chair, every word minuted, every resolution proposed and seconded. There are none of the long, discursive, cross-legged discussions of the kraals, discussions which end in unspoken understandings rather than punctilious agreements; here in Witbank, he says, this is truly occupied Africa.

My father goes out on his own to visit all the other black townships, and begins to make contact with the designated representatives of the chiefs back in the homelands, or *Bantustans* as they are referred to up here. On his first trip he meets emissaries of the chiefs – *kapteins* in Afrikaans – Mabooe, Mapuru, Mgibe, Dhlamini, and Mapoch. On one of these journeys he scribbles in his notebook some estimates of local demography: North Sotho, ±30%, Ndebele ±40%, Swazi ±30%.

In July there is a circular from the Chief Bantu Affairs Commissioner, requiring all Commissioners to ensure that Bantu spectators are not attending sports events in white areas, and vice versa. The facilities available to Bantus are quite adequate, he is told, and in some cases very good. Next comes a directive whereby Commissioners are to establish the full particulars, including numbers, names, ages, and ethnic groups, of all elderly Bantu residing in the urban areas. Thereafter it will be determined whether such persons can be resettled in the Bantu homelands, given that they are no longer able to perform useful work in the white areas.

My father writes back that his office's enquiries indicate the presence of many very old people, some of whom are infirm. I am concerned, he writes, that these elderly Bantu are to be rendered homeless, and respectfully suggest a review of the policy. Your urgent and sympathetic attention to this matter is requested, please.

His letter is acknowledged but it is indicated pointedly that the matter might remain under consideration for some time, as this is a policy matter, and not the preserve of officials.

In September, Commissioners are instructed to prepare to establish Urban Bantu Councils, in terms of the provisions of Act No. 79 of 1961. My father is asked to address the Location Advisory Board once again, as it will be subsumed into the new

Council at some stage in the new year. He says: Mr Chairman, Assistant Location Superintendent and all Board Members, as I said when I first came here, I have experience in rural areas but not in urban ones. So this development is as new an experience for me as it is for you. But I would like to say that by my coming here I have now learned two things. One, we cannot make progress for the people of the locations if a bad spirit prevails between the officials and the community leaders. Two, we have no choice but to make the Urban Bantu Council work smoothly when it is implemented.

To keep his own slender and precarious grip on sanity – a sore enough test even in the easier places – my father spends some of his free time writing about his experiences in the rural areas, and the lessons he thinks he has learned about Africa and its peoples. In early 1966, when we have been in Witbank for more than half a year and are beginning to find some equilibrium, he is invited by the local church to deliver a lecture. It is not a prestigious platform, certainly not a university, but he is delighted and puts his all into preparing the paper, working as hard as he would if he were going to address the League of Nations. The big night approaches and my mother, Chris and I will accompany the Commissioner to the church hall where he will deliver his remarks.

Before we leave the house, my father spends some time sitting alone, thinking carefully about the progress in life of his boys, especially those who are no longer in the home. Billy is now a fully employed adult in the Merchant Navy, called Safmarine; finally isolated South Africa mustered enough ships for him to find a place. From Ryan the end-of-year news from Natal is bad, if as predicted. He writes that the exams are over and he has definitely failed both Maths and Science; he knows this will disappoint his parents deeply. I'm very sorry, Dad, he says. He says he'll get his distinction in Art, but he's not going to make it to university just yet. He has been asked by a gallery to put more of his work on sale, though, which is something. My father simply does not know what to do about this boy of his. My parents talk about Ryan in whispers when I am out of the room.

At the church hall finally, we feel very proud as my father stands to speak, impeccably dressed and distinguished-looking, with his strong, kind, troubled eyes gazing out over a swathe of expectant white faces.

Ladies and Gentlemen, we live in a wonderful country – full of difficulties, divergent views, and interest. Every day brings its challenge and it is challenge that is stimulating. I am a Bantu Affairs Commissioner. My particular interest is in the field of language, Bantu custom and history. Things are changing very rapidly in our country and I must say I am not able to devote myself exclusively to these matters close to my heart, but I lay modest claim to being equally proficient in English, Afrikaans, Zulu and Xhosa, and I can understand and make myself understood in all the other indigenous languages. I hope one day to attain degree major status in Zulu and perhaps, in my later years, to be a lecturer in Zulu at a university.

Zulu is a marvellous language. Some may think the Zulus a primitive people with a simple language. They are not and it is not.

Iqaqa loqaqazela oqawweni
The polecat will quiver on the cliff edge
Iqaqa laqikaqikela kuqaqaqa
The polecat somersaulted on the lawn grass

Do you realise what you are dealing with in saying this? Firstly you are using a language as involved and as advanced as any on earth – with many more tenses than English, and more than twice the number Afrikaans has. Where do the beautiful clicks come from? Bushman. When the conquering Bantu armies came south they killed off the Bushman men and married the women. Bushman mothers naturally passed over clicks to their children and these eventually became part of the language.

Iqaobana lomqaqoba liqhawulwa ligqeshana
The little wild berry tree is broken by a small girdle

And still I have not used all the clicks. Let me demonstrate them.

C	*Q*	*X*	*KL*
CH	*QH*	*XH*	
GC	*GQ*	*GX*	*NKC*
NC	*NQ*	*NX*	
NGC	*NGQ*	*NGQ*	*NGQ*

Zulu is truly a beautiful language, capable of excellent poetry, onomatopoeic expression and idiom. And when you speak it and think in it, what deep understanding one is capable of. It is involved and almost mathematical in the accuracy of its structure. Do you know that a Bantu child does not talk ungrammatical baby talk? As soon as he begins to string words together they are correctly linked. This is because of the musical and rhythmic basis to the grammar.

> *Izinkomo zami ezinkulu zibaleke zayongena ezibayeni*
> My big cattle ran and entered the cattle kraals

The recurrent 'Z' is music and comes from what we call the concordial prefix *zi* in *izinkomo*, cattle.

> *Isitha sami esihle sithambe sazesafa*
> Here is the recurrent 'S'.

And so the ear teaches the child, until expressions like *Incuncu ephuza kwezide izizaba – ithi ingaphuza kwezifishane iqundeke umlomo,* can be used in the praise songs of a king and hold much subtlety of meaning. In this part of the praises of the late King Solomon of the Zulus, he was warned to uphold his station in life and not stoop to the common. But how it was said! Thus: a honey sucker (because of its long beak) must drink in deep pools – should it drink in shallow ones, it will blunt its beak.

How different are various cultures. Zulu lacks the word 'please'. You have to get round this by using a certain inflection in voice and saying something like 'will you' or 'would you'. *Ake*. There is no thank you – instead, you say 'I praise'. *Ngiyabonga*. No hello either, but the cautionary *sakubona,* we see you, and the answer 'we see each other' – *nyabonana*.

> *Lixabene ixolo ngomxhaxh' omxoxosi*
> *Lagxangxas' ingxungxu lixhom' isixhengxe*
> *Ixoxo kaloku lixhap' umxhafele laxobuk'*
> *Ixolo lixabana noxam'*

The bull frog fought because of the watermelon seen, and the grey buck interceded, hanging up the hatchets, because the bullfrog was licking foam from his lips and had lost some skin fighting the leguaan.

Actually most of the click expressions I have used are Xhosa, not Zulu. Xhosa is a cousin language to Zulu, as is Swazi. Xhosa is far richer in clicks. The Xhosas were in the vanguard of the Bantu invaders of what is now South Africa and met up with Bushmen in greater degree. The Swazi use the easier clicks and I venture to say that they are not as accurate or consistent. The following waves of Bantu – Tsonga, Venda and Sotho – have languages devoid or almost devoid of clicks.

You can enter a new world of meaning, a new world of understanding if you learn a Bantu language, and you can enter upon a most interesting study if you enter upon the vast sea of language. Africa has six hundred of the four thousand languages in the world.

My work has taken me all over southern Africa. I have had to do with the Zulu, proud of race, custom and language – a fascinating history of a tiny sub-clan of Zululand that under the 'Black Napoleon', Tshaka, conquered all Zululand and Natal, and sent people from present-day Natal to conquer and establish new nations – the Shangaans of Portuguese East Africa, the Ndebele of Rhodesia and the Transvaal, the Fingo of the Cape, and even the Zwagendabas of Lake Nyasa.

The Swazi as I know him is a very likeable and peaceable man, you could say the Swiss of Africa. During all the turmoil that took place in the *mfecane* they stayed right where they were, using diplomacy to its utmost.

The Hereros of South West Africa are proud to the point of arrogance. Perhaps arrogance is the wrong word, but certainly haughty with a bearing one could say was superior. And why not? Were they not the feudal lords of South West Africa who owned vast herds of cattle tended by the more numerous subject race, the Damara?

Bushmen. We supplied tobacco and mealie meal to border police posts for the Bushmen trackers, and after a few days salt, until eventually they would take porridge.

The Ovambos of South West Africa are of the purest of stock with a language basically similar to Zulu, but strangely with no clicks even though they have Bushmen living amongst them. This is because there is no history here of the killing off of the men.

The Basuto are a proud and in my experience an industrious race. Then the newcomers to South Africa – the Vendas, whose little stone cairns in the Zoutpansberg make me wonder whether they had a hand in the building of Great Zimbabwe. Could they have worked with the Queen of Sheba's artisans?

And amongst the Vendas the Lemba, who have no territory, no king – the priest tribe of the Vendas who install Venda kings and perform all religious rites without ever intermarrying with the Vendas nor eating with them. People who 'kosher' kill all their animals. How far have they come from, to have customs so like those of our Jewish people?

And last of all the Rain Queen. In all Bantu folklore there is the mythical rain queen. Every Zulu child hears fairy tales about her – but she is real. She is the Queen of the Balobvedu of Duiwelskloof, known as the Modjadji. The Modjadji never has sons – only daughters – and she never dies. Herein there is something like the traditional English announcement 'The King is dead – long live the King'.

I hope I have succeeded in quickening your interest in this aspect of life in South Africa. I believe you cannot understand South Africa without learning the history and the languages of the indigenous Africans. Many attitudes are assumed and bad decisions taken on the basis of ignorance. I cannot say more than that.

The evening is a mild success, though some younger members of the audience cannot help fidgeting during the long passages in a tongue they do not understand and cannot really see the relevance of, here in Witbank. My mother, Chris and I are congratulated by the adults. Of course I do not really understand it all, but I am watching everything, listening to everything, so proud that this elegant man is my father.

He is asked to make other speeches. This both pleases and alarms him – he is not sure that one with his moral frailties should be presuming to lecture others. But he goes ahead, and develops his theme of the dichotomy of ultra-liberalism on one side, and what he has long called the extreme *unperson* attitude on the other. He says, for what must be the thousandth time in his life: You cannot deal with a man unless he has pride in himself, his race, his traditions – and you yourself have sincere respect for that pride. He adds, unguardedly, that perhaps there is no solution to South Africa's problems. But, he says, perhaps problems themselves cause creativity. Nations can become lethargic when they think they have solved all their problems – perhaps The Problem, the challenge, is a talking point, a catalyst for thought, even a reason for our existing?

Then he muses: What is the real reason we whites are here? I cannot honestly answer that question, because it has defeated me most of my adult life. But we *are* here, that is a fact, and speaking for myself there is nowhere else I feel I belong or am loyal to, nowhere else I would want to go to, or perhaps could go to. So the question we should be wrestling with is that if, barring revolution or envelopment, we of European ancestry can contemplate being here as part of South Africa, what can we do to help our country, and every single person in it who calls it their country, grow and prosper and achieve their own human potential? Again I am afraid I do not have a glib answer, but I am sure I am right in saying that it is the question we need to be asking. I remain convinced that Europeans in Africa have a real responsibility at least, all of us, to promote balanced race relations, responsible training for all, and the creation of equal opportunities for all.

Through a member of one of his audiences, my father's thoughts come to the attention of the South Africa Foundation, in Johannesburg. He is asked to prepare a submission, which he writes by hand and which is lovingly and precisely typed by my mother. In it he revisits his ever-recurring theme: Love thy neighbour as thyself presupposes differences and a respect for who and what each person is, no matter their skin colour or language. Unless for each and every man pride in himself, his family, his clan, his race, his language and his traditions means something to him himself, then he is no neighbour but a contender, a maladjusted competitor and, at worst, an enemy.

By what means should the problems of South Africa be tackled? Educate, protect, lead. Two million Africans, being one eighth of the total African population, are attending school and all are being advanced in commerce, industry and agriculture. It should be the entire African population, and their education should be of the best. That would unleash in itself changes for the better of all that we cannot now dream of; that are beyond my meagre capacity to dream dreams.

On another platform he extemporises, uncharacteristically

explosively and witheringly: It is not enough to call yourself an African because of a geographical accident of birth. Sometimes I find myself despising white people who speak of their love for African landscapes, sunsets, African wildlife – but never the African people, not *the people*. Africa is not a film set!

He begins to correspond with a lecturer in archaeology at the University of the Witwatersrand in Johannesburg – they share an interest in the migrations to southern Africa from AD 800 onwards – and it is suggested to him that he introduce himself to a professor of the School of African Studies in Cape Town. He is pleased when he is asked to make more and more speeches.

Beyond the office hours, my father feels that he and his family are gaining a measure of respect and acceptance in the town. My mother's sense of alienation is slowly easing and she is making an effort to build friendships and learn to live in this place. She smiles when the local newspaper carries a special feature on the interesting Jamesons, who have travelled so widely in southern Africa. When we go to Uncle Barley Roseworth's golden wedding in the Natal midlands, it is reported as a news item; my mother's scrapbook is filling up again. The newspaper also carries a photograph of my father's Ovambo stools, bought with excitement all those years ago near the Okavango River. Africa has a great deal to teach European artists, he is quoted as saying, and he notes that Picasso himself had begun a lifelong study after noticing an African mask in a Belgian tourist office. In South Africa, my father says in the interview, the interplay between the African and European traditions is becoming readily noticeable in a most exciting way.

In this mood of enthusiasm, he writes in 1966 to the Chief Bantu Affairs Commissioner in Johannesburg, to say he has a personal and particular interest in Bantu migrations, racial affinities, history, language, custom and culture. In a document filled with historical detail and his own conclusions, he argues that in spite of the official policy which holds that all black people in white areas are by definition impermanent migrants, this flies in the face of both reality and fairness. Children are being born who have never visited their so-called homeland, he says, and it would be far better for black people to have freeheld homes, businesses and industries in the urban areas. He ends his proposal with another one. He reminds his superior that after the Bambata Rebellion of 1906, Dinuzulu, Paramount Chief of the Zulus, was banished by means of deportation to the farm Uitkyk, in the Middelburg district near Witbank. I venture a suggestion, he says, which I know may be wholly unacceptable to the Department, but which I believe may have in it sufficient merit for consideration. The suggestion is that a valued gesture may be made by the Republican Government of South Africa to the Zulu nation by proclamation of the place of detention and demise of the present Paramount Chief's grandfather, as a National Monument. In passing, says my father, I might mention the interesting fact that Miriam Mbata, daughter of one of the exiled Dinuzulu's personal servants, married Dinuzulu in 1910 and is alive and resident in the Old Location of Witbank, which falls under my jurisdiction. Other Zulu descendants of advisers and servants of Dinuzulu are to be found in this district, and members of the Zulu Royal Family are not infrequent visitors.

But he receives an opaque response: Your minute No. (0)N1/12/5, refers. Because of the many facets involved it is regretted that it cannot, as yet, be replied to.

He gets the message. For all his attempts to create new avenues for the thoughts he cares about and that interest him, the machinery of the system for which he works clanks and grinds on, growing bigger and more self-confident with each passing month; machines beget machines. He is reprimanded in writing by the Chief Bantu Affairs Commissioner for having approved, without authority, the application for employment in Witbank as a domestic servant of one Bantu female Christine Mtswali V/F 2681961. This is followed by another stern letter saying reports have been received by the Head Office indicating increasing incidents of crime by Bantu youths in the Witbank area. If this is unchecked, my father is told, drastic measures will need to be considered. He replies that he has investigated the matter and believes it has been exaggerated. In any event, he says, it will soon be the school holidays, when the mothers of the township will be able to take leave to spend time with their children. At this stage therefore, he says, I cannot see any urgency for considering the establishment of a Bantu Youth Service Corps in Witbank.

On the 1st of March 1966 my father receives from the Secretary for Bantu Administration and Development in Pretoria, Circular No. A5/2, addressed to All Urban Local Authorities In The Republic Of South Africa. It is an instruction to Bantu Affairs Commissioners that there will be a Festival to mark the fifth anniversary of the Republic, and the attendance of Bantus in each area is required. In pursuance of this, exceptional expenditure may be charged to a special account set up by the central Government. In addition, the Secretary says, the Government will donate a school bell embossed with the Republican coat of arms to each Bantu school that participates in the Festival. All functions must be concluded before the end of April 1966.

The matter dominates the proceedings of the Location Advisory Board. A Republic Festival programme will be printed, with the Festival emblem alongside the coat of arms of Witbank, to be sold to the residents of the locations. In Zulu, 1300 copies, in Sotho, 500. For the children, 600 packets of sweets and 600 soft drinks will be supplied at the Government's expense. One large ox will be slaughtered, and there will be 150 gallons of Bantu beer. The Mayor will address the Bantu attendees and there will be a march past of all school choirs, carrying flags. After an address by the senior representative of the chiefs, there will be a fly-past by the South African Air Force, and a fireworks display. The day will end with tribal dancing and a football match. My father grits his teeth through the festivities. But the authorities are satisfied with him again.

One evening toward the end of our first year in Witbank, my father comes home from his office carrying a familiar official envelope and a strange smile on his face. It is from the Honourable this confirming the decision of the Honourable that, he tells my mother, and then cackles disturbingly, like a hyena; laughs in a way we have never heard from him before. He reads her the letter, which says that so pleased with his work is the Honourable the Minister of Bantu Administration and Development, that on the recommendation of the Public Service Commission, he has approved a special promotion of Mr G M Jameson to the post of Principal Bantu Affairs Commissioner. This makes him junior only to the Chief Commissioner in Johannesburg. He will earn R4500.00 per annum, backdated to May 1st. Congratulations, says the Honourable, and we look forward to your further contributions in our important work. My father says to my mother: What would *you* do with this letter?

In June a Proclamation appears in the Government Gazette, which my father also brings home. It is titled Establishment Of Bantu Labour Control Boards, Proclamation No. 866. He reads it out at the dinner table.

> Under the powers vested in me by section 28 of the Bantu Trust and Land Act, as inserted by section 24 of the Bantu Laws Amendment Act, 1964, I, MICHIEL COENRAAD BOTHA, Minister of Bantu Administration and Development, do hereby declare that, as from the first day of the month following that in which publication hereof takes place, a Bantu Labour Control Board shall be established for each area specified in the Schedule hereto.

My father points to number three on the attached schedule: Witbank. That's me, he says. Here we go. He will be required to become Chairman of the Bantu Labour Control Board, which will do just what its name suggests.

His files of office correspondence become bloated as he battles to do the work he has to do. He is heavily understaffed, and complains regularly in writing to Johannesburg and Pretoria. In fact he writes thousands of documents, which are all carefully filed, and which he tries his best to forget as soon as they have left his desk. He composes a five-page proposal to the Chief Bantu Affairs Commissioner in Johannesburg, setting out a plan to merge the Bethal, Middelburg and Ogies district authorities with that of Witbank, and to establish and fund a Bantu craft centre. He receives a reply: The question is at present under consideration and the Bantu Affairs Commissioner of Witbank's request is, for the time being, held in abeyance.

Again he gets the message.

But for all the pacts of purgatory he has made with himself, my father has not given up on the dream of deliverance, no matter how thin it has worn. He reads a report in the newspaper, heart beating like an adolescent with a crush, about the establishment of a new Museum of Man and Science in the City of Johannesburg. He writes immediately to the director, Mr A S Beit, offering his services in any capacity at all, remuneration highly negotiable. Perhaps the Director smells the desperation on the page, perhaps he is just a kindly man, but the blow of the reply is softened by its civility.

Dear Mr Jameson,

Apologies for the delay in replying, but even at this early stage I am snowed under with correspondence. People with your qualifications and convictions will certainly be of great service to us when we are up and running, but that will still take a couple of years. Buildings don't get built that quickly and there is still a great deal of preparatory work to be done before we really begin. Nonetheless, your name and address is now on my list and, who knows, perhaps we will need you sooner than what we now think. Thank you for your friendly offer.

Another one for the collection, says my father bitter-sweetly when he receives the reply. I could publish a book of rejections – that's never been done before, so far as I know.

George, says my mother, that's just not funny.

To his own more modest library at our home he adds the just-published lectures – *Bushmen and other Non-Bantu Peoples of Angola* – of Antonio de Almeida, who is leading an anthropo-biological survey of Angola and has been working with Professor Tobias. My father talks briefly of writing to them, too, but quickly decides he cannot face going through the process again, with its seemingly inevitable soaring and dashing of hope. He says perhaps some other time he will feel strong enough to keep trying.

Ryan has written his last letter from Pietermaritzburg. His final results were as he forecast: distinctions in the Arts, failure in Maths and Science by irretrievable margins. He had discontinued his extra lessons in those subjects, he informs his parents peremptorily, because they were a waste of money and he was constantly being told he has to save money. He says he sometimes has a sick feeling, he doesn't know why, but he feels like a flying ant that has lost its wings. Accompanying this letter is one from his headmaster; in spite of Ryan's failure he is impressed enough by his talent to write a special commendation. As an artist Ryan is much more than an above-average student, he writes, he has exceptional ability. My father appreciates the trouble taken, but says to himself: no university degree, only talent in an entirely uncommercial field … sounds familiar. Billy still writes regularly, eager to find out all he can about our doings in Witbank, this latest clearing in which the tent of the wandering Jamesons has been pitched.

There is still time and space for some laughter in our home, even in these Witbank years. Chris, on being driven around the town in the family car to look at the sights, remarks in all seriousness: Dad, do you know this family in Witbank called *Kie*? They must be very important, because they seem to own part of every company and every shop in town. My father is initially nonplussed, but then roars with laughter: In Afrikaans, *en Kie* is the equivalent of the English *and Company*. On another day my father impishly explains to Chris, who has been asking for more pocket money, that the word restaurant originates from the phrase

Rest your rand – and that is why we hardly ever eat out; we have no spare rands to rest.

And I, already known within the family for asking strange questions, cause laughter too. After the Republic Day celebrations at which my father had to officiate, I ask him: If this is the *Republic* of South Africa we are living in, Dad, then where are the *other* parts of South Africa? Following my childish logic, inwardly smiling wryly, my father answers: Good question, my boy, good question.

Then in July 1966 the day comes finally – and it has taken longer than the ten years my parents estimated – when my father announces that their Overseas Account is full. For all that is swirling around in our lives, they are to make their aeroplane journey to the Europe they have read about in books and heard about at family firesides, but never seen. They pore over an intricately detailed itinerary, carefully executed on a manual typewriter, six pages long, from Rennies the travel agents. Chris and I look over their shoulders. Travelling Itinerary Especially Prepared For Mr & Mrs G M Jameson: Visiting Portugal, Spain, England, Ireland, France. Commencing Thursday, 1st September, 1966 At Johannesburg, Terminating Sunday, 2nd October, 1966 At Johannesburg.

My mother and father are beside themselves with disbelieving excitement and the atmosphere in the house alters completely. I whoop around the garden. I hear my father singing in the bath, his favourite Xhosa Click Song: *Igqira lendlela nguqotwane/Igqira lendlela nguqotwane/Ubeqabe legqithapho ahi uqo ngqotwane/ Ubeqabe legqithapho ahi uqo ngqotwane.* My mother is fussing around like a dainty bird fluffing its feathers. It is agreed that while they are away Chris, now fifteen, will look after me with the help of our next-door neighbours, the Goldmans. Those few friends who have travelled abroad before drop by with helpful hints and bring gifts for my parents to take on the trip. At long last George and Jean Jameson can make their small people's pilgrimage to the distant island in the northern oceans from which their forebears originated, once upon a very long time ago.

My father is so certain this will be a highlight of his life that he spends more money than he can afford to buy a large tape recorder with a separate microphone. My mother brings out evening wear she has not worn for years. My father proceeds to record a running commentary of the travels of the Jamesons of Africa through the Europe of the mid-1960s.

WE'RE at about twenty thousand feet, still climbing. The seats are very comfortable but it's hot. I counted fifty windows along the side and there are six seats in each row, so that must be three hundred, except of course for those First Class people who have only four seats, I think, in a line.

We only just made it because Jean was a bit slow in getting dressed. What a production that all was – I would have slept at the airport overnight if I'd had my way. When we were doing the final packing in Witbank Jean gave me hell because of how much I've packed. And I have to concede she was right: when I weighed the suitcase on the bathroom scale it was sixteen pounds overweight, and I'm lucky South African Airways were forgiving. I brought too many mackintoshes for certain, quite a few bottles of whisky – but they won't go to waste – and that portable massager machine for this bally rheumatism that I'm developing.

We'll get to Luanda tonight at 8.45. It's a Boeing 707 and drinks are just being served. Jean and I have ordered gin and tonics. After Luanda we'll sleep I hope. I don't quite know how to adjust this seat yet, but I believe it goes back. We get to Lisbon at five to six tomorrow morning, to our hotel by about eight. I wonder where we'll cross the Okavango River. Maybe we'll just tip through a portion of South West Africa. Of course we'll have to, because South Africans are not allowed to travel over other African territories – even at thousands of feet up!

I still can't quite believe we're on this trip. We seem to have been talking about it all our lives. I suppose it's when we first see a foreign town, a foreign country, that I'll realise it is true. We've got a window seat. It's dark, but there's a very pretty red-orange glow on the horizon. In just thirty days time, just one month, on the first of October 1966, we'll be coming back over this same country but in the other direction, back to reality.

I'm glad I bought this tape recorder and microphone. I know they're big and bulky and Jean is embarrassed by it all – she thinks I look very eccentric and unsophisticated – but I think one will get more out of it than by taking a lot of pictures which in any case you can see in *National Geographic*. And it'll be nice for the boys to be able to listen to these tapes one day. Although Jean says she'll be blushing her way around Europe what with me making a spectacle of myself, what I plan to do is to talk directly into it when I can, to describe things as I see them.

Jean says she refuses to speak on this thing unless she's given proper warning! I wish I could catch her voice now, she's sitting talking to this young Portuguese man and they're getting on famously. The steward has just brought along our gin and tonics, and it's so steady we've got the tonic bottles standing just like in a lounge. Cheers Jean! You know darling, I don't know why I haven't got the real thrill yet. I somehow don't feel yet that we're actually doing it. It's like going in a train, except there isn't that rattle-rattle. It's cooling down now. The Portuguese passenger is showing us some wood carvings that he bought at the airport, Jan Smuts. I don't know those woods. I think they look Rhodesian. Jean says he's got quite a sad story, his parents fled Portuguese West Africa when the changes came. Made their way as refugees with few belongings across the river into old Ovamboland in South West. Then to South Africa where he says they have not really settled. He is studying in Portugal, but wanted to go back to Luanda and the countryside to see something of his childhood. A bit like what we're doing, going to Chichester, though of course that's not about my own childhood, but rather about my ancestors.

I'm thinking now about my boys. Young Sam seems happy enough and I hope Chris is going to manage with him. Ryan went off with ten quid so perhaps he'll be all right for this month. Billy I don't have to worry about. There are at least nine children on the plane; I can hear some of them crying. Oh aren't we glad that we haven't got our children with us, and I don't mean that unkindly.

Give me an aspirin, won't you Jean, I feel a little bit headachy. But I don't need an air pill. We've just passed our first test! Jean says that a gentleman across the aisle asked her whether she comes from England; he can't quite believe we're South Africans. That's a good sign, because I certainly don't want to be explaining what a Bantu Affairs Commissioner is and does all the way through this tour, or in fact even once. I plan to forget that entirely.

It's cool now. It's a quarter past seven, and we should be well over the desert. Down below I see a big fire, I suppose it's a bush fire. The steward came by: Can I put your table down for dinner madam? It's an indented tray: steak, peas, carrot, two kinds of sweets, a bun, cheese, some biscuits. I don't know if I can get through all this. It's just been announced that we're passing over the Bechuanaland border. Coffee has been served, so I think we must be near Luanda now. I imagine that soon they'll be telling us to fasten our seatbelts, put our shoes on etcetera. It's getting bumpy and I suppose it's because we're starting to drop in altitude. What a wonderful aeroplane – it's about as long as a dance hall!

To think that fourteen years ago we lived somewhere near here, or down there rather. It's quite eerie, everybody quiet. I can hardly hear a thing, my ears are blocked. Fasten seat belts says the notice that's flashed on in front of us. I can see the lights of Luanda; a pretty sight is Luanda at night. We've got to set our watches back an hour. It's 71 degrees. Cameras not to be taken on to the airport because it's a military airbase. We must be about three thousand feet up now, from what I remember of my flying. I didn't think Luanda was as big as this. The stewardess has just said: *Maak asseblief u stoel gordels vas en moet nie rook voordat die paneel ligte afgeskakel is;* please fasten your seat belts and do not smoke before the panel lights are turned off.

•

Well I had to turn off the recorder there for a while. We went into the transit tea room and couldn't get out. It was as hot as you could make it. Engines are warming up now, we're still climbing, and we're over the sea. People are starting to push their seats back into the reclining position.

It's five o'clock now and we're all awake again. We've had quite a good sleep. Only half an hour before we get to Lisbon. Coffee is being served. I'm getting excited. I hope I have a window seat on the way back so I can see what I can see of Africa, perhaps even the Sahara. It's quite dark outside. Now there are the lights of Lisbon, can you see them Jean? Just like a string of pearls. It must be an esplanade along the coast. Look at that floodlit castle, my dear, and the pattern of the streets; just look at all of those patterns. We're coming down, now we've touched down. Jean, it's like Lourenço Marques – looks like it, eh?

Up to Room 317 in the Excelsior Hotel. The porters don't understand any English. I've just handed over ten escudos as a tip, apparently it's about a bob. Very nice and clean looking place. Strange looking things in the toilet, though – a rope contraption from the roof. We're going to rest for a while, and tomorrow we'll go on a bus tour, eat at a café, and have a night tour which is to cost us about four pounds I think.

I must get one thing about today taped before I forget it. Lisbon is really so strange, so old world, and we had a wonderful experience this morning because as I've said I've brought far too much luggage with me, like my greatcoat etcetera. Jean doesn't want to go through the embarrassment of remarks at every airport, bus station and hotel, so I've agreed to try to get some of it sent back to South Africa. Luckily Mr Batista, who's the Portuguese Inspector with whom I work in quite close collaboration at Witbank, gave me the address of his sister. So we went up to Rua Compalide. What driving, all on the right – you want to see these taxi drivers, I don't know how there aren't more accidents. And people are talk-talk-talking, running across the streets. It just doesn't look orderly. A very old town, Lisbon, very old buildings all over the place.

I don't know where we went to, over all these cobbled streets, past the old buildings. Then we got to one building – they have a funny way of numbering things here. We went to the first floor, we knocked at the door of the wrong side, and a lady came out – but just peeping and then after that she spoke over her shoulder and a man came out. Most helpful. The lady was a relative of the Batistas, but not the one we were looking for. Then she started on the telephone and the more we asked her to leave it alone, the more she insisted: sit down. She made three or four phone calls and eventually got another address; very complicated and my plan is evidently not going to work. So we'll just have to buy another suitcase and Jean will have to put up with the blushes.

To get the taxi we were standing outside when an old woman, who heard us speaking, ran all the way up the street and then eventually came back down with a taxi – I gave her ten escudos and she just about kissed me for it. And to think that Europeans speak of Africans as being primitive, meaning it badly. There is a primitiveness here in Portugal, but I would rather call it honesty. You can get very sophisticated people who are dishonest, don't I know!

Now we're on a bus tour outside Lisbon and I must say this part looks just like Tongaat in Natal and is just as hot. Pine trees and gum trees, poor and stunted, oleander, and some stuff that almost looks like Port Jackson willow. Some places are very green; they look like Durban. Driving on the right like this it seems we're going to have an immediate crash with every vehicle that comes along. Look at that, Jean, that really could be Tongaat. Have you noticed the big open spaces everywhere? Old military installations, old forts, but so much space that isn't built on. Last night we heard the *fado* singers, and Jean was most affected. It really is the singing of the sad soul.

•

I wasn't able to make any recordings on the trip to Spain – Jean wouldn't let me – but here we are now. It's the 3rd of September. We're at the Gran Via Hotel in Madrid. It's hot! I knew about siestas when I was stationed at Ingwavuma, but I never realised that in this climate they are not luxuries, but absolutely essential. We have seen Cascais, which has an atmosphere I will remember. Estoril is a fashionable resort, and there are some very nice places there – for a resort. But to me it doesn't compare with South African places; Durban, the Cape Town waterfront. It doesn't compare, I think.

When we were offered drinks at Estoril, I said I wasn't used to the wine and we should have something more South African. So we asked for a gin and tonic. Well, we were brought very tall glasses with huge blocks of ice and I should imagine at least a third full of gin, and a bottle of tonic was handed to us. We finished those drinks, though we shouldn't have – the biggest G & T of my life! Time is running out. We've been bathing and taping and we're supposed to be off to a bullfight. I think this is going to be wonderful. I'm so glad, so very pleased that Jean agreed to go with me – she knows how much I want to experience this.

Now I have my tape recorder hanging around my neck to look like an ordinary camera – or so I hope! – with the microphone in my pocket. It is inside the pocket so that I can operate the on-off switch. Canny, eh? But rather awkward to keep one's hand in a trouser pocket fiddling about, and I am getting some funny looks. Look, Jean is crimson – she thinks it's very rude! Now we're inside the building, going through the *sambrio*, the shady side gate, where to or what to I just don't know. I haven't been this excited since I can't remember when.

I've just bought a beer for three pesetas, very reasonable compared to home, and read up on how the bullfight works. It's a disgrace for the matador, apparently, if the bull is not killed in fifteen minutes. You will not believe this, but Jean has just told me the people sitting on our left live in South Africa! Excuse me, but let me get this straight: we are George and Jean Jameson of Witbank, and you are Karl and Francine Jacobs living in Johannesburg. Imagine that we are sitting together at a bullfight in Madrid! This is all fun isn't it? Jean says all fun indeed, especially for South Africans who've never been out of the country before!

Oh Jean look! Look! Here comes the bull for the matador. Oh, it's a pass! And here's the kill! That's it! It's right through him!

Well that was a very exciting bullfight, though the Spanish people sitting with us said the matador was very poor, and would never appear again because he had taken so long to kill the bull, and then done it inelegantly with the sword slashing horizontal and desperate. For us it was unforgettable.

Tonight we meet Wilbur Barns and his wife Dora from Newcastle – that's our Newcastle in Natal – for a sidewalk drink. In my case tea; I did enjoy tea last night, had two full pots and so did Jean – as I've said we're not used to wine in South Africa as they are in Europe.

The hotel is quite a madhouse. There's a congress of psychiatrists on at the moment. Felt like marching in and asking for a free consultation! In the dining room nobody seems to be speaking the same language: there are Chinese, Thais, Japanese, Germans, French, Swiss and any number of others. I speak a lot of languages, but I don't think these people would understand them!

•

England at last. We came on British European Airways, in a Comet. We're in London. We've got two bottles of whisky and two hundred cigarettes each. We flew direct from Madrid over Bilbao, the Bay of Biscay.

We are feeling very shocked. We went to the customs official feeling on top of the world. But when he discovered we were South Africans, he said: Have you heard the news? We did not know what he was talking about. He said Dr Verwoerd has been stabbed, assassinated. Really, what a strange welcome to the city we had waited all our lives to visit.

I've kept the British newspapers and all carried the biggest banner headlines: *Verwoerd Is Assassinated In Parliament: White man attacks him with a dagger*, and the like. The reactions are quite different. One paper said *Verwoerd, The Name Millions Hated*. I feel so confused, being here while this is happening and not being at home. I can't really explain it, but I don't want to talk to any English people about it, although naturally they do. They wouldn't understand, I think, the complicated feelings we're going through. We'll keep these papers for a long long time, anyway. Jean has written on the front page of the *Evening Standard*, September 6, to remind us: Jean/George landed at Heathrow London as news of assassination televised at airport before South Africa knew of it. Such a strange coincidence.

Jean is drawing my attention to the chimney pots of London, the Mary Poppins chimney pots. Today is the 9th of September, 1966, the anniversary of the Great Fire. There are parades, barges and fireworks displays on the Thames; for us a dramatic backdrop to the news from home. There's Trafalgar Square, look at those pigeons Jean. The birds of London, isn't it remarkable in a city like this. And did you hear how that lady just identified me as a South African?

•

Monday the 12th. Finally we went to Chichester to meet old Aunt Ethelworth, she's eighty-nine now, and to hear the stories about my family. Jean thought the train was very comfortable but didn't have the clean hygienic look of a South African train. It took us an hour and forty minutes. Aunt Ethelworth is seven miles out of Chichester and we took a taxi from the station. Her house is called Lebanon at Itchenor.

My Aunt said two Jamesons went to South Africa, originally. Lucas followed by Edgar. Lucas never came back, but Edgar did. Jean said it's a pity we didn't know all those names when we were naming our four sons. Aunt Ethelworth said did I know that my earlier ancestor, also called Lucas, had a castle around here, in about 1600 or so? Imagine that. Aunt Ethelworth also said my great-great grandmother had two grand houses near here. I like the old lady so much – she and her late husband were interested in archaeology, like I am.

Aunt Ethelworth said Itchenor is a very old place, thirteenth century, where her grandfather Stanforth lived from 1832 to 1865. She herself is a governor of Dover College, has been for fifty years. Our highlight was going to see Chichester Cathedral and the many stained glass windows for the Jameson family, so many of the names I know from the family tree hanging up on the wall back in Africa. I had asked Jean to read out the inscriptions, but she was still shy. I wrote down a couple. In the vault are deposited the remains of Martha Jameson who departed this life on the 2nd day of January 1784. Walter Jameson Esq, Alderman of this city, who departed this life on the 16th day of February 1801. Also in the same vault are deposited the remains of Edmund Jameson Esq, who held the office of Town Clerk of this city for forty-five years and who departed this life on the 13th July 1807 ... there were lots more.

In Itchenor church the communion rails were installed to the memory of Stanforth Jameson and the inscription was carved into the base of the rail. Above the family pew Aunt Ethelworth had another stained glass window installed, in memory of her marvellous husband Frederick Duckwood CBE, MBE (Mil.), Croix de Guerre, Rossall and Trinity College, Oxford, Master of Dover, Cheltenham, Eton, Senior Chief Inspector, Ministry of Education. It was sad saying goodbye to my Aunt. Of course we're unlikely to see her again.

•

We've had wonderful weather ever since we struck England. Today we're travelling along at about fifty, sixty miles an hour in a double-decker bus on a great big highway. Toilet, tea served, cigarettes etcetera brought around. I have a stack of newspapers. There's such interesting news. I think Wilson is being criticised very severely indeed. I think the Commonwealth is coming to an end. Splashed all over of course is the news of the new Prime Minister at home, Vorster. Ah, Coventry. This is where we are to eat. Makes me think of Gillooly's Farm in Johannesburg.

Now we're in Birmingham. It doesn't look a nice city so far. Blows a lot, there's litter on the sides of the street. Like the back streets of Johannesburg, End Street, Fordsburg, something like that. Bomb damage is quite evident here, twenty-five years after the War. I'm thinking of the gorgeous costumes of the Kirov Ballet last night. The whitest white skins of those Russians. I felt myself quite uncultured when various items were applauded in the first three acts. But in the last act I was completely taken. It was too wonderful. I shall never forget those scenes. This is a lovely bus. A little handbasin and the lot at the back of the bus. And we've just had the lady come around: Will you have some tea love? *L-u-v,* I think they would spell it.

Finally we're in Kendal, the Lake District. I think Umtata's far in advance of this! But it is delightful. We're on the third floor of a little hotel. Jean is explaining to a local man that Jan Smuts is our airport in Johannesburg. He says seeing we've travelled so far, are we going to see the Queen? I told him she hadn't invited me! We're going down towards Keswick, and the country around here is very much like Underberg. Windy, too – *nomanye,* what we call typical *nomanye* country in Zululand. When you look at how soft this land is, I think the 1820 settlers were really rather marvellous to have adapted themselves to the conditions round about Port Elizabeth.

Now Jean's just woken me up, we've got to leave here and go to Liverpool. It is so peaceful here, I could have slept right through. My God, I feel happy!

I'm so interested in the politics of the country, so in London I found myself buying three or four papers a day, as well as listening to the BBC wireless they supply in the room at the hotel. So I thought it would be interesting to get the local paper up here to see what their angle is on the dramas at Westminster. I got the *Lancashire Post,* and quite a surprise too. Oh, please! It's like the *Transkei Territorial News.* Very parochial. The first class coach – I've splashed out – on which we're travelling from Kendal to Preston, comprises twelve upholstered seats like armchairs. There's only one other person in this compartment, and I think he is one of England's upper-uppers.

Jean is reminding me about the guide on that bus tour in London, who asked where we came from. Well, when we answered South Africa, he came back with: Blimey, real foreigners! Then he said you're the next country to be thrown out of the Commonwealth you know, and soon you'll have no friends. I didn't really want to get into a political discussion with him as I could see he had his own assumptions about us. I didn't want to have to explain anything.

Time is really flying now. Last night we made the crossing to Ireland on the ferry and it was very quiet – we were lucky. A local man said it was particularly lovely because the Irish Sea can be notorious for its roughness. I asked him what kind of weather we could expect in Ireland and he said in his lovely accent, which I'll try to mimic while it's fresh in my mind: Oh in Ireland we describe this as a soft morning. Which is apt and to the point. It will go neither one way nor the other, so why worry?

Here in Ireland they are most polite; if they see you looking up and down the street they will say, can I help you? This chap told me in Ireland you take life easily and soberly. Soberly in the correct sense of the word – nothing to do with drink; it's a point of view, an outlook. You take life temperately. I like that a lot. When I asked him whether the country, which is very poor, could still be developed, he answered: Oh enormously, stupendously. He said the problem was not the people, but money and the lack of it. Said in history there'd been no country butchered by Cromwell as quickly as Ireland. He said the approach to the Irish had been like that he is hearing from South Africa and Rhodesia towards the coloured people of those countries; that they should not be educated.

The horses here are magnificent and there is a lot of breeding and racing. Yesterday we were in a town pronounced Nace, seems to be spelt Naas. Tipperary county! I know the song Tipperary. The courier said if we don't know it, we're going to walk home! So Jean and I sang it with gusto. I don't think I've seen one clock right in Ireland, but even in England so many of the clocks were wrong. We're passing a wedding. The courier says: He's a brave man, that. Oh Lord, another good man gone wrong. Then he makes the sign of the cross and winks at us. Here's the lordly Shannon again, it drains eighty per cent of Ireland, and there's an airport – all very new. This is the main parking area, about one hundredth of the size of the one at Jan Smuts. But it's a beautiful airport, most modern, and certainly with a far better restaurant than Jan Smuts.

In Limerick I saw a sign for petrol: five and six, save sixpence, special! High up in the mountains is a lake known as the Punchbowl. We had tea at Glengarriff on Bantry Bay. A very deep inlet. Along the side, strange fuchsias, a smaller kind and a very deep red. We passed the ruins of the O'Sullivan household, just in Cork. Here in West Cork all the signs are in Irish. We're going to kiss the Blarney Stone; we can't go back to Africa without kissing the Blarney Stone!

It's bustling, this small city of Cork, and we're in the Hotel Metropole, a lovely hotel. I'm not sure I got the gift of the Blarney, but I did kiss the first Irish girl I saw; her name was Christine. We've met a nice couple on the tour. They're from Massachusetts, USA. I had such fun with them in the pub because they asked me to speak in Zulu and Afrikaans, which I did. Soon all the people in the pub were listening and making me go on and on. Jean said afterwards that she hadn't seen me so relaxed and happy in ages and I think she's right. I told our new friends it had been a lovely four days, it really had, and thanked them very much for their friendship. I said 9 Mountbatten Avenue Witbank is our address, come out and visit us in South Africa. I didn't try to explain what I do.

•

We got back to London yesterday. Jean is writing a card to Chris from the Post Office Tower in London. It is 619 feet. It's broader, bigger, but not as tall as our own in Johannesburg. Ours is 747 feet. It's more interesting than ours though, because it's in the heart of the city; you can look right around. But it's surprising to note that Johannesburg has far more skyscrapers close together. Here they're just individual skyscrapers standing alone.

We were walking near Green Park. Men were offering to do a portrait of you. This would interest Ryan very much. They work very quickly, too. London is now the middle of the world, the centre of the world. Every human type is represented. There is every kind of entertainment. We went to the original Windmill Theatre, that theatre which never closed during the War, and saw a completely uncensored version of a play, *O! Calcutta!* which I'm sure you won't ever see in South Africa. I was quite shocked, actually.

For me it was a mistake to also go out on Saturday night. We got to Piccadilly Circus and walked around there looking to see where we might go into a bioscope; we'd have loved to see a flick in a foreign country. But I can't describe the sea of people coming into the central point from the many streets which radiate out, not in straight lines – they all bend away as it were. People coming in, going out, sinking into the underground, bubbling out from the underground. After a time I told Jean I am an African country boy and this is too much for me, so we came back to the hotel. Now this morning I am resting. Jean has gone off to Carnaby Street as she so wanted to. I'm going to watch the news programmes on television, still such a novelty for us South Africans with no TV.

Jean has just arrived back and says that our South African fashions are quite up to date. She says the very way-out hippie fashions of course we don't see at home, the long-haired jackets and the corduroy suits in vivid colours. But the slimline slacks she's seen at Bevans in Johannesburg, and just as well cut. She says the long collared button-down shirts our boys have been wearing for about a year already. It's only the really way-out clothes that we don't find at home.

We spent a most enjoyable evening at my relative Bill Jameson's house on Epsom Downs. A new house in lovely surrounds; we went to Box Hill. I see in this paper of the 27th of September, that fifty thousand more immigrants are to go to South Africa. But everything is being dominated by the crisis between Mr Wilson and Mr Smith in Salisbury. It seemed last night that Mr Smith had made arrangements to end the deadlock with Britain, but this morning the story is quite otherwise. An article in the paper talks about the difference between what they call the shallow-bedded Rhodesian – I suppose that's the industrial Rhodesian – and the deep-rooted ones, that is the man who has made his home there and intends to keep it there forever. If forever is a word, in Africa or anywhere else.

•

We're in Paris now and I'm doing this recording under rather cramped conditions. A double bed, a shower, ordinary toilet facilities and a bidet; that's the sum total of our room in the Burgundy Hotel. In London the day before yesterday I went to the History of Natural Science Museum and I was in heaven. I spent most of my time at the cases dealing with the evolution of man in Africa, and I bought some magnificent books on the Neolithic revolution for my collection. I got back for lunch, and in the afternoon we went to the Vaudeville Theatre on the Strand, Dame Sybil Thorndike in *Arsenic and Old Lace*. We walked along the Embankment right to Westminster, crossed the bridge, and caught three underground trains back. They are wonderful; even a Babanango boy can't get lost on them. In the evening we saw a wonderful musical, *Hallo Darling*, at the Old Drury Lane. Yesterday, having counted my cash, I joined Jean shopping. It was wonderful to go through Marks & Spencers, Littlewoods and Selfridges. The prices for wonderfully made quality goods are a good deal better than ours. We shopped and shopped and I saw more cash go west, until eventually at about three o'clock we had lunch in one of those traditional English pubs. And are they wonderful. Later we saw Dame Peggy Ashcroft in *Days in the Trees*; superb acting.

Rennies saw us to the terminal. Eventually we got into a British Trident, that is an 88-seater, and a forty minute flight it was into Paris. We landed there, and straight in trouble. The French are not kind or helpful in any way. When I got onto the bus I realised I had, I suppose foolishly, not had time to change cash into francs. So the driver bundled us off the bus, and our luggage was thrown out. That was our first experience and from there on it's been very similar. Whether they don't like English as a language, or whether it's because they're not very appreciative of seeing Englishmen visiting their country, I don't know. You can't walk around with a sign saying I'm not English, I'm South African, now can you? I'm considering talking to them in Zulu, Xhosa and Afrikaans!

So this is close to being the end of a wonderful, delightful holiday with wonderful experiences. But I'm feeling a little bit homesick now, and my thought is that I've seen enough of these foreign countries. From now on I think my visiting will be to the parts of Africa I don't know yet.

Jean, ever the sergeant major, says we have to be ready at two, as our bus picks us up at half past. We are to visit the Louvre, Notre-Dame Cathedral, the Vendôme Square, Tuileries Gardens, and the Pantheon.

I asked Jean what her favourite thing was this afternoon. She says she liked Notre-Dame, but the biggest surprise was the Mona Lisa, because she'd never been very impressed by that picture – thought it insipid and ordinary. She'd always wondered why everybody raved about it, but then seeing the original today really shook her because the eyes follow you wherever you go. It is a masterpiece, and she never recognised that before. I agreed that the Mona Lisa's eyes followed me right round until I felt like running away from her! Her whole face changes.

Now it is evening and we are walking in the wrong direction, instead of coming to the Rue de la Madeleine. We'd better hurry as we're entitled to a free supper at the hotel tonight, after which we have got to find an underground to the Folies-Bergère. Thank God I brought this whisky from London, or we'd never have been able to afford a spot in Paris. Another couple who are tourists staying in the hotel told us they went to a striptease restaurant – very risqué – ordered three drinks and were charged eighteen francs a shot. That's the equivalent of eleven dollars, which in English money is over seven pounds – for three highballs. Witbank, here I come!

At the Folies we were offered programmes. Now I find out that you can apparently get a programme for three bob, but we were socked fourteen francs, twenty-two bob. I said I think you're right Jean, not a penny more from us into the French economy, not one franc or centavo or whatever they call it. We'll just get out of this place. They caught us at the toilets too! It seems to be daylight robbery against anybody who speaks English. Though the show itself was lovely, wasn't it Jean? Spectacular, beautiful, and they weren't nude – at least not entirely. So I'm not as much of a prude as some people think. Those acrobatic turns; I've never seen anything like them. Breakfast this morning was two rolls and butter and bitter coffee and that cost ten and sixpence. It's no wonder I've got no more cash. I apologise to the American tourists, who I first thought were so rude and brash in a country that isn't theirs. But now I understand that the only way to get through this place is to push and to push damned hard, and be rude and demand everything you want at the lowest price possible. Beautiful city, but why be made to feel so unwelcome in a place? But we mustn't regret coming to Paris, Jean, I think that it was necessary for us to appreciate the world.

Goodbye Paris. We are flying directly over the city. I had confirmation of the French attitude this morning when I thought I'd tell the courier what I thought of their inhospitable behaviour. He said don't take it personally, they're like that. I'm a Spaniard, he said, I just work here.

•

We can be proud of what Mr Krawitz from Pretoria, who is on the flight with us, says about South African Airways. He says it's as good or even better than Pan American or BOAC. I missed passing over the coast of Africa because of the route we're taking, but here we are over the northern parts. It's dry but there are patches of cultivation. A salt lake, and then mountains, could be the Atlas range. Oh am I so thrilled to see something of this part of Africa. I so wanted to see it, and I know we're very high, but I'm sure I'm going to gain impressions all the day. There's some afforestation here, roads; thrilling to me. This will be Algeria. Razorback edges to these mountains, no lee side. What a moonscape! It's bumpy now, very misty under us. The fasten seat belt sign has gone off, and Mr Krawitz has given me a cigar – very decent thing to do, and I feel quite grand. Look at these cloud formations, Jean, I can see two arms, a leg, an opera scene with a girl.

We're flying in a four jet DC8 and I can read on this one engine nose Pratten Whitney Aircraft Engines. Actually from the flight information they've just announced it seems I'm wrong and the plane is a Douglas Super DC. Landing time at Brazzaville is 18h05. I've just taken a picture across the wing; the light is intense, I've never taken such a reading. There's the Congo, the snakiest river I've ever seen. There are actually two rivers, one with a big bend in it. Perhaps we're beginning to strike the equatorial forest area. It's four o'clock, and we've another two hours to Brazzaville.

Jean says one feels very small when one sees how vast everything is from up here. I think one feels great. When one thinks of all the trouble that's been happening on this continent, and it looks so peaceful from here. There are mercenaries down there – including South Africans fighting somewhere in those bushes and valleys. If you went over Nkandhla at this height, and the Qudeni Forest, it would look a lot like this. If there was a door here I feel I could easily just open it and walk out; it just gives you the idea of relativity, how it is that through space the world is travelling at eighteen thousand miles per second. It makes you consider that everything, everybody, is in relation to you. It makes you feel at once great, humble, and most of all, responsible. But perhaps that's just the whisky talking – I have been rather generous to myself on this flight.

So one of my great wishes has been answered; I have seen the Congo River. It's an immense thing, with great big islands. I saw the lights of Leopoldville on the other side of the Congo. Mr Krawitz says it's in a pitiful state. The Belgians just got out of their cars and left them. We're in Brazzaville aerodrome now and it is very nice indeed, but stiflingly hot. I was a little surprised to see that in the transit area there were only Europeans. I wonder why that is. We've filled in a pile of forms to get back to South Africa and we've crossed the Limpopo. In half an hour's time we'll be home, or should I say in Johannesburg, on our way home. I will finish this last tape by saying we have had a wonderful time, but it's a warm feeling to be returning home, to the place I belong. I said to Jean I realise that I have not had really any bad episodes in this whole month, which is really something to think about, isn't it? And I've already stuck out a year in old Witbank.

Jean is being cheeky now – she's also been enjoying the whisky – and says for someone who's supposed to be shy, I've done quite a lot of talking in the four weeks we've been away. She's enjoyed that very much. I wonder if we will ever do this again?

THEY seem different people, younger people, my father and mother as they spill off the plane at Jan Smuts Airport in October 1966. From the airport viewing deck where I stand with Chris they look like strangers – loud, laughing, laden, arms around each other and waving goodbyes to the other passengers.

We are driven back to Witbank by Uncle Arthur in his silver Wolseley. My parents are bubbling with excitement at being able to tell their tales and show off their souvenirs. My father is especially talkative. Oh how we missed you, he says to Chris and me, then winks at my mother: Didn't we Jean? They smile when the smokestacks of the town first come into view, and when finally we swing into Mountbatten Avenue my father says Ah, our very own Champs Élysées! And there is chez Jameson!

That night in the house Chris tells me he feels like he has been transported back to the better times, before Witbank. They have brought presents for us: mine is a British Bobby with a removable truncheon. My father puts on the lights in all the rooms and goes out to look at his garden; my mother does not take him to task for wasting electricity. Nor does she notice where Chris has tried to clean stains from the furniture, products of a party he held in the house one night while I slept. My father produces the last of their holiday whisky and it seems like the family disciplines of a lifetime are suspended. We are patient with him when he insists that we start listening to his tape recordings, from the beginning. Nobody remembers to tell me to go to bed.

This mood lasts for some days. When he returns to his life as the Bantu Affairs Commissioner of Witbank, with 1966 drawing to a close, my father says to my mother: only four years to go. Even by the year's end, it seems the glow of the travels is still with him, holding him up, lighting the house. He follows the unfolding drama of the Unilateral Declaration of Independence in neighbouring Rhodesia. Since the trip abroad he uses his tape recorder a great deal and records, from the radio, speeches by Ian Smith, John Vorster, Harold Wilson, James Callaghan, Lyndon Johnson. He patiently explains to me who they all are. He says he is intrigued as to how this will all end. He says a Rhodesian Republic seems the inevitable next step now that Mr Wilson is going to the United Nations for mandatory sanctions, and that no one will back down. He cannot see there being any but one eventual loser, he says; except that when men will not compromise, everyone affected will lose in some way.

He records the New Year's radio message of the dour, jowly new Prime Minister of our country, in office since the assassination of Verwoerd. This is the feared Balthazar John Vorster, known as BJ, who has a darkly biblical oratorical style, building slowly to deep pauses, dragging them out, then building to thunder. This speech, at a tense time when there are concerted moves to declare apartheid a Crime Against Humanity, isolate South Africa and impose sanctions, is a self-righteous epic, and it alters my father's mood. He plays it back several times.

Fellow South Africans, in spite of the cold and cynical world we are supposed to be living in, our people still walk before God in all humility. We prepared to meet the onslaught against us in the international court. The reaction of the adolescent and communist States we expected, but the reaction of the other States came as a great shock. The General Assembly of the United Nations has made a clearly unlawful and senseless decision. Whilst we must not allow this decision to worry us unduly, we must face the fact that it will create certain problems. Also, towards the end of the year Britain saw fit to place the domestic issue of Rhodesia in the hands of the United Nations, and in doing so the peace, quiet and stability of southern Africa was placed in jeopardy. The Security Council simply accepted that the action of Rhodesia more than a year ago constituted a threat to world peace, and mandatory sanctions are now called for. Let me say plainly that I don't know of a single threat to world peace which is brewing in southern Africa. All that I do know is that adolescent African states to the north are openly plotting the downfall of my country and southern Africa. I know that those selfsame African states have as yet made no contribution to world peace, nor have they got the courage or the means to attack us themselves. What they want to do is to inspan the world organisation. Their motives as well as their plans are obvious. Like spoiled children who have always got their way, these and other States are abusing their voting power, which is out of all proportion to their strength, importance or contribution, to create a sort of world government often with complete disregard of existing rules. It is clear that the year 1967 will find the peoples and nations of the world, including ourselves, confronted by the naked realities of ill-conceived decisions. I cannot minimise this problem. The year 1967 might be a year in which we too get hurt. We might be bruised. But I verily believe we will not be broken.

My father listens distractedly to the round-up of the other biggest news headlines of 1966. They have to do with a perilous drought – the Vaal Dam dropped to 23.8 per cent of its capacity – shock as South Africa's most famous racehorse, Sea Cottage, is shot by a gunman on Durban beach, and the conviction of Advocate Bram Fischer, scion of a famous Afrikaner family now in the forefront of the struggle against apartheid. There is an editorial comment on the State-run broadcaster that causes my father to sit up and take notice. The year 1966, says the commentator, saw the first appearance of terrorists in South West Africa. Twenty-three are known to have crossed the border, and seventeen of them have been arrested. The search for the other six is being carried out night and day. The Commissioner of Police has issued a statement: The possibility that further groups may follow during 1967 cannot be ruled out. But the South African Police are organised to trace and arrest every person who receives training in terrorism as soon as possible after his return to this country. This is the only threat to the internal security of our country at present, and it is not a dangerous one.

My father shakes his head in mute disagreement. He says he can feel the faintest of tremors, the beginnings of an earthquake deep down on the seabed; the sound of war in the far distance. Chris and I become alarmed as we listen to him speak this way. We try to get him to talk about Europe again, though by now we know all the stories. We appeal to my mother to help, but the spell has been broken.

He begins work in 1967 with foreboding in his heart. The year looks long from here, he says to my mother, and the returning strength he had felt is fading. He does his work. It is getting no easier; nor any more palatable. Early in the year the Department issues a printed card, to be given to all white employers in the urban areas. Retain This Card For Your Own Convenience, employers are to be told. Will you just look at this madness, says my father.

> Whenever you require a Bantu male or female employee, you must report the vacancy at the local Labour Bureau. Should a Bantu report to you for work you may not employ him/her unless he/she produces proof that he/she has been sent to you by the local Labour Bureau. Should you employ a Bantu you must within three days register the service contract with the Labour Bureau, and enter your name and address in Part B of the Bantu's Reference Book. Only in the case of Bantu males must the reference book be signed monthly. On discharge you must sign off Part B of the Bantu's Reference Book, and inform the Labour Bureau of this fact on the form supplied to you for this purpose on registration.

In May he becomes embroiled in a flurry of correspondence that he brings home each evening. He has had a request from the Witbank Golf Club Committee for permission to allow their course to be used for a one-day Bantu Golfers' Tournament. After all the mounds of memoranda, recommendations, and appeals to the national authorities, he has to write to the honorary secretary of the Witbank Golf Club. Dear Sir, I regret to advise that the Town Council of Witbank has informed this office that it refuses to give permission for Non-Europeans to use sporting facilities in the European areas. Under the circumstances I regret to say that I feel it will serve no purpose to pursue the matter further. My apologies.

The work is gnawing at him again but he spends as much time as he can with us, and we experience him at this time as a sad, rather than an angry man. We begin to give him a wider berth and I speak to him only when spoken to. Still he applies for any vacancy he sees advertised in the newspapers, or hears of through his colleagues. He tries for the post of Legal Adviser to the Town Clerk of Johannesburg. His friend Fanie Aucamp, the Manager of Non-European Affairs in Witbank, writes the reference this time. It is sincere and heartfelt; he is the one at work who best understands the predicament of my father's working life, and he wants to help him to get out.

The collection of rejection letters swells by one. The work grows worse, and grows and grows. My father begins again to experience the momentary immobilising spasms my mother says he first came to know in Duiwelskloof, and tries as best he can to hide them from us and from his staff. But he is losing the struggle again, slipping backwards and downwards. Three and a half years start to seem to him like an age, perhaps too long a time to last out after all. He and my mother begin to argue again, a great deal now, about things big and small – about anything, in fact. Chris experiences this most directly, though he is too old now to hide under a pillow. I do not understand what is wrong with my parents.

In June 1967 they celebrate their silver wedding anniversary. It is quite an event in the small town, and the many celebrants are genuine in their liking for the Jamesons. Our house comes briefly to life again. There are flower arrangements all over the place, unexpected visitors, and telegrams and cards flow in from all over the country. Congrats on silver, keep on heading for gold! reads the message from my father's brother Gary and his large young family on the farm in Zululand.

We miss Billy who is at sea aboard the MV Lubombo. My father says he is doing well as an engineer, but Billy has written that he does not think this will be the life for him in the long term – he is a landsman after all. He is engaged to his girlfriend in Port Elizabeth, and I am excited about a party that my parents keep mentioning. Billy sends me postcards whenever he docks in ports around the world and I keep them on a bookshelf, dreaming of exotic places. I miss Ryan too, but do not hear from him. I gather from eavesdropping on my parents that he has disappeared into a murky and dangerous life in Johannesburg, and is being characteristically creative and feckless by turns. He says he is looking for a job. Chris is making his mark at Witbank High, and he always has time for me. Though he too is beginning to display the rebelliousness of a teenager, it is said in the house he is likely to be the first of our family to go on to get a university degree.

I had thrived in my curious situation at the convent and received a glowing report card, with distinctions in all but Arithmetic. I am installed at Robert Carruthers Primary School. I like my grey blazer with matching grey cap, the letters RC emblazoned in red on both. My mother and father are amused by a letter I write to a friend back in the Transkei. Dear Paul, it reads. How are you and your family. How is the school at Libode. Did you know I did grade one at the convent. It was all girls, and me. There is only one thing I don't like about school, that is sums. I also have a nice pair of shoes now. Here is a diagram of my new house. Love in Xhosa from Sam.

Precisely one week after the silver wedding festivities, which go off well, what my father has feared since 1959 comes to pass. He is in his office behind his huge Government-issue desk, the one for Commissioners of the Principal rank, writing one of the innumerable bureaucratic memoranda that his secretary will type in the Departmental style and circulate to other white men perspiring in suits, sitting behind slightly smaller desks in smaller offices in smaller places like Middelburg and Ogies. This is how what are known as the Pass Laws are actually applied. Mr Pistorius, his willing but limited assistant, has just given his report on some labour troubles at Springfield Colliery, and has gone down the corridor to his own room. My father must prepare to chair the Labour Control Committee, made up of Commissioners, senior police officers, and lesser officials, later in the day.

He stands up to stretch, then falls like a stone to the wooden floor. The loud crash brings his secretary running, and thereafter there is a confusion of activity and noise, culminating in the sound of a siren, and an ambulance tearing up the tarred road to the offices of the Commissioner. A crowd gathers on the pavement under the jacaranda trees; there is not often excitement like this in Witbank.

Nervous breakdown is the phrase used in these days for such occurrences. The staff whisper the words because they are not nice words and can mean only bad things for their likeable leader, Mr Jameson, who is always so polite and takes the trouble to speak to everyone in their own first languages. But they are reassured to be told that the Commissioner is suffering from extreme exhaustion brought on by stress, and that a spell of rest at the Lynnwood Nursing Home in Pretoria should see him right. They hope so. Mr Pistorius says he will do his best as a stand-in for Mr Jameson, until he recovers.

The intervening weeks are awkward and tense in the house but my mother says we should be relieved that medical experts are helping our father. It could actually turn out to be a good thing, my mother tells us, as she's been saying for ages that he needed to see a doctor and his pride wouldn't let him. Perhaps this is going to fix your father's problems once and for all, she says, and means it.

A month later, at his own insistence, my father returns home, and to his office. Within days he realises, sadly and with fright, that his problems are not fixed. He forces himself to go through his working motions for all of July, all of August, all of September, and into October. Chris and I can see the lines of effort etched on his face, as if he is on a forced march that never ends. The letters, memoranda, minutes – thousands of them, on the official note-paper – swirl before his eyes in a nightmare treadmill, speeding up and spreading out. On the 5th of September he sends a reply to the Johannesburg head office regarding its instruction to repatriate one Buthi Mngomeni to his homeland. Unfortunately, writes my father curtly, your order cannot be acted upon as neither we nor he know where his homeland is. He signs the letter with a trembling hand.

On the 4th of October he has to prepare, for the Secretary of Bantu Administration and Development, a detailed reconciliation of accounts for 1967, to be sent as a formal Minute to Pretoria. On the 15th of October he calls his staff together to start preparations for the Annual Report. On the 23rd of October, late in the afternoon, he prepares to circulate to all his staff and the officials of the town the Secretary of Bantu Administration and Development's new regulations governing the Bantu Residential Area of Witbank, regulations which he says are so hateful that he briefly considered destroying them. By the time he has finished composing his covering letter it is dark and all the typists have gone home, so he reluctantly leaves the work unfinished on his desk.

The next morning, the 24th of October 1967, at his office in the town, the dam breaks again in his brain. There is another siren and the screech of tyres as the ambulance comes once more for the Commissioner. The staff say nothing to each other this time; they just look at the departing white vehicle and wonder whether poor Mr Jameson will ever come back.

The doctors insist that my father must be flown immediately to Durban, to the Wakesford Nursing Home, where specialist treatment is available. My mother rushes home from bridge as soon as the doctor calls. George, she says, I told you that you'd come back from Pretoria too soon, so let's learn that lesson once and for all. This time you must listen to the doctors – it doesn't matter how long it takes, this time you will get well. I will be fine with the boys, though we'll miss you awfully. She means everything she is saying. Chris and I, bewildered and with staring eyes, hug our father and say come back soon please Dad. He looks at us and says only this: I am very, very sorry my boys.

The following day, when he has gone, a bolt of lightning strikes the roof of 9 Mountbatten Avenue, Witbank; the only direct hit in the town. On the 1st of November, my mother goes out to work again after twenty-five years as a housewife. She begins her battle to hold together what is left of her family, while he begins his to hold together what is left of himself. She writes to him constantly, and he replies whenever his mind is clear enough. Chris and I go off to our schools each day. We do not talk to our friends about what is happening at home. Then a day comes in December of 1967, shortly before Christmas, when my parents hold separate conversations in Durban and in Witbank. My father talks to a Mauritian man in the Napier mental ward. My mother visits her next-door neighbour in Mountbatten Avenue.

THEN

Bedroom, 1968

HE does get out of Durban before Christmas. He does leave the mental ward and the Mauritian man behind him. His parents do fetch him to make the long journey home. He does not take the train via Babanango and Glencoe to Witbank. He gets instead on to a flight from Durban direct to Johannesburg.

He arrives at the airport and they drive home. Ryan and I are there waiting. He does feel happy, within the constraints of the circumstances. It is Christmas Eve.

We do have a lovely roast chicken for Christmas dinner. We do not mind the absence of a tree and presents. We feel immense relief at being together, even though my mother's dream of the whole family being under one roof is not realised on this night. My parents drink wine in a toast to Billy on the sea, who will be with us in a fortnight, and to Chris, on holiday at our grandparents' house on the oceanfront in Ballito Bay. Ryan smokes a cigarette at the table. I drink Seven-Up from a plastic glass. My parents talk about years gone by and do not talk about this one at all.

We do have Christmas Day together, and we go to church in the morning. Before we leave the house my father makes good an old promise to my mother and composes, using a tripod, a slide photograph of our street with its avenue of jacarandas in such riotous bloom that the surface of the road itself turns purple in the brilliant African sunlight. The process requires complicated calculations with a light meter, and my father parks our family car, the black Dodge Lancer, in the foreground just alongside the street sign. Ryan has to stand at the stop street and prevent cars from turning into Mountbatten Avenue while my father fusses and fiddles with the equipment, right in the middle of the road.

When we arrive at the church the whole congregation is pleased to see him back with his family and the priest even mentions it in his sermon, saying it is itself a Christmas present of a special sort. People are at their kindest at that time of year.

He does feel better and he does feel a small flood of hope. He is withdrawn as an injured animal and inarticulate as a stranger who does not speak our language, but still soft and gentle with my mother, and with us. His eyes are wet as filled basins, but he always leaves the room before they overflow. He tells us he is not quite ready, but when he is he will sit with each of us in turn to hear about all our doings while he has been away, about what we think the new year might hold in store. He shows no ill temper, not even with Ryan, and seems to me in some ways as serene as I remember him in the Transkei.

We have Boxing Day, and the day after, and four days after that still, until New Year's Eve arrives. They are peaceful days, quiet in the empty town. My parents agree that they have never ever been so glad to see a year consigned to the past. On New Year's Eve, 1967, they embrace 1968 quietly, greedily. They say that seeing it is burning summer weather in the coal town and this is holiday time, we should all go on an outing. They settle on a drive to the

Loskop Dam and we spend New Year's Day swimming and fishing. We all put on our swimming costumes, Ryan proudly showing off his young man's physique and olive skin that seems to tan instantly when exposed to the sun. I, much fairer, have to endure my mother spreading layer upon layer of cream on my face and limbs, but it is all worth it as we are together and I have the undivided attention of my father for more hours than I can ever remember.

My father goes back to his office the next day, but quickly concludes it is too early for a full return and makes the necessary arrangements. On the third day of the new year he begins to turn his mind to eventual re-entry into normal life once everyone streams back to their houses and offices. Although he is clearly not ready, he does feel hopeful that his strength will return and starts writing out a *Things to Do* list for the day he will go back to the office. He will ask the temporary additional assistant to do him a report on all that has happened while he was away.

On the fourth day of the new year, the tenth since his return, a Thursday, in summer, in the small box-like house at number 9 Mountbatten Avenue, in Witbank, in the Transvaal, in South Africa, in 1968, in the morning, he sits at the dining room table and composes a letter to his employers. He recapitulates in scrupulous detail the time he has been off, attaching medical certification, and does a reconciliation to show that his time allocations have not been exceeded. He thanks them for their forbearance. He says although he is not in a position to resume his duties yet, he does not expect the delay to be more than eight weeks, after which he is confident there will be no need for further sick leave. He records his thanks to the Acting Bantu Affairs Commissioner of Witbank in his absence.

He sets out his priorities for the coming year and says he believes much can be achieved. He suggests a series of possible dates for particular meetings. When he is finished writing this letter he goes to the sideboard and finds a stapler in a drawer. He staples the letter neatly, folds it in two, and puts it to one side. His secretary can type it up on the official notepaper and post it for him to the head office in Pretoria.

Then he writes a letter to his psychiatrist, marked *Urgent*.

Dear Dr Lukic,

Enclosed please find a form of application for extended leave and also a copy of your previous certificate and an official letter in this connection. My memory is very bad and I was quite unable to recommence work on 2 January 1968. This leads to periods of depression. Please authorise my absence from duty at least for February 1968, as I doubt whether one month will suffice. If you consider that I must return to hospital I am willing to do that, although I have not told my wife that I think this might be necessary. I would be glad of inclusion of the word amnesia in your report, and the return of the form to the Acting Bantu Affairs Commissioner, Witbank, as soon as possible.

Yours sincerely,
G M Jameson

To the letter he attaches a copy of the medical certificate dated 30th November 1967. Re: Mr G M Jameson. This is to certify that the abovenamed has been under my treatment since 30.10.1967. He is at present in hospital suffering from a Reactive Depression and it is expected that he will be fit to resume work on 1.2.1968. A J Lukic, Psychiatrist.

Also a letter to the Chief Bantu Affairs Commissioner.

We forward herewith the following documents relating to Mr Jameson. 1. Application for sick leave duly certified by specialist psychiatrist for period 24.10.1967 to 31.12.1967. 2. Certificate by specialist psychiatrist indicating that Mr Jameson should be able to resume duty on 1.2.1968. 3. Application for vacation leave by Mr Jameson for period 1.2.1968 to 28.2.1968. Mr Jameson attended office on 2.1.1968 but found that, because of amnesia, he could not assume duty. His specialist is in Durban and it is to avoid any possibility of his being considered absent for duty without leave that he has submitted the application for vacation leave.

This set of papers my father puts in a large envelope, addresses it to the King George V Hospital, Durban, and places it and the others on the sideboard.

Then he takes a pad of lined paper, the personal and not the official type, and begins to write something new with his fountain pen in the elegant sweeping strokes he developed during his school days. What he is doing looks strange on the page. All the way down the left-hand margin, in bold capitals which he goes over twice to make the letters thick and heavily inked, he writes his name, and leaves enough space between them so he can set out his intentions clearly alongside each one of the thirteen in turn. This takes some time, as he takes great care over each letter.

When he has finished it looks like this:

G
E
O
R
G
E

J
A
M
E
S
O
N

He looks at his handiwork thoughtfully. Then he takes from his pocket the list of twenty-two points he drew up that evening in December in Durban in the sleeping room at the mental hospital. He is pleased with himself for having written these for precisely this purpose, and doing it in such a handy way – it is like a card for a prompt in a play. Starting at the top of the fresh sheet, he begins to fill in neatly the blank lines opposite each letter. This takes some time. Occasionally if he gets stuck he skips a letter and comes back to it, as one does with a crossword. Twice he scratches out what he has written – against the first O, then the second E – and writes alternative words in the space above.

When finally it is done he reads it aloud to himself.

Give your own account of yourself; on that are you judged
Every day now passing must be used to regain strength
Obviate all danger of suicide
Remember the conscious mind creates the subconscious
God's methods are not for you to question
Every member of your family depends on what you do now

Just do that for which you have been trained in your service
A person like you can still contribute to your country
Make yourself count your blessings
Even suicide is too simple to close something intricate as life
Slow down, ease your pain, quiet your mind and heart
Overcome too great awareness of self, which may be conceit
Never again partake in exacting competition

He finishes reading it out and sighs deeply. He leaves this sheet of paper on the dining room table along with the notepad. He is alone in the house. My mother has gone back to work. Billy is still making his way to Witbank. Ryan is working at the Curzon's bottle store. Chris is still with Gran and Grandad and his cousins in Natal. I am playing with a friend, a few blocks away; the start of the new school term is still some way off. Enoch is on leave, back in his village. The cats are sunning themselves in the front garden near the big loquat tree.

He stands up and walks down the corridor past the small bedrooms on the right; on the left the single bathroom we all share, and the separate toilet. He is dressed in casual trousers, slip-on shoes, and a plain open-necked shirt. He walks back up the corridor and turns through the dining room into the lounge. He looks around, noting that the furniture he made with his own hands nearly ten years ago is holding up well. He opens the front door and crosses the partially enclosed veranda, walking down the red painted cement steps and on to the lawn. Then he starts to traverse the small garden slowly, covering carefully every inch of its perimeter, starting at the loquat tree where the cats roll on their backs and present themselves for scratching. He passes the fuchsias, the vines, the flower beds with their daisies, the jumping beans, the fruit trees; he passes and looks at every single thing he has planted in the close to three years of life we have lived in this place.

When his tour is finished he re-enters the house from the backyard through the kitchen door. He goes back to the dining room where he has left all his papers, picks up the pen and, leaning over the dining table but not sitting down, scrawls on the side of the lined pad: It's all wrong, all of it.

Then he goes directly to their bedroom. He opens his cupboard and reaches up to the top shelf. He takes out a cardboard box and a bundle wrapped in oilcloth. He sits on the neatly made bed. He opens both packages. He works with the contents. It is sunny in the room. The sounds of the suburb are muted. It is 10.30am. He completes the loading procedure. He releases the safety catch. He places the barrel in his mouth. He pulls the trigger. The bullet does what bullets do when fired at point-blank range into a human head.

Backyard, 1968

IT is Ryan who makes the discovery. It would have to be him, who else, pursued by furies all his own. He comes home from work to a silent house. The cats have not moved to investigate the shot which rang out earlier. Dogs would have done so, but not cats. Some neighbours heard it, they will say later, but had no idea where it had come from or what it meant.

Ryan lets himself in through the front door. He calls out to see if anyone is home. He thinks he will get himself a beer from the fridge and have a cigarette. Something makes him walk from the kitchen down the corridor past the bathroom and toilet on the left, and the small bedrooms on the right. Something makes him open the door to our parents' room, the only one that is closed. Something bangs in his head too when he looks inside.

I am dropped off at the garden gate in the middle of the slate waist-high front wall which my father built himself, and the house is not silent any more. It is filled with people as never before, though they are all talking quietly. There is a white vehicle with a cross painted on its door and lights on its roof, in the driveway next to the grapevines and the fuchsias. On the street there are two police cars, two-way radios crackling just like in the radio programme *Squad Cars*. There are people on the small veranda including, I can just make out, my elder brother. I can't see my mother or father. I stand for some moments at the gate holding my satchel and looking at our house which doesn't seem to be ours any more. Then I run up the path to the veranda, and all the grown-ups turn to look at me strangely – as if I am not expected. They seem confused about what to do, when Ryan pushes through and puts his arms around me.

I am silent for a time and then start to scream, just one word over and over. What? What? What? *What! What!* I am tearing at myself with my hands, my arms are flailing and it looks like I am having a fit. Ryan holds me tightly and says, come with me to the backyard.

Where is Mom! I shriek. *Where is Dad!* The adults who are strangers and are moving around as quietly as fish in the ocean look away from me and suddenly I go limp, allowing my brother to drag me by the hand through the lounge, dining room, and as far as the kitchen. From there I can see the familiar corridor leading to my parents' bedroom, and I wriggle free and run. I am stopped, kindly but firmly, by an ambulance man stationed outside the bedroom, but not before my eyes register a dark wet spreading stain seeping out from the bedroom carpet behind the closed door. Something bangs in the head of yet another Jameson just then. I let Ryan lead me out into the backyard.

In that yard under the mulberry tree from which I feed my silkworms, my brother, nineteen years old, looks at me and says ever so gently, his usual cocky manner entirely absent: Dad has gone away.

Again? I say, quieter now but with tears streaming down my

cheeks. He can't go away again, he's just got home. Where to this time? And for how long? And why are all these people here? Why are the police here? And where is Mom?

Dad's gone away forever this time, Ryan says. He won't be coming back. He got very sick and he died.

I begin to shout again. But I saw him this morning! And he wasn't sick at all!

Mom is very sad and upset, Sam, says Ryan, and we've got to let her do what she has to do. I'm going to take you to the Goldmans, okay? And then you're going to need to go away for a while. Just till Mom has done what she needs to do, okay?

Ryan and I, two brothers, never again discuss this conversation, or what we have seen on this day.

AFTER THEN

Highway, 1968

MY mother's actions take on a robotic quality. It seems preposterous that this tiny, bird-like woman is all that is left standing on the ground, holding together these broken people flapping and straining like damaged, diaphanous kites in a fierce wind. What can she do now, what can she be now, but an automaton? She can set herself to tasks but not think beyond them.

From the moment Miss Sybil Walls put through the call from number 9 Mountbatten Avenue to my mother in her cubicle at Mr Bernstein's offices, she has frozen all her emotions and concentrated on physiological strength alone: there are things to do and she is doing them, methodically, determinedly, coldly.

The day is ending. I am sleeping next door, where I am to stay till the funeral. Ryan has shut himself in my old room. My mother sits, as is her lifelong habit, at her portable typewriter in the dining room and begins to type lists. The funeral service and a cremation to be arranged. Family, friends, associates to be informed. Notices to be placed in the newspapers. Acknowledgement of telegrams and cards. A compilation of the estate, such as it is, and an assessment of the family's catastrophic finances. A decision on the house; how and where to live after that. How to contact Billy, travelling on a train from the south. What next for scarred, scared Ryan. Where and how to complete poor Chris's schooling when he returns from the coast. Me to be sent to Durban to live with Aunt Emma and Uncle Keith as soon as it can be arranged; to be adopted by them permanently, or not, she will decide later.

Four boys are cast to the winds and they will scatter. Of one thing they can be certain: from this day they are each of them on their own in the world. Each will gather up all his strength for his own coming battle of survival; they will love each other but not rely on being carried – and tiny Mom can carry only so much more. Bang bang, Dad's dead. Bangs all round in the head.

Things happen very quickly from the day after. The train Billy is on is stopped outside Caledon so that the station master can inform him of the news from Witbank. Some kindly official in my father's office must have pulled strings. Chris is at a teenagers' party at the Ballito house with his friends when he sees, to his confused amazement, Uncle Keith from Durban arrive and talk secretively to Grandad, pointing at him. Then the father of his best friend in Witbank, who is holidaying in Durban with his family, arrives too. They are all in the wrong place, out of context; my brother thinks there must be some mistake. They take him aside and tell him he must come with them immediately. From different corners, the remains of the Jameson family converge on number 9 Mountbatten Avenue.

An obituary appears in the newspaper and though she cannot bear to read it, my mother reflexively places it in the scrapbook box, just on top of the souvenir programme from the bullfight in Madrid, and the notes from the trial of Tanase Ntabaka in

Kentani in 1957, which she has found in my father's bedside drawer while trying to sort through his belongings. The obituary is straightforward.

IT is with sincere regret that we report the death of Mr George Jameson, Commissioner of Bantu Affairs, who died very suddenly at his home in Witbank on Thursday. Born in Zululand in 1916, Mr Jameson's career was a distinguished one. He was a Zulu and Xhosa linguist and was loved and respected by all the Bantu communities. Having distinguished himself as a Captain during World War II, he entered the Department of Native Affairs and held a variety of senior posts.

Mr Jameson is survived by his wife Jean, and four sons Billy, Ryan, Chris and Sam. His parents are Mr and Mrs M F Jameson of Ballito Bay, Natal. His passing leaves a sad gap in the lives of his many friends, acquaintances and fellow workers by whom he was held in high esteem for his sincerity, friendliness, and dedication to the task at hand.

We extend our deepest sympathy to his family.

There is a separate notice: A memorial service will be held on Monday, January 8, at 4pm in the Anglican Church, Witbank, prior to the cremation which will take place at the Pretoria crematorium on Tuesday, January 9, at 11am. No flowers by request. Donations in lieu thereof may be sent to the Homes & Orphans Fund, Box 8021, Johannesburg. Friends kindly accept this intimation. Conradie & Miller, Funeral Directors & Florists, phone 63, Witbank.

With Billy, Ryan and Chris now at home and me still in my next-door protective exile, my mother sits with the pile of telegrams and letters which has been growing so quickly that she has been quite unable to keep up with it. Now she can try to concentrate and absorb the outpourings of those who cared for him in some way, had been touched by him in some way.

My father's parents were shopping in Stanger when it happened, and arrived back at the Ballito house to be confronted by both the shocking news and the blunt fact that they could not get to Witbank in time for the funeral. For all that has gone before, my mother's heart opens to them as she reads the old people's hasty scribbles, the familiar handwritings themselves now writhing in pain on the page. Gentle old Milton Jameson of Babanango's effort looks as if it will slide right off, and he can write only in gasps: Words fail me. God rest his soul. Stand together. Shocked parents. Will write when I am more normal. Dad. Even fearsome Grandma Enid, always so controlled and precise, looses her streaming consciousness, as when she releases her mane of hair from its tight bun: Sad God knows how sad we are Oh God. Oh God's blessing to you all and help in your great need Oh! Oh! Gran. From New Zealand, there is an almost disbelieving letter from my father's favoured cousin Lucas, the one named for the ancestral patriarch.

Dear Jean,

It is very difficult to express myself to you. I will say first that it is nice that the boys have, each in their own way, so many characteristics to remind you of George. They will be a comfort to you, and thank God for that. Alayne and I are remembering our stay with you in Libode, and your kindness, and that young boy Sam, such a happy child and hero-worshipper of his father; the apple of George's eye. And I am sorry to say this, but I am asking myself how it is that if even I could see what tremendous ability and zeal George put into his country and its people – if I as a bloody New Zealander can see how much he gave to South Africa – then Dear God how could he not see it himself? I am sorry to lose control in this way, but I am just so angry at what has happened. If you want to come and bring your boys to New Zealand we will fetch you and we will look after you as our own family. You are Jamesons.

Yours sincerely,
Lucas Jameson

My mother writes at the bottom of the letter: Why not! Why not get out of a country that poisons even its best souls! It is the raw sincerity of the angry ones that touches her the most, almost but not quite making her feel something like emotion in her frozen state. Lane Jameson, another cousin, writes from Zululand, his entire letter like a question mark.

> I can't help wondering why should it happen to someone at the peak of a successful career? And yet on the other hand knowing George was not in good health perhaps we should just wish him peace. He was someone who was very understanding and fair, conscientious and knowledgeable in a wide variety of subjects; cherished by every different kind of person you could hope to meet. He loved his country and its people and he always believed he would live to see them become one nation. What a shame, what a shame. You give those boys a chance in life if you can.

From a kraal in a valley in Pondoland, two nuns, sisters named Florence and Edna Mbete whom my father had befriended: We have heard on the radio. What actually happened to him? Did death come unexpectedly? Oh the harder that would be. The best always seem to be taken first. We suppose God needed him for important work wherever he is now. The Lord be with you and be your guide and Father until you meet one day Mr Jameson again in eternity! You must know that we know what a good man walked this earth.

After a while some of the letters begin to merge, fluctuate, become incomplete and disjointed in my mother's mind, shards of English rather than full sentences. Remember the best years ... Nkandhla with our young families ... George so good to me and my young family when my husband died ... Kind and understanding ... Carefree times we must treasure ... Did a great deal of good to so many people ... Tremendous shock to you all ... So much better than a long illness ... Went quickly and quietly while you still remember him in his prime ... Wish you were able to leave Witbank with happy memories ... Remember we are your friends always ...

My mother concentrates again when she comes to a letter from her own cousin. My mother should try, she writes, no matter how difficult it might be, to keep all her boys together as a family. She knows that relatives have generously offered to adopt the small boy because my mother has too much to cope with, but she is sure that in time she will realise she will be much happier if the family is kept intact. As regards the boy Sam, she says, it is amazing what understanding children of his age can show. They accept things better at that age, even if the price of real understanding, when it comes later, will be very heavy. She and her husband had tremendous admiration for George and what he was doing, even though they used to argue about politics and attacked him for working for the Government. They used to say to each other that even with these terrible policies, if South Africa had more people like George, approaching their work in the way he did, the country would not be in the disastrous position it is in now.

Doreen Harries of the Duiwelskloof days has been told the news by the local magistrate, sitting in the offices my father had refurbished eight years before. At least now George is at peace, she writes; he must have been desperately unhappy in his work to do that, as he was so devoted to his family. She says poor little Sam will miss his father in a way that thankfully he cannot yet understand. Be off to start elsewhere just as soon as you can, and remember we are here.

Then Rina Goldman, my mother's most important friend: I suppose one always wonders why, because we are just human beings and can't help ourselves. But try not to torture yourself, Jean. Think of all the wonderful and happy memories you have. I am so glad you went on your overseas trip before it was too late.

My mother appreciates the trouble taken by Marius Marnitz, their doctor friend, in writing from Libode.

Do not give in, Jean. You were a wonderful wife to him and I know you had many trying times over the years with his illness, so please do not look back, because a better and more understanding wife and friend he could not have had. I feel sure he is now resting peacefully. His friends will remember him as a very dear person. My daughters thought the world of him. It has been all over the Xhosa news. He is remembered by the Xhosa people as a good and understanding person to them all. You have good sons who will always stand by you, Jean, so to the future and your health we must now look, as the boys will look to you for guidance. Have strength Jean.

Most startling of all for her, even the frail hand of a now very elderly Mr Pendlethwaite, a name from so long ago; a letter that trembles in her grasp for the lost time it holds.

Dear Mrs Jameson,

I truly do not know what to say or how to express the shock I experienced on receiving the news of George's passing hence. On reading the first part of the newspaper report, I knew at once that something serious had happened, but when I came to the part telling of what had actually happened, I could not read further. I am old now and I am afraid I cried out, 'Oh', and frightened my wife.

You may not know that not only did I hold George in high esteem; I was deeply fond of him. He was my personal appointee when he commenced his official career at Ingwavuma. I very soon realised he was destined for a high position in the Service (as it used to be called in the old days) and I mentioned to the Governor General that he should keep an eye on him. I had hoped he would become Chief Commissioner for the country – South Africa could not have done better – and one day take my own place as Secretary for Native Affairs.

But then everything changed, including for me, and I could not help George any longer. My goodness he would have served with distinction in the highest office! But we all know what happened. Politics was brought into the Public Service. One of the new Cabinet Ministers at that time, just before I was removed, said to me brazenly: All things being equal, I will always appoint an Afrikaner.

I am not making naïve or self serving accusations – I am too old for that and too aware now of my own faults and those of my kind – but that is what suddenly happened at that time. These are my own opinions, Mrs Jameson, and I know I can entrust them to your secrecy.

I am now well on in years and as the years roll by, the old friends are fewer and one naturally fades away into the background. But it was not so with George. He never failed to call on us in our retirement on his visits to Zululand. His friendship to old people like me and my wife – though he knew I could no longer help him in any way – was something I very, very much treasured. In fact I will treasure his memory for however long I still have left. We fully understand how perplexed you must be at present, but you have the love and support of your sons who will help you to bear the sorrow. There is a beautiful Norwegian poem (which of course cannot be translated without losing its full beauty) written by a man about his friends passing away: He left a rainbow over his grave, and glory over his coffin. I salute the passing hence of a fine man and a dear friend.

From a sincere friend of the Jameson family,
R S Pendlethwaite

PS Your husband was to me like the son I never had. Our professional circumstances meant that I could not express myself to him in such personal terms in those days.

My mother receives telephone calls confirming that my father's death has been a news item on the radio in all the languages of the country. There are calls from Babanango, Kentani, Tsumeb,

Duiwelskloof and Libode, as if the message is being drummed mournfully from hill to hill, like in the old days, across the breadth of the land. It even reaches Mauritius, over the Indian Ocean, and a note arrives from Port Louis, in imperfect English: Mrs Jameson, I just want you to know how hard he try. God help you and us all. Maurice.

We wear black to the funeral, my mother flanked by all four of us straight-backed boys, well trained in the Transkei, two on either side, in descending order of height. She has us all under one roof as she had hoped, but it is the wrong roof, the wrong building. The church is packed to overflowing. The hymn is The Lord's My Shepherd. We do not remember the service as having taken very long, and thereafter choose not to remember it at all. The *Witbank News* covers the event, and the clipping finds its way into the scrapbook box. The report says a large number of Witbank people, including all the dignitaries of the town, high-ranking officials from Pretoria and Johannesburg, and senior foreign diplomats, attended Mr Jameson's funeral, which took place at St Margaret's Anglican Church on Monday afternoon.

After a few days – none of us can distinguish between these days, which are smudged – my mother sits down again at her typewriter in the dining room. First she lists meticulously every single message of condolence that has been received, from whom, when, and from where. One hundred and nineteen messages have come so far, from forty-three different places. When she has finished these chores, she moves to another. It is time to think with herself, and no one else, about what has happened.

She has carefully separated out from the others those letters that confront directly the manner of her husband's death. Her caring aunt from Benoni:

My dear girl,

Remember what I told you – that when the brain is involved or affected, we must not blame them. There is still so much that our doctors have to learn affecting that important part of us. We have spoken about this many times.

From friends of the South West Africa days:

Oh Jean; dear, dear George. How thankful I am that his troubles are over and that he has found peace. We have lost such a good friend and feel bereft, but to wish him back would be pure selfishness. I know of no one who did more for other people. Such a blameless, good, constructive life he led – surely his rewards will be rich. With your courage and that of your fine sons, you will take up the threads and carry on the pattern as George would wish. If this burden of life was too great to bear, I believe he had the right to lay it down, for all your sakes, as time will surely prove.

Jan van Doorn, my father's friend and clerk from the desert years:

What a shock to learn of the tragic news. How empty and lonely life must feel for you folks. It is impossible to understand these things, I think. But the aching void must be filled even if the sorrow appears insurmountable. Just at the time this must have happened, we were preparing to leave for Cape Town. We had not been reading the newspapers, and moreover we are no longer moving in the old circles. But when we heard, I felt I must drive out to old Mr and Mrs Jameson at Ballito Bay, which I did. The poor old folks were very cut up and just could not understand. I told them one's mind cannot be explained – it can take so much, and then something snaps.

I believe that while we are well enough, it is essential to take stock of ourselves; it is necessary for us to stop and consider, so that we can get a real sense of values. I believe that if I had not been able in the past to do this myself, then when I was down I would have gone the same way as George – and I was not a sick man like him. George's action has shocked me into taking true stock of myself, and of how much I have flouted; how great are my shortcomings. May God be very near to you and help you and Billy and Ryan and Chris and Sam with your very heavy burden.

And from George's cousin in the Natal Midlands:

My dear Jean,

Fay has tried and tried again to take up her pen and write to you, but she cannot. Her hands are shaking and she says her mind is numb. She says she can find no words to embrace or give comfort in the face of such incalculable heartbreak. So I am writing, and I say to you only this: As godfather to one of your sons, I forgive George.

Then my mother takes out some books and articles she has collected, and writes in her neat hand, with headings:

THE CHRISTIAN CHURCH

Life is essentially a test to determine an individual's eventual destination – Heaven or Hell. So the man who takes his own life is in a sense dodging the test, and flouting God's Will.

THE JEWISH FAITH

A man was created in G-d's image, and hence to destroy himself is to commit sacrilege by destroying G-d's image. But we do not condemn the man who is driven to suicide by insanity, or by great pain or mental anguish.

These last words she finds comforting, and is grateful that throughout their lives they have enjoyed the closest and most loyal of friendships with Jewish people. She finds other things to write down. She copies out from a book: A man taking his own life usually does so with a clear head. In that last final step he is not thinking about chickening out, because he has thought it through and made up his mind that this is the logical – the only – thing to do.

She has taken new clippings from the newspapers, which she now rereads carefully. The first is a reader's letter:

> Sir – On numerous occasions I have walked past the Town Hall on Saturday mornings, and have seen a group of people with banners asking the Government for an inquiry into mental healing in this country. As a citizen of this town, I salute them. I have often asked myself: What happens behind the walls in these institutions' padded cells? Why don't people recover in mental homes? Why do some psychiatrists use such torture as shock treatment? Why do they use shock treatment when it does nothing but harm to an individual?
> *Citizen of South Africa*

This has drawn a flurry of responses. My mother takes some comfort in the realisation that she must not have been alone in her situation; that others have shared their suffering. A psychologist replies:

> Sir – Your correspondent deplored the use of shock treatment in South Africa. I must agree. More and more thoughtful people are protesting against the use of electric therapy. In most countries in the Western world, many psychologists (and some psychiatrists too) are certain that electric shock is harmful, not useful. Yet in South Africa it continues to be used – I believe because of the snake-pit atmosphere in our country these days.
>
> It is not generally known that electric shock produces a violent rigidity in the muscles, that back and neck injuries and even fractured vertebrae are common. Small errors in the giving

of the shock sometimes result in death or permanent injury. Other damage done is loss of memory (sometimes permanent) and the fact that once a person has had shock, he usually gets worse after a time and is eventually permanently hospitalised.

Few cases who receive shock several times do not become mentally incapacitated and deteriorate. It is almost unbelievable that such antiquated and unproven practices can be permitted. An inquiry should definitely be launched to discover the facts of the matter. Perhaps the families of the unfortunate people who have suffered this 'treatment' will speak out in your columns, giving their own observations.

The last of this correspondence she covers with asterisks and underlinings. It is from a reader in Springs.

Sir – I can hardly describe the shock with which I read the article 'Shock Treatment Does Not Shock'. I have been associated with mental health for 15 years – much of that time overseas – and my observations of the results of this dreadful and entirely unpredictable 'treatment' have led me to conclude that the sooner it is discarded the better. Even Russia no longer employs this barbaric treatment of the mentally ill or disturbed.

Statistics on the subject are for some reason carefully obscured, but I managed to learn in Brisbane, Australia (which boasts the largest mental health hospital in the southern hemisphere) that in 1960, 10 per cent of patients died soon after shock treatment, or what they call Electroconvulsive Therapy (E.C.T.).

Electroconvulsive therapy was introduced in Rome in 1938 by U Cerletti and L Bini. I quote from a technical work which describes it: The technique is essentially the passage of alternating currents through the head between two electrodes placed over the temples. The passage of the current causes an immediate cessation of consciousness and the induction of a convulsive seizure. Following a course of treatment there is usually an impairment of memory, varying from a slight tendency to forget names, to a severe confusional state.

I have known several cases who wished to commit suicide during and after such treatment. And pray answer this question: if electric shock is so benign, then why is such a furore created when instances of employing similar methods to torture prisoners are alleged?

Finally my mother copies out fragments from an article headlined There's Nothing Left To Live For.

At least two thousand people will die by own hand in South Africa this year ... No one left to prevent last fragile link between life and death being severed ... Figure could be much higher ... Many covered up by relatives or suicide victims themselves ... Difficult to probe causes, discover real reasons ... Suicide often last event or circumstance in series of crises and disturbances, over many years ... Too few trained psychiatrists in SA ... Situation getting worse ... Few who take own lives are mentally deranged or psychotic ... Suicide in SA spread evenly among race groups, genders.

She notes the expert definition of a suicide motive:

The normal circumstances or ordinary crises which the average person has to face, and with which most of us succeed in coping, but with which the suicide feels he is unable to cope. A suicide is a person who has failed in some degree or other to succeed in life, or to make life meaningful. The act of suicide is contradictory to one of the most fundamental urges of human life – the urge to preserve life. It is, therefore, a desperate act.

My mother places the articles in her scrapbook box and, at the end of these pained meanderings, writes: Enough. Oh God, full of compassion, grant perfect rest beneath the shelter of thy divine presence. Shelter him evermore under the cover of thy wings.

Then she decides she cannot keep going through all the letters and messages any longer; she is too drained. Some will have to wait for another day. For now she wants to put her typewriter to a different use. Sitting there in the dining room at number 9 Mountbatten Avenue, alone, my mother writes a poem to give voice to her lament. She will never show her guileless verse to anyone in her lifetime, but will secrete it along with everything else within her box of memories.

Blue eyes enrapt and awed
gazing with wonder as we stood under
The Tear of St Peter
This to remember for years
This to remember through tears

Blue eyes excited and wide
The thrill of the heat
The crowd on its feet
Watching the picador ride
Saluting the Matador vain
Never again to see Spain

Blue eyes untroubled and clear, soft and loving
Watching the sparrows so clever
Feed from my hand
This memory to treasure forever
Blue eyes laughing with joy
Drury Lane, Dolly's banquet again
Lifting carefree hearts higher, to wander back
Hand-in-hand through the crowds
No thought of shrouds

Blue eyes content and enthralled
Loving Ireland,
Poor, green, and everywhere walled
Unearthing a history, lapping it up
Giving joy where he went and filling his cup
This to remember for years
This to remember through tears

Blue eyes closed and at peace
No longer to look on pain, sorrow and strife
Perfect release from this troubled life
This to remember for years
This to remember without tears.

Hardly Keats, she would have quipped in better times.

Days later she receives a formal letter of sympathy from the Secretary for Bantu Administration and Development, and then the Chief Bantu Affairs Commissioner, my father's direct superior:

I just want you to know how high was my regard for your husband. We had our differences, but I always knew I was dealing with a man of principle. It is an unhappy enigma of life that one realises, usually too late, that affection for others should cast aside pride when differences arise.

There is a courteous telegram of sympathy, too, from the Anglo American Corporation, saying that Commissioner Jameson was one of the most impressive officials the company had dealt with. There is an unexpected letter from the University of the Orange Free State, asking if the papers of this prominent figure in our country might be housed in its Department of Political Archives.

One day the postman tells her, not unkindly, that she is getting more mail than the rest of Mountbatten Avenue put together, and he alerts her to the fact that in that day's batch, there is an envelope addressed to George himself, rather than to her. Of course not everyone can have heard the news Mrs Jameson, he says, and I thought I'd just point it out. Back in the house she opens the unfamiliar envelope.

Dear Mr Jameson,

When I wrote to you about a year ago, I really had no idea or even hope that I might be able soon to offer you better news. Well, I cannot overemphasise my joy in being able to say that Mr Harry Oppenheimer has come forward – this was entirely unexpected – and has undertaken to underwrite the new, additional post of Deputy Director: Museum of Man and Science, City of Johannesburg, to help us move things along more quickly.

I have told our Trustees that I think I know just the man for the job, that he is in Witbank, and I am certain he would be happy to travel to Johannesburg to meet us. So please do use the telephone number at the head of this letter to be in touch just as soon as you can!

Kindest regards,
A S Beit

My mother is baffled at first, but eventually remembers how this correspondence might have come about. She makes a note to telephone Mr Beit to tell him he is too late.

On the 24th of January she receives a telephone call to tell her she can report to the office of the District Registrar of Births and Deaths, Witbank, to collect a Provisional Death Certificate in Respect of a Person Who Presumably Died From Other Than Natural Causes. This certificate, for which a payment of 25 cents is required, is issued in terms of Act no. 81 of 1963. It is needed so that the lawyers can begin to process the estate. The certificate notes: Legal proceedings are being instituted in connection with the death of this person and on completion thereof the death will be registered and a death certificate will be obtainable. Into the scrapbook box goes another piece of paper, to lie there dormant for thirty-five years.

Now she is free to go. The last days at number 9 Mountbatten Avenue are taut and cold. She becomes, and will remain for the rest of her long life, a committed but despairing and martyred shepherdess for her sundered and scattering flock, to the exclusion of all else. Though she is but forty-four years old, no man will again share her bed, or give her a lover's embrace, for the rest of her days. Those parts of her humanity are placed on ice forever. Brightly energetic in appearance and in company as always, she develops but disguises the private stare of a concentration camp survivor. Occasionally it is captured in photographs, when she does not know they are being taken.

Billy has gone back to sea for the last time. Ryan has vanished once more into the wildness of Hillbrow. Chris continues his schooling, distractedly now, because he knows he will not matriculate at Witbank High after all. I remain in Durban with my relatives, stunned each morning to find myself going to Durban Preparatory High, a school I do not know, and coming home to a family I do not know.

My mother's sister Helen, who is secretary to the head of Premium Milling, an important company in Johannesburg, says she is sure that Mr Francken, her kind and powerful boss, will help my mother find work of some sort if she moves from Witbank to Johannesburg. And she and her husband Arthur are childless and so can provide some support for the refugees, lifts to school and the like. My mother agrees and puts number 9 Mountbatten Avenue up for sale, saying she will accept the first offer she gets as long as it is enough to pay off what is still owed to the bank. Chris can go to a cram college in the big city to complete his schooling. She can fetch me back from Durban, 'readopt' me, and I can be put into a new primary school, an affordable Government one in Rosebank. She can rent a small flat, the first of our lives, in a suburb of Johannesburg that is at least not so very poor as to embarrass her. My father's estate will take time to wind up, but soon she should receive his Civil Service pension, and should be able to get by as long as she can find work herself.

A few weeks after my father's death, and having made a special effort when asked to do so by the influential Mr Bernstein of Witbank, a local accountant delivers to my mother an Inventory of the Estate of George Milton Jameson, the material remains of his fifty years of life on earth. It is a short document.

INVENTORY OF ESTATE: G M JAMESON, ESQ.

Immovable Property, Erf 805 Witbank	R5 000.00
Movable Property, Dodge Lancer	R300.00
Cash:	
Current Account, Standard Bank Witbank	R567.13
Savings Account, United Building Society Pretoria	R13.36
S.A. Mutual Assurance Society	R442.74
Department Bantu Administration salary portion	R49.96
Total value of Estate:	R6373.19

At the bottom of this sheet of paper, my mother writes: There may be other things I have forgotten about, or don't know about. The bank will also take their slice, but the mortgage has been settled and these amounts above are with that already taken off. I must make sure I have enough for meat/telephone/rates/lights/water etcetera each month. And some pocket money for the two boys. Pension payout will take six months. Estate at least a year. Note that of the cash in the current account, my October/November/December salary payments are included – and unfortunately frozen along with all the other accounts.

Her certain instinct, that she must escape the house and Witbank as soon as she possibly can, is deepened by reports from Durban of my increasingly erratic behaviour. I have become a chronic, and dangerously inventive, sleepwalker. In the darkness of the early hours of consecutive mornings, my exploits are downright frightening for my hosts. First I have to be hauled, in sodden pyjamas, from the swimming pool next door – seeking second baptism, or suicide, or just a swim, no one can know. I do not remember it in the morning. The next night my uncle and aunt are woken to the sound of shattering glass, and they run to the dining room to find me, eyes wide open but fast asleep, having hurled a crystal decanter against the wall. I am led back to bed and again do not recall anything in the morning; they do not press me or remind me, but quietly lock my bedroom door from then on, once I have fallen asleep. I become noticeably quiet and introverted for the first time in my life, given to hours of unmoving brooding in their back garden.

I am sent to a child psychologist, who asks if I know what has happened to my father, and why I now have only one parent. The psychologist eventually tires of my wild made-up stories about a Spitfire pilot shot down in the war, a sudden cancer victim, a magistrate drowned while heroically trying to save a woman in the Wild Coast surf, a stylish highwayman hanged in the bush; answers from cartoons or my imagination. She tells me to draw pictures instead. I produce a tightly packed page of childish outlines: dozens of guns and bullets, nothing else. I write to my mother: Mom, if something happens, surely something else unhappens? She is troubled enough by my question to make a note of it in her diary. She knows I am thinking what she is thinking – is it not possible to take back a bullet, at the instant it leaves a barrel, like an intake of breath, and therefore revert to the instant before the instant?

At the February monthly meeting of the Labour Control Board, it is minuted that the Chief Magistrate himself has travelled from Johannesburg to Witbank to observe a minute's silence for the Committee's esteemed former Chairman, Mr G M Jameson, who died suddenly earlier in the month, and whose contribution would be sorely missed. An official letter is written to my mother to say that at a meeting of the Board, all members unanimously expressed their deepest grief at the death of Mr Jameson and wished to convey their sympathy to the family.

The house does not sell quickly, and my mother settles for an agreement to rent it out from the 1st of May, which has become her deadline for leaving. Privately she hopes that the tenants are not aware of what has taken place in this house. She sells my father's old black Dodge Lancer, and buys a small light blue Peugeot in which she will undertake the migratory flight down the long highway to Johannesburg, City of Gold, to see if we can start life again.

When at last she is ready to leave Witbank, my mother is still in the sedative, relieving, trance-like state that has enveloped the family. In this condition she fixates on fulfilling one very last, very important task, after which she can go and never come back. She gets into the small motor car and drives the short distance from Mountbatten Avenue to Voortrekker Road, where Witbank's single branch of the OK Bazaars is located. There she requests, in her characteristically authoritative way for someone so very small, that she be able to speak to the store manager. He recognises her, and expresses his condolences. He says she must have been touched by how many people were at Mr Jameson's funeral. What can he do to help her in this difficult time for her and her family?

What she needs, she says, is the biggest and sturdiest cardboard box that the store can spare. She has some precious documents that must be transported to Johannesburg, where the family is relocating, and it is important that the box is big and strong. It is going to have to carry a lot. And she also needs, please, a roll of the strongest sealing tape that is available – the kind the removal companies use.

The manager of the OK Bazaars, Witbank branch, says that will be no problem, it will be his pleasure, and there will be no charge. He tells one of his store-packers to find the biggest and best cardboard box in the place. He has it taken out to the car for Mrs Jameson, where it has to be folded to fit in the boot, and he explains how simple it is to reassemble. He hands her a roll of heavy duty glued sealing tape. He waves from the store entrance as she drives off, feeling sorry for that poor, nice, harmless family that had such a terrible thing happen to them; the town has been talking about nothing else since the news came out.

When she is home, my mother rebuilds the box in her neat, patient way. She is most satisfied with both its size and its strength. With Chris at school, she sits cross-legged on the lounge floor. It offers a wide, flat expanse, and she begins to sort through her collection going back to 1916. My father's birth certificate from Babanango is the earliest document, and will end up at the bottom of the box. His death certificate from Witbank will be on top.

The work is not unlike that she used to do in the little library she founded in Kentani. Over several hours she places everything that went before into the box carefully and logically, at pains not to crease flimsy papers or have photographs stick to one another. When all is complete, she is pleased to note that it fits just as if the box had been specially measured up for this purpose. She takes the roll of tape and wraps it around the box; around and around and around as if to throttle it, cut off its oxygen.

Now she can pack up the rest of the house and they can go and try to start over somewhere else: it is after all, she reminds herself, only the very beginning of her youngest boy's life. As soon as she has unpacked in Johannesburg she will drive to Durban to fetch me, and she determines to then block off forever everything that has happened up to this point; she will treat it as the day I was born. There will be more boxes to fill. But this box, this one right here in front of her eyes, she has sealed and will never open.

IV

THREE summers have passed, and two long winters; finally I am done with my mother's box and it with me. I have my story now, and I feel grateful for her meticulous preservation of memory triggers. It has allowed me to replace the shard that is my lost father's reflection in the mirror of my country, and to begin to fill in the void it has been in my own. I am glad I did not stop.

In its final days the story shaped and revealed itself to me as a parallel, crepuscular universe, unwinding and uncurling intermittently. Slowly, indistinct dots joined themselves together into some order I thought I could follow. It expressed itself at times as a reverie, a lament; at others as just a family saga which I now finally own like everyone else does theirs. Whether I have told it just as it happened – whether, in that sense, it is true – I do not know. It is my version, anyway, and if nothing else, I now know more about how I came to be here.

Along the way I often felt like I was in a San-like trance, the meditative condition quite pleasant, and I hummed, over and over and over, lines from an old song that sustained me in the wrenching 1970s: *Into this house we're born; Into this world we're thrown.* I shut myself in my study on countless nights while my small family slept, a faded photograph of a happy George Jameson in our Libode garden watching unblinkingly from the wall, and read through the papers and listened to the hours of tape recordings: My father's voice. I wept gently for unbroken hours, amazed that the fluid kept coming, as if somehow attached to me was a giant reserve tank that had collected the dammed tears of decades. I thought also of my brain as containing a series of locks, like those in rivers, all full of brine and blocked by the one in front, the one containing the memories of everything up to the 4th of January, 1968. It is unblocked now. When the tears came they were calm tears, soothing more than painful, warm and soft. They'd aged well in the bottle of my body, had been ready for pouring.

Later in those nights I would lie half awake, in middle age awash and adrift in the sounds and smells and colours of childhood times so long lost and denied; not always unhappily, often with a safe sense of being transported back in time to complete an obscure mission. When finally I slept I dreamed as the secure, happy boy I had been in the Transkei, and marvelled at the fact that the screaming sleepless nightmares that had for more than thirty years shared my bed unbidden, all over the world, were replaced – as if a stubborn tape had finally worn itself out and there was a new one to put in. All of it made me think about my own life after the cataclysm, naturally enough, but I reminded myself this was George Jameson's story, not mine, and he had earned the right to have his retold; not all lives deserve that.

I am a lawyer, a commercial attorney with a respectable practice, fairly successful I suppose by the measures of these times; but nothing really special or someone who will leave much of a legacy behind. I am ordinary in most ways – you would not look twice at me in the street. But I have a family I adore and they do not seem disappointed with me, bless them, though my wife worries when I go into my black moods. I am getting close to reaching the age my father was when he died, which is an unsettling assignation, and I have also come to the surprising stage in life where I find myself thinking of retirement, though it is still quite a few years away, and in a sense the prospect is a relief. Clearly the years have tempered my ambitions of old. Like my father, I wonder whether mine has been a worthwhile life. Like him, I am not sure, and I don't know by what standards I should judge myself. Perhaps everyone has these thoughts in middle age, and mine are just being heightened by this delving into the entrails of the past. Still the thought pesters me that it might not be too late to try to do something more meaningful – for myself, my family, my country? What, I don't know. I realise how soft, at least materially, have been my generation's adulthoods by comparison to my father's – though in other ways, especially in the struggle for values and against shame and guilt, I think they have been just as hard and inconclusive; for we were left a wicked inheritance.

The box caused me to wonder how it can have been that my brothers and I never talked about our father's story, how I could have spent my life pretending it did not exist, running away from it, trying to keep ahead of it. This was a very un-African response, I think now, to true trauma. But perhaps it was just that, like our father, we did not want to be pitied, but loved.

My long immersion, almost-immolation, also makes me realise I have never publicly displayed the supposedly mandatory and precise paroxysms of anger, blame, shame and guilt that are said to attend a suicide in a family. In the fashionable phrases of the contemporary world, I suppose this would be called denial, or internalisation, or suppression. I recognise that my own approach has been to avoid volunteering my secret to people, unless they asked directly. I have never offered the information, but neither have I lied. If asked about my father, my stock response has always been: He died when I was very young.

My own depression has been episodic and not nearly as catastrophic as my father's. I have also had a lot more luck in my life than he did in his. I cannot claim that my life has been unhappy because of what happened; it is not a true conclusion, and not one I wish to reach. Rather: I have a condition that many people have, that can be managed, lived with constructively like other diseases; you can build a structure around flawed scaffolding.

I wonder whether the story I have pieced together – whatever it is: true, false, invented, sanitised, exculpatory? – will one day help my own son and daughter to understand their lives and identities better. Or just make things more complicated for them. The English-Speaking White African, the European-African; a riddle still not unravelled after all this time, being left unsolved again by us, for our children to wrestle with one day.

Of the four brothers that once were, two are indeed still white Africans in Africa, bringing new Jamesons into the world in this new century my father tried so hard to conjure in his mind in the Libode house in that long-lost time. These are Billy, the eldest; and me, the youngest. Of the other two boys, Ryan left Africa for America as soon as he could, and it must be no surprise that he was eventually not able to survive any longer in the world. The third boy, Chris, went east a full quarter of a century ago to start a new life on the farthest side of the hemisphere.

Of course I wish my father could come back, so we could talk at last and perhaps see if we could find some of the answers together. But I know well that this is the one thing I can never have, no matter how hard I work and run and fight in this life I have lived so ridiculously quickly and unreflectively. I am a father now. So I prefer to remember the Zulu greeting he taught me: *Nyabonana*, We See Each Other. At least we have seen each other at long last; I have that.

On the day I decided I had at last sucked out all I wanted from the accursed and blessed box; when finally it was so empty and light that it could never again drag me down; when I said to myself

1968 is a very long time ago now and it is time to let go of it, I walked alone to the dining room in my own house on this African shoreline, and sat at the table.

I took out a pad of lined notepaper and a pen and began to write. What I was doing looked strange on the page, but also familiar. All the way down the left-hand margin, I wrote my name in capital letters. It looked like this:

S
A
M

J
A
M
E
S
O
N

I began to fill in the blank lines opposite each letter. Occasionally I scratched out what I had written, and put alternative words in the space above. When it was done I read it out loud to myself.

Stop being afraid; you can stop running now; slow your heart
All your skills can benefit others; put them to better use
Make your home a place of safety, love, honour, happiness

Joyously give thanks you lived to see justice in your country
Absolve through your contribution your children from guilt
Make an effort to control your tendency to self-destruction
Exhibiting kindness and love is the greatest quality in a human
Stop trying to climb every mountain; seek serenity rather
Open Ryan's box; tell his story and all the others too
Never fudge a moral choice, or it will trap you and kill you.

When I finished, I laughed. I felt a dizzying lightness of heart. I took the new sheets of paper on which I had written, in my hand. I stood and walked out over the wide veranda and down the steps, across the lawn to the garden gate that looks like it opens into the very ocean itself. I followed the rough seaside path to the cellar. The door opened easily. When my eyes had adjusted to the light, I placed the sheets inside another box, in which there was a mound of carefully ordered paper and memory trinkets I had been collecting all my adult life; my magpie's work.

Acknowledgements

The writer would like to thank the following people for, variously, expert editing, belief in the book, helpful suggestions, research assistance, emotional support and the like. At Penguin Alison Lowry (name in bold, underlined); and Jeremy Boraine, Pam Thornley, Claire Heckrath, Hayley Scott. At home my darling, clever and supportive girls Stefania and Luna Johnson. And elsewhere in my life, alphabetically; Mike Adler, Cheryl Arthur, Bridget Astor, Richard Astor, the late David Astor, Jonathan Ball, James Barty, Claudia Bickford-Smith, Vivian Bickford-Smith, John Boorman, Ben Bradlee, Michael Brophy, Felicity Bryan, the late Alan Bullock, Letitia Calitz, J M Coetzee, David Cohen, Jenny Crwys-Williams, Jakes Gerwel, Pumla Gobodo-Madikizela, Peter Godwin, Paul James, Margaret Jay, the late Joan Johnson, Barry Johnson, Craig Johnson, Suzy Joubert, Andrew Kidd, Alistair King, Gary Lubner, John Maytham, Niall Mellon, Patrick Nairne, Sean Naidoo, Gavin O'Reilly, Sally Quinn, the late Anthony Sampson, Mark Solms, Dusanka Stojakovic, Susan Thomas, Melanie Whitfield.